Country in Ruin: 1865

by

David Lee

of

Hatton Cross Steampunk

ISBN: 0615763677
ISBN-13: 978-0615763675

DEDICATION

I'd like to dedicate this book to my daughter, author JM Lee (Jessica) and to my wife Michaela. Both of whom inspire me in so many ways that I cannot begin to list them. I shall however make an honest attempt.

To Jessica; your own accomplishments in the literary world have completely blown me away. I am constantly amazed at the creativity you possess. Your accomplishments at such a young age have been an inspiration to me and yes, my genius daughter you are the inspiration for Priscilla. I have no doubt that you are capable of making "epic" changes to this spinning rock we call home.

To Michaela, my gorgeous wife; you have been my compass, always pointing and guiding me in the right direction. Without you I likely would have been complacent enough with mediocrity and a boring life. It is very likely that I would have accomplished little more than the bare minimum. I attribute most of my success to the fact that I wish mostly to make you proud and to provide for you and Jessica. You are the inspiration for both Esmeralda and the German Duchess, Eloise von Strombeutel. You are my gypsy dancing beauty and my little bag of electricity, my "Strombeutel."

To my brother Joseph who is the inspiration for Declan O'Sullivan. While I embellished a tad on his ferocity, I feel it important to note that he truly is a bad ass. A former Army Ranger and veteran, he truly does embody the hero. He is never one to brag but when the stuff hits the fan, he is definitely the guy you want on your side. Always dependable and constant when it is important, he is someone I truly admire.

To my friend Richard who is the inspiration for not only Lord Paddington Aldwych but also Lord Wesley Chamberlain. You have been a refreshing change to a town not yet enthralled in the magic of Steampunk. If there were ever a perfect example of a fun-loving, lovable English nobleman, you Sir would be it.

To Richard's lovely wife Angela who is the inspiration for Agatha Foggybottom I state here publicly (or to the 12 people that will likely buy this book) that I took no liberties with your character. This is exactly how Angie is, loveable and tough as nails, not to be trifled with and someone I am honored to know and call friend.

To my parents Tony and Darla Lee, my desire to be a gentleman and display chivalry and admirable behavior comes directly from you. When I am not trying to impress my wife and daughter, I am trying to make the two of you proud. For those of you that will not find my humor funny, I am sorry but I get that from my Dad. We share the same humor and sarcasm gene.

To my brother in law David Hoffman, the inspiration for President Lincoln. It may seem weird but it is your steadfast devotion to your family, country and common sense that inspired me to write in the character of President Lincoln. David is also my technical sanity check to which I have sent a constant barrage of emails asking how to make the science work. He is my human internet search engine.

To Jacque Kilduff, Jacque took on the decidedly insane role of being my first editor. Through countless hours of being frustrated with my horrible grammar, she was able to help me flesh out areas that needed more of the story and to rearrange the story so that the reader would be more engaged from the beginning.

To Alan Braden, my second editor who helped me

focus on the content and story plot. Alan, your insight has been invaluable and I truly appreciate your help as well as your friendship.

Foreword by Alan Braden, aka: "Professor Upsidasium"

As Professor Upsidasium it has been my honor and my pleasure since 2009 to seek out interviews with the men and women inside the Steampunk genre for the Visuatronic Audiographic Steampunk Archive. At this point in the early history of Steampunk (right on the edge of mainstream recognition if the standard media is to be believed), we are still a subculture of people expressing our selves through hard work and hard-won creativity. Just like any brand of fandom that has come before us, our tools and props are not easily found in stores. Everything that Steampunk has in the modern movement are works of fashion, art, and literature that we are making ourselves. We are all beginners here, even the "trade experts" who are writers and artists in their regular lives, leveling out the playing field to where anyone can participate.

I met David Lee for the first time at a convention in Upstate South Carolina where he hosted a panel on the art of converting household items and spare junk into functional and interesting genre props. David and his group, Hatton Cross Steampunk, create artifacts small and large, amazing and amusing, on a frighteningly regular schedule. Just in the same way that David has created this book from the ether with ideas both small and large, amazing and amusing.

It has been my honor and my privilege to read an early rendition of this work, and I'm hoping you'll follow along in the journey of this new idea as David (in true Steampunk form) tweaks and twiddles with concepts and history in ways that I don't believe have been done before. Creating a complete revision of early American history involving mysteriously prodigal children, mutated zombies and plasma weapons?

Yes, indeed, that's Steampunk.

Enjoy.

Country in Ruin:1865

PREFACE

This book is my first attempt at story telling. I've been making up creative stories the better part of my life. Most people are content to call that lying but I prefer "story telling." I distinctly recall learning about the Civil War in the third grade. I tried to correlate a tie to General Robert E. Lee and even went so far as to say that we still had his horse. This lesson was my first in getting caught and embarrassed. Instead of learning, I got better at research, but I digress.

This story is my first structured attempt and it is a direct result of my awesome published sixteen year old daughter, JM Lee. I am hopeful that you will find it amusing and be inspired to pursue the arts of Steampunk, science, invention and all around gadgetry.

To me, Steampunk is simply fusing science fiction with our romanticized notion of Victorian era life. It is taking the old fashion approach to how a man should behave; to the manners he should posses, as well as paying tribute to the nineteenth century's age of exploration and inventiveness. It is a growing love of science and engineering which I have combined with my love of tinkering in my cluttered garage building neat Steampunk junk. I also enjoy seeing my daughter and wife dressed in frilly, flowing dresses enhanced with bustles and fancy hats. I realize that the average man and woman in the 19th century lived a miserable life working in horrible conditions, in poor health and a distressing environment. Like today's reality though, this presents the unique opportunity to display a romanticized notion that is very much obtainable. I feel that we should not settle for mediocrity but rather strive towards a higher standard, even the impossible.

I have attempted to 'write' Declan and Finnegan's Irish accent into the dialog. I have purposely spelled their dialog out phonetically so it will require you the reader to use some imagination. As you read it, I hope you'll hear the accent in your head, even if it sounds like the cereal leprechaun, and that it will enhance the images and story I am trying to convey.

That being said, I hope you are entertained and that you enjoy this story. If you are not a Steampunk fan then I hope that you become one. As you 'invent' gadgets for your persona, research scientifically plausible explanations for how and why they work. You will come up with a story about 'who' your character is. You will likely be amazed with just how smart and creative you can be. Before you know it, you'll be writing your own novel and contemplating quitting your day job.

Enough preaching, start reading! Enjoy.

Chapter 1 – The Fort is lost
Fort Monroe Virginia, 1865

Sergeant Milton Rogers sat at his desk, his elbows hurt as he leaned forward, resting. The stack of papers was nearly complete and his schedules for the next week's shifts were finished. They merely needed to be re-written thanks to that bumbling klutz, Private Jacobs and his propensity towards spilling the Sergeant's coffee. It was as if he took a sick pleasure in spilling or breaking things. Surely no one was that clumsy. Hell, a good monkey would be of more service than that buffoon. While the good Sergeant was grateful for the desk job at Ft Monroe and for the fact that he was no longer out on the battlefield, watching his fellow soldiers die, he did find this kind of stress to be very taxing. This monotonous stress of mundane paperwork and schedules was very taxing but it was safe. He breathed a sigh of relief as he thought of returning home. He was hopeful this would all be done soon and he could get home to his family. He could hang this blue coat up in his closet and never look at it again save for the times he imagined he'd be sitting at a pub with all the other old men discussing the horrors that they had survived.

The Confederate President Jefferson Davis was imprisoned there at the fort and all that remained of the rebels was rapidly surrendering. All the madness would soon be over and he could go home to his loving and patient wife and their eight children. Milton was a good soldier and a good leader of men. He looked into a small pocket mirror at the reflection that stared back. He stared into the blank stare and thought that he looked old and tired. This war had taken so much out of him, from his soul. He looked at his hands and thought how soft they were and how dirty and rough they used to be working in the fields. His wife Betsy always insisted on soaking them in some milk to make them softer. A faint grin appeared on his worn mustached face as he thought about holding her again.

He sat at his desk and allowed himself the luxury of reminiscence. He could almost hear the angelic voices of his daughters as they sang hymns and the sounds seemed to dance around the room adding warmth and happiness. The house would be full of the smell of chicory coffee brewing on the stove and the sweet scent of burning cedar chips. His sons liked to put the cedar shavings on the fire as they carved toy rifles and knives. Occasionally they would wrap the thin strips of dough the girls had made for them earlier around sticks and cook them in the fireplace.

As Sergeant Rogers sat in the stiff, unforgiving wooden chair in his quarters, he imagined himself sitting in his comfortable old chair and soaking it all in. His wife had threatened to burn that chair many times, claiming that it "stunk to high heaven". He would simply chuckle and gesture her to sit in his lap. Her cheeks would blush and she'd turn away so as not to have her children see her flustered. This was what life was about. This was what he'd given up for the past four years only to be replaced with the horrors of warfare. He shuttered and closed his eyes as terrible memories invaded his thoughts. The pain of these memories rode into his thoughts like a heartless General on a giant steed. He'd seen his fair share of action over the duration of this war. He'd managed to survive Shiloh and Gen. Johnston's surprise attack. He recalled the horror and chaos that followed that initial attack. As they established their positions at that sunken road they all called the "Hornet's Nest" they fought for their lives against overwhelming odds. It was the longest day of his life and he could not recall ever having prayed that much. His prayers were however answered the next day as reinforcements came and brought an end to the massacre. Nearly 23,000 soldiers lost their lives those two days of fighting and for what? Only to be repeated again, over and over again.

He next saw battle at Antietam under General McClellan. He lost over twelve thousand of his fellow soldiers that day. Every time they thought they had the Rebels in retreat it seemed reinforcements would show up and push the Federal forces back. Of all that happened that day he could only remember that smell. It was the smell of the dead, a pungent stench of burnt flesh and hair mixed with the haunting cries of those about to join them.

At the Battle of the Wilderness under Grant he again watched nearly eighteen thousand of his fellow soldiers die only for the hell to continue to Spotsylvania where they lost nearly nineteen thousand more. He felt as if he were cursed. He did not understand this madness nor did he want to. He was a simple man who enjoyed the simple pleasures of life and he quite simply wanted to go home.

He stared off at the corner of the room. He sighed heavily, the corners of his lips turning down as he remembered just how far away he truly was from the comforts of his quiet family home. He was no longer able to enjoy his smoke and he set the pipe down on the table. His thoughts tormented him with horrific sights, sounds and smells of the last four years. He rubbed his forehead slowly as if attempting to massage the thoughts away. It was no use however; those thoughts would never leave him in peace. They would accompany him till his dying day.

Today had been particularly stressful as the Fort had received nearly 50 civilians earlier that evening in search of medical care. It was normal that they come to the Fort as many doctors were serving in the war. This left many towns in Virginia without the luxury of a doctor. The civilians were stricken with some sort of illness and it had set Milton with a great uneasy feeling, there was something not right. He could not say exactly why but he had an overwhelming feeling that he should run away as fast he could. It seemed completely irrational but he had learned long ago to trust his gut feelings. Doc McGee had quarantined them to the Casemate infirmary to keep it from spreading to others in the installation but it did not seem enough.

Milton protested and asked that they not gain access to the Fort but Doc McGee was confident that it was nothing to worry about. Despite his protests that idiot Major decided that the Doctor knew best and allowed them entrance to the Fort. It was always the same in his mind, the officers made decisions that ended up costing good men their lives. He could not shake the feeling that this was a similar circumstance.

Sergeant Rogers face glowed with a warm yellow light as he lit a match and held it to his pipe. The sound of the match strike still seemed to echo in the tiny room. Shadows danced around behind him as he puffed the sweet tobacco. He shook the match extinguishing it and the shadowy figures disappeared to their lonely corners. The smoke began to lurk and linger around the room with the scent of cherry and molasses. Milton continued with the last of his log entries. His quill pen dipped in the ink bottle and returned to the parchment as he wrote in the last of the watch schedules with the names of the tired and weary.

His evening smoke was his only pleasure here and he was determined to enjoy it. The war had taken nearly everything from him and this seemed to be the only thing that kept him grounded and allowed him the tranquility required to truly appreciate thoughts of home.

As Milton wrote the last entry his hand slipped, smearing the name, thanks to the startling and annoying clanging of the watchman's bell. Its rhythm was frantic instead of orderly like they had been instructed. It's carelessly and erratic noise served as a warning that something was definitely wrong this night. He decided that it must simply be one of the newer soldiers and that he would need to beat some sense into him.

"Damn fools! It ain't difficult, slow and consistent for ships, fast for troops. How many times must I beat it into their thick skulls? Sounds like monkeys are swinging from the bell" he moaned. He was going to put someone on the dirt for this. No one interrupted his smoke without serious consequences.

He swung the exterior door with clenched teeth and all the intent of hurting someone. As the door crashed into the wall he gasped in complete horror. As he looked out into the courtyard of this heavily fortified fortress, all he saw was the eruption of chaos. The giant grey stone walls of the fortress became grisly prison barriers locking in the terror that Milton saw before him. His soldiers actually shot at one another. At first he thought that the fortress had been infiltrated by Rebels but everywhere he looked, he only saw Federal troops. As he squinted and attempted better focus at his surroundings he noticed several of his men crouched over another actually tearing at him like an animal. They were biting him and the poor fellow fought with all his might but he was no match for the vicious and barbaric nature of these…these men. It was as if Hell itself had unleashed its hate upon the fortress and all the poor souls locked inside. He scanned the area and located a large group of his soldiers that had managed to establish a line of defense.

Without haste, Milton grabbed his Spencer repeating rifle and his black leather ammo belt. It was brand new and lacked the character of his old one. He thought of the irony of a statement he made earlier that week. "Brand new ammo belt like this will make my wife think I never saw any action." As he charged into the chaos towards his men he thought that this would be the least of his problems and he secretly prayed that he would in fact have the opportunity to see his wife again. He charged to his men hoping to help them. He had come back from overwhelming odds before but it was never like this. Either way, his men needed him. For a split second he felt a tingle of cowardice as the thought of hiding in his cabin entered his mind. This only made him run faster towards his men. They had formed a line four men deep and about 100 across. Behind them was a corner where two massive stone walls jetted up towards the heavens. He surveyed the possibility of getting to higher ground but it was useless, they were pinned in good and their only hope of survival depended on their discipline and teamwork. As he ran through the lunacy, he was forced to raise his rifle on his own men. They ran towards him in frenzy. Their eyes were blood red and their faces grimaced as if in excruciating pain. He only needed one to lay hands on him before he realized that there was no hope of reasoning with them. The soldier's rigid hands tore and clawed at him like an animal. Milton slammed the butt of his rifle striking the man in the forehead with a sickening thud that dropped him to his knees before slumping to the ground dead. He made his shots count as he raced towards his men, each time placing a bullet into the forehead of his would be assailants.

As he ran through the fray, at times leaping over dead bodies, the smoke of burning buildings and burning flesh scorched his nostrils and nearly caused him to vomit. His stomach convulsed yet he pressed on. With each assailant he sent to God, he recalled their name in his head. These were his men damn it, what could possibly have brought this upon them? He dashed left and right, at times leaping over piles of the dead. As he fired each round he thanked the heavens for his Spencer repeating rifle. Had he been reduced to a muzzle loader, he would never have made it out of the front door.

As Milton approached his men, several pointed their weapons at him preparing to fire. Milton could see the look of pure horror in the young men's eyes, many barely old enough for service. He held his weapon high and shouted "Don't shoot! Let me through!" They made a path and let him through all the while firing their muskets. He was proud of their composure. At best he could expect them to fire off 4 shots a minute under the best circumstances. This was an enemy that was running full speed towards them. It was easy to fire at a Rebel line but this, this was different. Despite the extreme circumstances they did as he had trained them.

"Maintain your composure gentlemen! Make your shots count, aim for their heads! Then make way for the second column to fire as you reload! Then the third row, then the fourth, just like we train." The thick pungent smoke filled his lungs as he barked his orders. The air was now thick with the gunpowder adding to the chaos. Had it been daylight, perhaps they would have stood a chance. There were simply too many of them and they were too fast, too vicious.

As he did his best to keep the men together and to keep the attackers at bay, he knew defeat was inevitable. There were just too many of them. He'd seen battle, he'd seen horror and he'd seen death but he'd never seen anything like this. He couldn't let himself admit defeat if he hoped to inspire his men to survive this night. He noticed that the left flank was holding their own, where as the right started to weaken.

"You there, fourth row, get over to the right and help them out! NOW!" he screamed. The men rushed over to their new fighting position and the onslaught balanced. He watched as his men hit their targets. The attackers heads splitting and exploding at such a close range. There was a building on fire about 50 yards behind the attackers which helped with visibility. The orange glow of the fire backlit the red misty clouds that exploded behind the heads of their attackers. Despite how well his men were performing, the attackers pressed on and ate away at their lines (quite literally). A young man turned to retreat back as he reloaded his musket. Milton looked him in the eyes and saw the terror that consumed the young man. He didn't get a single pace before he was grabbed round the ankles and pulled backwards into the mass of attacking mob. Milton fired several rounds in his direction hoping to give the boy a fighting chance but it was no use, he was lost amongst the pile of ravenous monsters. The center of his line was collapsing and he needed to balance the lines again.

"Fill in the center! Hold the line Damn you!" screamed

Milton at the top of his lungs.

His shots were becoming frantic and he was losing control. His men were holding on but he could tell that it would not last much longer. He needed something to rally them, something to provide hope, the kind of hope that inspires men to achieve great things. He needed something, anything!

As if his prayers had been answered by God himself, Milton noticed that a small contingent of Calvary men charged towards their position. Their sabers glistened in the firelight and seemed to possess an angelic quality. The small group of Calvary men, numbering approximately 30 men charged with a feverish assault that rivaled the ravenous monsters that decimated his lines. For the first time this evening, Milton actually thought they had a chance. The Calvary charge drew the brunt of the attackers off of Milton's men and towards the horseback angels.

Milton saw the reaction of his men and shared their joy. They began to regroup and reload, hoping to provide good cover fire for the Calvary. A young man walked around loading weapons and handing them to others to fire. He was quick, very quick and there was an abundance of weapons lying around as their dead numbered at least 50 of their original 100. The young man loaded another rifle and handed it to his comrade when one of the attackers leapt through the air landing on his back. His attacker bit into his neck, ripping the flesh back and exposing the vertebrae underneath. The young man didn't even scream, he couldn't, his lifeless body dropped to the ground. For the first time Milton was overcome by emotion and he paused. His stomach twisted and turned at the gruesome site and his heart ached for all of them. A rage overcame Milton and he began to fire his weapon into the carnage. His barrel was hot and he had little ammo left.

Among the Calvary rode a woman in a long navy blue dress. Her golden locks bounced almost in slow motion as she charged with the others. She wielded a saber and hacked and slashed as good as any man there. Milton decided to focus his fire at the attackers around her. He could not bear to see her fall to the same fate as the others.

What seemed like a good idea at the time turned out to be a very useless attack as the Calvary men, and woman, were swarmed by hordes of attackers. They could not amass significant casualties and one by one they fell. Milton's golden haired angel was no different. Her screams pierced his heart more than anything else that night as he watched her being dragged down to the horde of monsters.

It did not take very long for the horde to refocus their attack on Milton's soldiers. Slowly but surely his lines dwindled to a handful. He knew that he would never again sit in his home and watch his children play. He would never hold his beloved wife close to him and kiss her. Milton had but a handful of ammo left and would soon be forced to resort to bludgeoning his attackers with his rifle. As his vision scanned the scene for a way out, everything slowed. Motion crept to a standstill almost and the scene gave way to mirage. Just beyond the attackers Milton could see his sons playing by the creek near his home. He could see his wife off in the distance waving to him, beckoning him to come home. This gave Milton that last bit of rage as their images dissipated and all he was left with was the site of the hell that was tonight. He fought like a madman possessed but there were just too many of them. He hoped and prayed that this was all a horrific nightmare but try as he might, he could not wake.

In a matter of minutes the entire garrison of Union troops had been reduced to raving lunatics and the dead witnesses of this horrible night.

Sergeant Milton Rogers swung the empty rifle at the approaching monsters. He hit the first in the head, splitting it open as he fell to the ground. His body ached yet he ignored the pain. Adrenaline fueled his every move and the visions of his family fueled his anger. He swung his rifle striking two more in the head and kicked a third in the chest knocking him to the ground. He swung frantically hitting anything he could as the hordes of monsters engulfed him. His muscles ached but still he pressed on. His barrel jabbed like a sword and became lodged in an attacker's eye socket. He tried to free the weapon but it was lodged too deep. He then resorted to throwing punches and kicking, anything to survive. He could not give up, he wouldn't. His back was nearly against the cold stone wall now and he had nowhere to run. There was no escape only a horrific death.

"GRAB THE ROPE!" a voice screamed from above

and behind him.

As Milton desperately fought for his life against impossible odds a twisted bloody rope dangled a foot to the left of him. Without hesitation Milton leapt for the rope. He stepped on the heads and bodies of his attackers as he was lifted to safety. A large man stood on the wall high above and desperately attempted to raise Milton to safety. It was old John Moore the mess hall cook! The blood soaked rope was slippery in Milton's hands. He wrapped his hands around the rope in a desperate attempt not to fall.

"HANG ON! IT'S SLIPPING!" screamed John Moore. He tried with all his might to hang on to that rope and to pull his friend to safety but he simply could not. The rope tore through his bloody hands and he watched in horror as Milton fell back into the horde of attackers. Despite the overwhelming number of attackers, Milton managed to get to his feet and continue fighting but was eventually overcome. As he was pulled to the ground he even resorted to biting his attackers. He kicked and clawed but was smothered by them. His body felt as if it were on fire. Milton gazed one last time into the night's sky. He peered between his attackers and the smoke at a small patch of stars that shone through. As he admired the brilliance of the heavenly bodies a shooting star passed and he found himself making a wish. He wished for it all to be over, to rest. His wish was granted as his consciousness faded into darkness. The pain of the tearing and biting slowly numbed away until he felt nothing.

Chapter 2 - A "boring" machine
Hartford Connecticut, 1855

Sam Colt sat in his oversized, leather chair and watched his young protégé Finnegan erupt into another of his foul-mouthed fits. The leather creaked obnoxiously loud as he shifted his weight to the left, resting his left elbow upon the soft arm of the chair. His protégé's outburst was directed towards the factory Foreman, Mr. Eli Root. Colt's Patent Fire-Arms Manufacturing Company had just received word that Mr. Eli Root's patent had been accepted for the "Lincoln Miller", a universal mill machine invented under the direction of a one Mr. Eli Root. Pre-orders were already coming in and the company was looking at a significant sales profit. This was a circumstance that young Finnegan was not pleased about. He felt that he deserved an equal share in the profits. The two had worked on previous milling machines and a factory such as this required multiple machines, each for separate jobs. Finnegan had devised the single milling machine design, which could perform a variety of functions saving valuable space and time. With the help of Mr. Root, they built the first model calling it the

"Universal Miller." Finnegan claimed that Mr. Root had promised they would share all aspects of the new invention.

As Sam Colt observed the "discussion", he observed Mr. Root with a very guilty look about him. This only made Finn that much more furious.

"Ya son-of-a-bitch!" screamed Finnegan. "Nowhere on dis patent is me name listed!"

"Now Finn, we've discussed this before, all ideas conceived while under my employment are the intellectual property of my company. I dare say you would not have been in the position to contribute were it not for my generosity" retorted Sam Colt.

"Mr. Colt, you gave me a chance some years ago and I am deeply grateful. Me brother and I have always been loyal ta ya but this is going too far. He may be the best mechanic in da state but he has clearly stolen me idea, hell, he even took me name fer it!" pleaded Finnegan.

Samuel Colt was not a man that entertained 'discussions' regarding his decisions. He had learned over the years that this bred weakness and caused decay. You had to snuff these things in the bud and with total authority so that others did not get similar ideas. The only difference here was that Finnegan and his younger brother Declan did have a history with the entrepreneur, similar to that of father and son. However, just like a father subdues his unruly son, he feared he may have to do so here. The men that worked for him knew this and all abided yet here he sat, listening to the young man's complaints.

As he prepared his response, he took a deep and heavy breath. His eyes met with young Finnegan and the past flooded his thoughts like a dam breaking. As many men his age are prone too, his thoughts drifted off to earlier days.

Samuel Colt first met the boys in 1851 after a business trip to London England. His visit was in conjunction with the grand opening of his factory in Bessborough Place, London. Earlier in the visit he led a grand demonstration of his firearms in the Crystal Palace for her majesty, Queen Victoria. His demonstration was very well received and the orders were already flooding in. Sam had boarded the ship earlier in the morning and prepared for the long journey home. He recalled that day when the ship's Captain held the young stowaways by the scruffs of their necks and asked what to do with them.

“We should trow dem o’er board Sir” snorted Captain Nathaniel. He was a rough man with an abnormally large nose. His skin was weathered after a lifetime on the open sea. It was easy to assume he was a man in his 70’s but with these sailors, you could never know. It was just as likely that he was a man in his 30’s. “Mr. Colt, what do ya want me ta do wit’ dem?” the gruff Captain asked again.

“Now Captain Nathaniel, I think we should find out a little more about these lads” replied Sam Colt. “What brings you lads aboard my ship?”

“We’re orphans Sir, haven’t a place to lay o’er heads. I only be try’n to take care o’ meself and me little brudder” replied the older of the two boys.

His Irish accent sent cringes down Sam’s back and was nearly reason enough to ‘trow’ them overboard right away. Sam had dealt with many Irish over the years and he didn’t have a whole heck of a lot of use for them. They tended to resort to thievery and crime the second things didn’t go as they expected. They were generally nice people but leaned heavy toward the drink which only complicated their ‘loose morals’. His run-ins were all with adults however and as he pondered what to do, he thought to himself, perhaps they can become fine upstanding citizens with the proper influence and guidance.

"Sir, please let me werk fer ya, to pay fer o'er passage to America." pleaded the oldest brother.

"What's your name boy?"

"Finnegan O'Sullivan Sir, and dis is me brudder Declan."

"How old are you son?"

"14 years I am Sir and Declan here is 12." Finnegan stated with a definitive amount of pride. "I can build most anyting and I'm real good with me hands. AND I'll work fer a fair price!"

"A fair price you say? You're not in much of a position to be making bargains young man. I do admire your gumption though." He paused for a moment and thought on it. "Let's start by working for Captain Nathaniel here. If he doesn't throw you overboard by the time we arrive in Connecticut, perhaps I can put you to work in my factory."

"Sir, tank you very much Sir. You won't regret it, I swear!" said an elated Finnegan. "Did ya hear dat Declan?

We're gonna be Americans!"

"Don't ya ferget dat I have da option o' trowin ya o'er board. You'll be doin' hard work and I'll not be hearin' any whinnin' er cryin'. One werd and o'er ya go" warned Captain Nathaniel. His left eye seemed to bulge compared to his right eye. It exaggerated his already comical appearance.

"No Sir, not one word!" answered Finn.

Just like that the boys were put to work. Captain Nathaniel did not relish the idea but Sam Colt was paying a pretty penny for this voyage and therefore was able to call the shots.

The voyage home was rough and Captain Nathaniel worked the piss out of those boys. Not once did Sam hear a single complaint from either of the boys or from the Captain Nathaniel. In fact, upon arrival in port, Captain Nathaniel offered the boys jobs on his ship. Sam had to laugh as he recalled Declan's response to the offer.

"I'd sooner kiss y'er datter than work one more day on dis shite bucket!"

A feeling of dread came over Finnegan and he punched his younger brother in the arm. He quickly looked at Sam Colt to plead for forgiveness. Sam released a bellowing laugh that resounded throughout the harbor. “You boys are going to help me make a lot of firearms with that kind of spirit.” he said. He didn’t want Captain Nathaniel to know this but his laugh was primarily due to the comment regarding the Captain’s daughter. She was indeed one of the ugliest girls he had ever seen.

“Well gentlemen, fetch your things and apologize to the good Captain. You’ve got a lot of work to do today and we don’t have many hours left.”

“Sorry Captain Nathaniel, I didn’t mean to disrespect yer ship” apologized Declan.

“And what about me daughter?”

“He’s sorry for that too” stated Finnegan quickly, knowing that something foul and mean was about to come from his little brothers lips. He covered his brother’s mouth and quickly dragged him off to fetch their things.

“What da hell ja go an do dat fer? You can’t ruin dis little brudder, even if dat man’s datter is ugly as sin!” laughed Finn.

~~~~

The thought of that day made Sam chuckle, the kind of
~~~~

chuckle one has when reliving fond memories. He shifted his weight again causing the leather chair to creak as if to moan and groan under his weight.

"What ar ya laughing at Sir?" asked a baffled Finnegan.

Sam was instantly brought back to the present day. This young man that only a few years ago was a wide eyed child was now a very skilled mechanic with a very bright future ahead of him. He had every right to be angry towards him and Eli Root. They would both make a fortune on this machine and none of it was to go to Finnegan O'Sullivan.

Samuel Colt cleared his throat and gave his best stern face. "Finnegan, you know the deal and there is nothing that you can say or do to change it. These are the rules and we live and die by rules. Perhaps we can come to an accord though. You and Declan have always wanted to get out and explore this grand country. What if I offered you both work as Jobbers? You'd be working for my best agent, Agent Ezekiel Cooper. He's a good man and heading for the Kansas Territory very soon. I'd even be willing to let you keep 5% of your sales, plus your salary."

This offer was very generous and Finnegan was quick to realize it. Finnegan must have looked quite comical as his jaw hung open with surprise. A Jobber worked for an Agent and traveled around selling Mr. Colt's firearms. He didn't have to be very good in math to know that 5% could add up to a lot of money, maybe even enough that he could start his own company someday.

He hesitated for a mere moment then replied "I'd be happy to take yer offer Mr. Colt."

"Excellent! Agent Cooper will take care of outfitting you and getting you up to speed. You'll be heading to the Kansas Territory. Be sure to check in with him tomorrow after lunch. Now if you'll excuse us, Mr. Root and I have business to which we must attend."

As Finnegan and Declan left the room, Eli Root noticed that Declan's right hand had been behind his back the entire while. He knew that his hand rested on his trusty Bowie knife and he also knew that he did not want to test Declan's skills with the blade. Eli had heard stories enough to know that, while only 16 years old, he was more than capable of splitting him open without losing that grin. No other 16 year old scared him more than

Declan O'Sullivan. As Declan passed by him to leave the room, he flinched and made Eli jump about a foot in the air. Declan quickly turned to Sam Colt and tipped his hat gesturing with a short bow.

No sooner than the two had left the room, Eli Root pleaded with Sam Colt. "Five percent, have you gone mad? Those two are unstable and should have been thrown overboard four years ago when they stowed away on your ship!"

"Unstable? No. Tough as nails; yes. These two are exactly the type of men that I need with my agents. I need young men that I can trust and that can kill a group of thieves or bandits without much difficulty, skillfully or morally. They must protect my merchandise. Those two boys will give any potential thief one hell of a run for their money and I likely won't lose a single firearm. Besides, what do you think they would have done when they found out that I just took the company public and am awarding you shares? You'd be lucky not to be gnawing on that giant knife of his."

Eli Root stood there looking at his friend of 26 years. While he admired Sam for his ingenious ideas he did not always agree with his methodology. One thing he did possess was the ability to evaluate a problem and quickly devised the best way to solve it. He had made a lot of money by working for Sam Colt. He was right; Finnegan and Declan O'Sullivan would be good at Jobbers and would likely make the company a good deal more money as 'convincing salesmen'.

"For 26 years I've been backing you and you haven't let me down yet. I suppose the two will do a fine job and I know how much they mean to you" added Eli. "Best of all I won't have to watch my back with those two."

He recalled the day that Sam and he first met.

It was a dusty morning, nearly a hundred degrees which was unusually hot for Chicopee, Massachusetts. Eli had come to the fair solely to see a new device demonstrated. He had heard it was an underwater bomb that sank ships and he was most curious as to the method of detonation. What was even more impressive was that the inventor was a 15 year old boy.

There was much hustle and commotion as Eli neared the demonstration area. The scent of homemade pies danced about the air and mixed with the less-than-desirable smells of the livestock. Eli looked at the small pit that had been dug and filled with water. Off to the side, he observed a thick black cable running into the water to what he imagined was the device. He was immensely curious and chuckled to himself as he noticed just how close the crowd was to the water pit. 'This should be good' he thought to himself.

Sam Colt emerged from behind a large sign and acknowledged the crowd. Eli thought he gave a very articulate speech and sat captivated as Sam Colt explained how his explosive device could be submerged underwater and wait for passing enemy ships. Despite Eli's own enthusiasm, he was amazed at how little the crowd seemed convinced. Sam Colt pulled a large red level and a string raised the explosive device out of the water for all to see. He seemed to think this would garner a reaction from the crowd and was consequently discouraged by the lack of response. He would not let them sit for very long, arms folded and scowls upon their face. He smiled, however subtle, and went for the gusto. He lowered the device back into the water and depressed a second lever.

What happened next was as humorous as it was

impressive. It worked, boy did it ever! As Sam Colt's invention exploded to the heavens the crowd was doused with an enormous amount of muddy water. Sam's triumph was doused, much like the crowd, as they erupted into a rage. Eli quickly grabbed his arm and ushered him behind a wall of large advertising signs. Eli placed his hat on Sam Colt's head. When the angry crowd approached both young men yelled and pointed off in the distance stating "he went that way!"

Eli had to laugh as he recalled that day and then beamed with pride at the man the fifteen year old boy had become. As far as Eli was concerned, Sam Colt was his own younger brother, even though he was his employer.

"Fine, just as long as those two leave Hartford and I do not have to deal with them" Eli concluded. He did not like the idea and would have rather thrown the two out on the street but he respected his friend and looked forward to the day when he did not have to look over his shoulder.

Chapter 3 – The surprise
Hartford Connecticut, 1855

It was 1855 and so far, America had been everything that the folks back home in Ireland had said it would be. However fun it may be, one did not need to resort to crime to make your way or your fortune; just hard work. The "Land of Opportunity" was actually living up to its name. He was not 18 years old and Finnegan O'Sullivan was earning a decent living working for Samuel Colt. Despite his idea for the Universal Miller being stolen by Eli Root; Finn at least had a new job and a great one at that.

A Jobber worked with about 10-20 other Jobbers for an Agent. Together, the crew would travel their respective markets and solicit large bulk sales to stores, companies, lawmen, military garrisons or 49-ers. Honestly, whoever coughed up the cash became a client. It was a bit dangerous as thieves and bandits were always looking for crews to rob. He actually thought this to be one of the fun aspects of his new job. He liked the sense of adventure and danger.

Finnegan was 6' 4" tall; much larger than the average man so he stood out wherever he went. His nature was such that people usually felt comfortable around him, despite his abnormally large size. He was usually joking around and could be accused of needing to grow up at times. He had an odd beard that only covered his chin which he felt quite unique and fashionable. He couldn't stand having a mustache and the full beard just didn't suit him. His hair was brown and short, often matted down by his hat. He loved that hat. It was a grey top hat with his trusty goggles resting on the brim. His hat was adorned by pheasant feathers which some felt too "Dandy" but Finn felt it added that whimsical touch that said he was a man of action as well as fashion. When Finn looked in the mirror, he preferred to see his reflection wearing nice things such as a waist coat and sharp trousers. He wanted people to respect him and he figured that dressing the part would only help.

His was a modest life. He did not consider himself a ladies' man. In this day and age a man had to establish his career before he even thought of marriage. There was one girl however, that he really had a soft spot for. Her eyes were a golden brown that glistened in any light and when Finnegan looked into them he was powerless. She had a golden tan complexion and long, dark brown hair. The problem was that she belonged to the Zott band of Gypsies. They had been just outside of Hartford for nearly a year. Many of the locals hired them for their craftsman skills while even more were lured in by the entertainment. One thing Finn could say for sure was that they knew how to throw a party. They had the best whiskey and the best food. He visited their camp however for the primary reason of seeing Esmeralda Zott. As previously stated, she was the center of Finnegan's world. He craved her and often thought of nothing else than being with her. They met as often as possible. Theirs was a passionate love, as most young loves are. It was equally ill-fated as it was passionate. Sadly enough Esmeralda's father did not approve and had forbidden them to see each other. Finnegan was not stupid, well, perhaps a bit, but not stupid enough to challenge the leader of the Zott band. He knew that it meant his death for gypsies were known for their skills with a knife and their general lack of fear of the local authorities. Everyone knew that the coppers would look the other way either from fear or from bribery. Still, despite his better judgment, he longed for her and desperately searched for a way to earn her father's approval. He was determined and oblivious to the dangerous path that lay before him.

Her father, Bizyam Zott was quick to boast of his ancient blood line. His heritage was of great importance and touted frequently amongst his band. The one and only time that he had a conversation with Finnegan, he proudly touted:

"I am the descendant of Izjaq Zott, who founded the first Roma state on the banks of the Tigris River. He did so at the request of the Persian Shah 'Bahram Gur'. For over one thousand, five hundred years my family has led this tribe and I'll not have my only daughter marry a "Gadge"" [*non-gypsy*].

They had tried to meet secretly several times but really only succeeded twice. Finnegan knew that if they did not end this, both of them would end up dead and he could not bear to think of Esmeralda being hurt on his account.

As he contemplated the tragic notion of never having his love by his side he was forced to distract himself with his work. Finnegan was anxious to join Doc Cooper's crew. It was widely regarded as the top crew in the country and was led by a legend. Agent Ezekiel Cooper was a spindly man who didn't talk much. He was real quick on the draw, definitely the quickest Finn had ever seen. No one that ever knew him ever thought to challenge him as they knew the almost certain result. Most had heard the story and many variations existed but Finn loved this one the best. As the story went, Agent Cooper was at one point an actual Doctor. He reportedly changed professions at the request of Mr. Colt. It was rumored that he lacked bedside manner. Finnegan could see it now, "You gonna die deal with it like a man!" Yeah, he couldn't quite picture "Doctor Cooper" being even the slightest bit sympathetic. The story says that Doc Cooper once tended to Mr. Colt. One day Doc ended up in jail for shooting a man. Seems they had a dispute over the man's bill. Sam Colt became very interested when he heard the shooting involved his firearms. The story boasted that Doc Cooper put six slugs in the man's chest before he could even fire one shot with his Adams revolver. Sam Colt went right down to the jail and bribed the judge for Doc's freedom. He put him to work the very next day as the first Agent.

Who knew what was true. It sure did make for a good story though, not to mention that it instilled a certain degree of fear towards Doc and the crew. They were definitely not to be trifled with. They called themselves the "Gabriel Crew." Much like the Angel Gabriel carrying messages to people in the Bible only they carried Samuel Colt's message to the everyday man.

"God may have placed us in different stations in life but Sam Colt makes us all equal." Naturally this wasn't Sam Colt's official slogan but they sure did like using it. Seemed nothing inspired a man than the thought of taking control of his own destiny.

Finnegan sat in his chair, smoking his favorite pipe made of African Purple Heart. The weight of the dense wood sat comfortable in the palm of his hand. The whiskey flavored tobacco filled the room with an intensely sweet aroma. His chair creaked as he leaned back. He felt relaxed; on top of the world even.

As if he knew that Finnegan was totally and completely relaxed, Declan burst into the room.

"Ah little brudder, … care fer a smoke?" asked Finnegan with a smile on his face.

"Maybe later. Got word from da gypsies. Seems that pretty one you used to mess around with has something to give ya. She wants to talk tonight an' she ain't takin' no fer an answer. She said to meet her at da pub."

Finnegan's felt a lump gather in his throat making it difficult to swallow. The only thing worse than slighting Doc Cooper, he thought to himself, was to slight the gypsies. He wondered if Esmeralda's father had found out about their secret meetings and if she was alright. How long had it been since he last saw Esmeralda; four months, five months, longer? Maybe it was best to slip off with Doc to Kansas and avoid any and all contact with them. There were two problems with this solution. The first being that the Gabriel crew wasn't set to leave for another two weeks and the second being he was not a coward. Besides, his heart began to beat faster as he thought of seeing Esmeralda again.

Finnegan was anxious to see Esmeralda. He did not know what she had to "give him" and he hoped it was not a gypsy trick. They were sneaky that way and he wondered if he wouldn't be met in the pub by a group of angry Zott hell bent on carving him up like a Christmas ham. He was not a cowardly man by any means and certainly not accustomed to running away from a problem.

Later that night, he sat at sticky table in the corner of the Blue Bonnet Tavern. An ice cold pint sat before him. Its golden color reflected the dim light of the oil lantern to his right. He took a large gulp as Esmeralda approached. She was every bit as beautiful as he remembered and carrying a small bundle of cloth. He thought that it might be a weapon so he readied his gun hand. She did not look happy at all.

"Here you bastard, she is yours!"

"Me what?"

"Your daughter you fool! My father will not let her stay with us and is forcing me to leave her here with you" Esmeralda stated in between sobs. Apparently it had been longer than four months since they last saw each other.

"I can't care for a child, I am about to head out to the frontier land; to Kansas!" protested Finnegan. He could see his brother Declan at the bar, grinning ear to ear. His shoulders bounced up and down and Finn could tell that he was laughing. He debated on shooting him in the back for laughing but decided to focus on the matter at hand.

He turned his attention to the bundle o' baby before him. There lay the most beautiful child he had ever laid eyes on. Her eyes were big and her gaze was familiar, as if she already knew who he was. From that second on, he would not let her out of his sight. The bond was true and he knew his place was by her side and he would protect and cherish her at any and all costs.

"I'll do it, I'll care for her. You don't need ta worry Ez, I'll care fer her. What is her name?"

"Priscilla"

That was a fine name he thought as he picked her up. He had no earthly idea how he would care for a child but he did not care. He knew that he must. He wanted to more than anything. Esmeralda took off and Finnegan wondered if he would ever see her again. His heart ached as she disappeared from sight. He stood there, torn between the desire to chase after the woman he loved or to figure out how best to care for this darling little girl.

"Cute brat ya got der brudder. Now all ya have ta do is sprout some tits ta feed her."

Declan was never short of insults but Finn knew that in his own way, he was just coming over to see the little addition to the O'Sullivan family. As he held Priscilla up to get a better look, Finn noticed that they both had red hair. Declan must have noticed the same thing and quickly shot back at his older brother.

"Don't even tink 'bout it, I's never laid with her …. just her two sisters."

"I tink she looks like o'er muther, do ya remember her?" Finnegan asked, ignoring his brother's crude humor.

"Na, but I'll take yer word for it. So … what we gonna do now?" Declan inquired.

"Do you remember that nurse … Agatha? Where does she live?" The fire in Finnegan's eyes flickered more intense than the lantern next to them. As he left for the door, Declan chugged both pints down.

"Der be no wastin' of alcohol here ya fook. First day as a Da and you've already lost yer priorities. Next ting ya know you'll be wearing a dress an' a bonnet."

"Come on ya lush, we need ta find Ms. Agatha Foggybottom" said Finnegan as he rushed out of the pub in a hurry.

Chapter 4- Agatha Foggybottom, nurse extraordinaire Hartford Connecticut, 1855

Finnegan went door to door, asking the whereabouts of Agatha Foggybottom. He did not care that it was nearly two in the morning; he only cared that he get help for Priscilla. He couldn't explain it but he felt a purpose stronger now than he ever did in his young life. He was only 18 but for the first time, his life had meaning.

When he finally found her door, he anxiously knocked praying that she was home and would be willing to help.

"Bugger off YOU!" The shout echoed through the rough hewn wooden door and overpowered Finn's frantic knocking. Undeterred, he persisted.

"I said … BUGGER OFF!" She swung open the heavy door grasping a large meat clever in her hand. She had a fire in her eyes that clearly stated her intentions to do bodily harm but Finnegan only looked more pathetic. He did not care. He looked at the woman before him who was known for her cold, stern nature and extremely dry sense of humor. She had a rather foul mouth to boot and was known to have a fist fight or two in her day. All this aside, she had helped care for more babies in this town than anyone he knew.

Ms. Agatha Foggybottom was the widow and fourth wife of the late Archibald Foggybottom, cattle salesman for Hartford. Agatha was much younger than Archibald so it came as no surprise to anyone that she had outlived him. It was rumored that she was 40 but no one dared to ask for fear of that cursed meat cleaver, or even worse, her sharp tongue and to what it might reduce you to. Mr. Foggybottom did not leave Agatha much in the way of finances to sustain herself so nursing and taking care of young ones helped pay the bills. Finnegan was hoping that she'd be willing to help.

"Evening Agatha, er, I mean Mrs. Foggybottom."

"Evening? It's clearly morning ya twit! I was sleeping and having one very juicy dream about Mr. Knowles again … 'til you came and mucked it up."

"Mr. Knowles is a married man!"

"Not in my dreams he isn't!" Agatha said with a grin.

"Never mind dat, I need yer help. Dis is Priscilla. I am to head out to Kansas territory for Mr. Colt and can't take care of her by myself. I … I need your help!"

"What the hell do you want me to do about it?" she protested.

Finnegan was desperate. Agatha just looked at him; no doubt still dreaming about an indecent Mr. Knowles doing God only knows what. When her gaze dropped to Priscilla, she could not help but smile. You could see the wheels turning as her heart softening to the little baby and she replied, or rather declared:

"I am coming with you! Always hated this town and now that Mr. Foggybottom is no longer with us, well, got no reason to stay. Besides, Mr. Knowles is married and I ain't the waiting kind. Come on in; let's get that little one out of the cold."

Finnegan breathed a sigh of relief. His problems were, for the time being at least, lessened. He had no idea how he would convince Doc Cooper tomorrow that their party just increased by two. He would just have to deal with that hurdle tomorrow.

Declan didn't say much, just shook his head and went back to their place near Mr. Colt's mansion. He too wondered how all this would play out. Regardless, he would have his brother's back and destroy anyone that got in their way.

"Dis calls for anudder pint me tinks."

As Declan walked the lonely, quiet streets towards the pub he grinned. He heard an all too familiar sound in the distance. The shadows stirred with life as the sound of shuffling feet hinted at their owner's devious intentions. He knew that someone was going to try their luck and he was more than happy to ruin their night.

Four men appeared out of the shadows and the big smelly one announced their intent.

"Yer money chum, and yer time piece if'n ya got one."

Declan just grinned and replied, "Not tonight fellas, I'm afraid I am a bit partial to me belongings."

"Oh shit … I'm sorry Mr. O'Sullivan. We's didn't know it wer you" the once mighty giant stated. His mannerisms now reduced to those of a timid boy.

"Now boys, you's come fer a fight and now ya got one." Declan slowly drew his signature knife from his belt. It was a good 14" at least and razor sharp. The handle was made from the jawbone of a black bear. Some said that he killed the bear himself, others speculated that he took it from an Indian during a fight in New York. Either way, no one ever wanted to see it, especially under these circumstances.

As the knife cleared the sheath, it made a slow dragging sound that sent chills down the spines of the men. Robert Tuff was the biggest and truly dwarfed Declan. He was the first to drop to his knees and beg for forgiveness.

“Mr. O’Sullivan, we truly didn’t know it was you. If’n we had, we’d asked if we could walk wif ya. Please let us buy ya a pint an’ apologize!” The man pleaded as he trembled.

“Why gentlemen, a pint at this hour? What kinda lush do ya tink I am?” mocked Declan.

“No Sir, we’z not sayin you be a lush, we just thought we make, ya know, a peace offerin.”

“Fine dan, a pint it is but none of dat cheap shite. I’ll be havin a few o’ dem German brews. Da strong stuff that makes ya look at ugly women.”

Declan was quite amused with himself. He rarely had to fight these days having made quite a name for himself over the past few years. Folks weren’t too used to seeing a teenager at a pub, much less handling thugs like they were school children. He had to think about it before he realized that he never had actually cut a man with that knife. Didn't need to, there were all sorts of story's around about him fighting off a dozen Indians, killing bears bare handed. His favorite was that he had helped Allan Pinkerton to found his detective agency after Declan ended a small riot. Never mind that he didn't even get to America until a year after Pinkerton established the agency, nor that it was in Chicago. It didn't matter, folks could say and speculate what they wanted as long as they respected the fact that he would not be pushed around or toyed with.

The night was young and he had four lads payin' his tab. Who knows what stories they'd be telling tomorrow!

The five men walked down a cobblestone street and disappeared into the shadows. Their images gone long before the sound of their off key singing.

Chapter 5 – Doc has a soft spot?
Hartford Connecticut, 1855

The room was large and opulently decorated. Mr. Colt used the room for business meetings and Finn felt greatly underdressed. He noticed that all the other Jobbers in the room seemed a bit uneasy as well. Their mere presence in the room felt as if they were a stain on a new shirt, that at any moment some snooty butler would enter and shoo them off like beggars.

The ceilings were easily twenty feet high and the windows seemed to go on forever. A tremendous amount of light shone through the ceiling to floor red draperies. Every wall had at least one large mirror embellished with a golden ornate frame. Crystal chandeliers hung from the ceiling and little shards of light danced around the room creating a very magical effect. It was very quiet, until Doc Cooper finally decided to get young Finnegan's attention.

"You Sir are a Jobber, not a dern nanny!" Doc Cooper chastised. "I can't believe that you are suggesting that we bring a baby and a nurse with us. Do you realize how dangerous this job is? What are you gonna do when bandits are upon us? How will you care for the women folk and do yer job? Yer sole purpose is to protect Mr. Colt's merchandise so I can make sales."

"Doc, as fer bandits; do not worry. I'll kill any man who even tinks 'bout robbin us. Hell, Declan here may even kill 'em before they realize that they be tinkin' bout robbin us. As for da nanny, believe me, she can fend fer herself. No man in his right mind would mess wit her."

Doc thought for a moment, his left eye seemed to bulge and the tiny blood vessels seemed more agitated than normal. He had a wild and crazy look about him. He raised a weary hand to his face and wiped it as if wiping the stress of the situation away. He sighed, slowly shaking his head. "Sounds like my kinda woman. … Bring her in and let me meet her. This nanny, she better be able to deal with traveling! And be able to shoot a gun!"

"Don't know 'bout da shootin' part but she sure is handy with a meat cleaver!" Finnegan was now hopeful.

"Meat … cleaver … did ya say?" Doc gulped and seemed nervous all of a sudden. It was completely uncharacteristic of the man and it almost made Finn laugh. Did Doc know Agatha? If so, why was he nervous?

Agatha Foggybottom entered the room with her head

held high. She was wearing what you might call a 'mixed outfit'. She wore brown pinstriped pants and knee high leather boots. A wrap around skirt with ruffled edges gave the impression of a lady from behind but all business when viewed from front. A white ruffled blouse with a high collar lost all femininity thanks to the leather shoulder harness that sported two Colt revolvers, one under each arm. On her head she wore a brown bowler with little glass bottles affixed around the base near the rim and a peacock feather. Her pace was fast and deliberate. She was not going to let any silly man tell her what she could and could not do. No Sir, she never did and never would. Those that had tried in the past were quickly reduced to sniveling school boys drowning in a wake of destroyed egos. As she geared up with a whole mess of insults aimed for this so called "Doc" she stopped dead in her tracks.

Agatha Foggybottom and Doc Cooper just stood there and stared at each other. There was an awkward silence between the two the likes Finnegan had never seen. Neither spoke a word for what seemed like an eternity. He wondered if this were a good thing or a bad thing. 'Speak damn-it! What is going on here?' he thought to himself.

"This woman is fine to come with us. Ready your gear. We leave tomorrow morning at dawn" reported a shaken Doc Cooper. He cleared his throat and left the room, head held low as he looked at the floor.

Finnegan could hardly believe it. He looked over at Agatha and it felt as though his jaw was dragging the ground. She had a devious grin on her face and Finn wondered what exactly he had gotten them all in to. At this point though, he didn't care. Whatever the circumstances that led to this decision were, all he knew was that he had his job, his daughter, and they were off to Kansas tomorrow.

He could smell the money … and the diaper.

Chapter 6 – The stranger
Lawrence Kansas, January 1865

He was here again. This time he stood across the dusty street and watched them. He was careful to be inconspicuous but Finnegan knew without a doubt that he was watching them. Question was; who was he watching? Finn was fairly used to crooked lawmen and criminals scoping out their operation. It was a fairly frequent occurrence to have a shipment come under attack and consequently the men of the Gabriel Crew were well versed in spotting shady characters.

This man seemed different somehow. Finn couldn't help but fear that that stranger was actually watching Priscilla. Finn was quite capable of maintaining control and remaining calm through an ordeal. It was what kept you alive in tough spots. This however was pushing him to a rage. The mere thought of someone coming after his little girl pushed him to the brink of walking over there and shooting him without a warning.

Who was this stranger and what could he want with Priscilla? Finn's suspicions were obviously shared by

Declan who slowly leaned into closer range to his brother's ear shot.

"How's about ya circle around out da buildin' den back up so's we can find out what dis bloke is up ta?" suggested Declan.

Finn's gaze slowly shifted left to his brother. "Dat's a good idea little brudder. You stay here with Priscilla?"

"Sure ting. While ya be in der, how's about sending another shot o' whiskey dis way?" Declan said with a grin.

"Always da sly fox. Just keep yer eyes on me girl"

Finnegan got up and headed into the saloon. He quickly ducked through the kitchen motioning to the cook to keep quiet. As he exited through the back door he went about a block up the street so to stay clear of the stranger's view. He began to cross the busy street full of carriages, pedestrians and puddles. As he worked his way across Finn kept his eye on the target. He could still see the stranger sitting on the bench across the street from Declan and Priscilla. He seemed to be looking around nervously. Perhaps he noticed that Finnegan had been gone too long. Finn decided that he had better be quick so as not to lose the stranger and broke into a dead sprint towards the man.

His heart thundered in his chest as he got closer. He gritted his teeth with anticipation at the thought of questioning the stranger.

As Finn got within 20 feet the man turned to his left and with a wide eyed, terrified look, ducked into the storefront. Finn drew his sidearm and prepared for a fight. He heard commotion as Declan hopped the railing of the saloon and ran to his aid.

"NO, YOU STAY WITH PRISCILLA! I got dis!" shouted Finnegan. He did not want a chance of something happening to his girl while they were distracted. It was a common ploy to use a distraction to draw away the team so that a second or third person could get to the target.

Finn leapt the short stairs that ascended the front porch of the storefront. As he came to the door he was blinded by an intense blue light emanating from the storefront as he kicked the door in. The door flung open and crashed against the interior wall causing a good deal of broken glass. Finn was surprised to see the store empty and the stranger gone. He searched for a back door but none existed. He then looked for a trap door in the floor or an open window but again, none existed. The stranger had vanished into thin air without so much as a trace that he had ever been there. Finn wondered if he had gotten confused and perhaps the stranger had actually gone down the alley behind the building. After a close inspection of the storefront he apologized to Mrs. Joyner. She had actually closed for lunch fifteen minutes prior so she had missed the whole ordeal. She did not miss however, the opportunity to scold Finnegan and quickly presented a bill.

"Yes Mrs. Joyner, I'll take care of it right away."

Finnegan crossed the street. The stares of his fellow citizens had him guessing his sanity.

"Did ya see him enter the store? I must be loosin' me mind" expressed Finnegan with concern.

"He did enter, saw it plain as day. But where da hell did he go? All I saw was that strange flash of blue light." said Declan.

"Dis is odd, very odd." Finnegan had an uneasy feeling and decided that he would have to make sure that Priscilla was never to be left alone. He began to wonder where his obstinate, meat cleaver wielding, sidekick had gotten off to.

Chapter 7 – A dead man for sure...
Lawrence Kansas, January 1865

Declan sat on the porch. It was late at night and he was enjoying the peace and quiet. His glass had been recently topped off with his favorite bourbon and he had three more smokes that he had rolled earlier in the evening. 'This is nice' he thought to himself as the amber glow of the match illuminated his face. The glow of the match was soon replaced by the grey wisps of tobacco smoke as it swirled around his face and hat.

The pungent smoke slowly danced across the porch as the breezeless night offered little disruption. The glass of bourbon glowed and eerie golden hue in the moonlight.

Declan's attention was suddenly interrupted. He was unsure of the reason but he suddenly felt as if something was wrong. His eyes scanned the horizon but saw no evidence to support his concerns. It was as still as things got.

He tried to shrug it off; figuring that it must be God reminding him of the late hour. As he drew his pocket watch from his waist coat a brilliant flash of blue light startled him. His body jerked backwards causing the chair to thump on the side of the house. His feet shuffled slightly and the wooden boards below creaked as his weight shifted forwards as if a cat ready to pounce. The light appeared to come from the workshop. It was followed by a sound that resembled the crackle of lighting yet it was no storm threatening the night's calm. This was definitely odd and Declan slowly stood to investigate. As he stood, he crouched as if a cat ready to pounce on some unsuspecting prey. He inched towards the edge of the steps that descended downwards to the pathway leading to the workshop. The silence was deafening and Declan's pulse thundered in his chest. The anticipation of what he might find was charged by a mix of adrenaline and bourbon. This made for a dangerous combo for Declan and God help whomever he caught in the workshop this night.

The volatile warrior crept slowly to the first step when the front door behind him swung open violently and was proceeded by a deafening scream. The shock of it caused Declan to lose his footing and tumble down the four steps into the dirt. He clumsily drew his knife and with vengeful eyes searched for his assailant, ready to thrust the blade into their gut. Rather than a villainous assailant however, there stood Ms. Agatha Foggybottom preparing for an enthusiastic burst of laughter. She doubled over, her face bright red with that silent pause before the laughter is able to catch up to the body's actions.

Declan was furious and debated on throwing the knife despite the fact that it was Agatha. "Shut yer face ya stupid git" yelled the humiliated man. His warning went completely un-heeded as Agatha burst into laughter. It was so amusing to her that she actually flopped down into the chair causing a loud thump as the back slammed against the exterior wall of the house.

~laughing hysterically~ "Declan O'Sullivan, you are quite the fool. If you could have seen your face, you'd be laughing harder than I am right now!" taunted Agatha.

"Laugh it up ya git. One of dese days I'll repay ya ten-fold."

Declan arose from the dusty ground and began walking towards the house. He brushed off the dust and dirt that had gathered on his clothes as a result of the fall. His pride was hurt and he felt that he would have to teach this woman a lesson. Clutching his knife firmly in his hand, he debated his next few actions.

Agatha's laughter was disrupted suddenly, not by Declan's revenge but rather by the screams of Priscilla inside the house. Both Declan and Agatha sprung into action rushing into the house. Priscilla was not prone to nightmares like other children so for her to scream like that meant something was wrong. Declan was faster through the house and burst into her room. His vision was somewhat blurred as he scanned the darkened room.

"Over here Uncle Declan! I'm over here!" shouted Priscilla. Her voice cut the tension in the air and Declan rushed to her aid. She leapt from the bed into his arms, clearly distraught and terrified.

"What happened to ya little one?" he asked.

"There was a man in my room. He touched my head with something metal and hurt me" she whimpered.

"A man was in here? Which way did he go?" yelled Agatha.

Finnegan rushed into the room, clearly fresh from a deep sleep. He was somewhat confused and incoherent. "What's dis about?"

“Priscilla says der was a man in her room and he hurt her head” answered Declan.

“Daddy! I was so scared!”

As the family frantically searched the house for the intruder Declan announced his intentions to his niece’s assailant.

“Here little rabbit…..come out and play. Ya know when we find ya we’re gonna cut ya up and have ya fer breakfast.”

The tension in the house was suddenly interrupted by the flash of an intensely bright blue light and the same sound of crackling lightening outside.

“That’s the sound I heard before he came in the house!” Declan proclaimed.

They searched the better part of the night and even encompassed a one mile radius of the property but found nothing, not one single shred of evidence that he had been there. Finnegan could not help but think that this was the same man from town earlier that week. Being creepy on Main Street was one thing but breaking into his house meant something altogether different. This meant war and Finnegan was prepared to take it as far as he had to end this. This man was not going to live long; he just hoped that he could end it before anything happened to Priscilla.

More than a week had passed since the stranger had broken into their house. The group was very tense and on edge for a few days. Each day was spent searching for that peculiar face in the crowd of residents and each night was spent with an uneasy sleep, fully dressed, and fully prepared to kill that SOB. Eventually however, life returned to normal and the family carried on with life as if nothing had happened. Both of the brothers were certainly prepared and maintained a degree of protectiveness but they eventually allowed themselves to carry on with life.

Finnegan sat at the table and looked at his little girl. There she sat, doodling on a piece of paper with a charcoal pencil again. Her hands were black with soot and her tongue protruded from the side of her mouth. She had shoulder length cropped hair that had a beautiful red/ brown sheen. He remembered when she was little and all of the things that they had been through in her short life. She was fine featured and loved dressing like the proper ladies in town. Even though she was only ten years of age, she had an obsession with dressing far beyond her years.

Finnegan often felt as though he were sitting with a miniature woman. She loved to dress like the finer ladies of town with multiple layers of skirts, sometimes using as many as eight. She always looked beautiful and her spunky spirit shone as bright as the sun. He could tell that she was going to be a handful as she got older yet he rather looked forward to it. For now, she was still his little girl and she was intensely scribbling on her sheet of paper. She had been acting peculiar ever since the incident with the stranger. It was time for curiosity to get the better of him.

"What are ya working' on love?"

"Plasma storage and a generator design" answered the 10 year old, matter of fact like.

"What is dat?"

"It's the fourth state of matter silly. If I pass a spark through condensed gas, I can convert it into energy."

"Okay ... what can ya do wit it den?"

"Well, it's kinda like lighting. You could … light streets or houses or … even cut through steel. You could do lots of stuff really" answered Priscilla.

Finnegan watched as the words came from his

daughter's mouth but the whole conversation seemed a bit too surreal. It was as if someone else was talking through her.

Declan looked at the drawing and let slip a smirk and a chuckle. "Looks like a gun to me. Dats me little niece! Other girls be drawin' ponies an flowers while mine be drawin' guns. I luvs it I do."

"I just have to figure out how to control the storage, sustain the charge, and the discharge of excess energy. Then perhaps it could be a gun." answered Priscilla.

Both Declan and Finnegan looked at each other. Neither man was stupid but clearly this conversation had already taken a direction that was beyond their comprehension. Priscilla had started to do this lately, displaying a "matter of fact" way of intellect that should not come from a 10 year old. Finnegan's reaction was torn between extreme pride and that of concern. Perhaps it was more a curiosity than concern but ultimately, he did not know what to think of it all.

His daughter had always shown a significant amount of intelligence but nothing quite like this. This was a display of advanced scientific knowledge. He truly had no idea where all of this had come from.

"Like I said, looks like a gun to me." Declan repeated.

Perhaps he was onto something. Just because they didn't understand Priscilla didn't mean that there wasn't something of great value there. Times were tough. Sales of Colt's firearms were down as both the North and the South seemed to be out of money and credit was never a good thing if you couldn't collect. It was January 1865 and many people agreed that this war would be over soon. The reports were that the South kept losing and shifting forces here and there. While this was a great thing for the Union, Finnegan often wondered how his job security would hold out if the sales and production of Colt's firearms came to a halt. Technically speaking, as long as they moved with the westward expansion, they should be able to sell firearms to pioneers, law men, criminals, etc.

Both Finnegan and Declan had made a good deal of money but had also lost a good deal of it back in '63 during the sack of Lawrence Kansas. Finnegan massaged his temples as he recalled that stressful time two years ago.

Declan had warned him to keep their money in a

larger, safer city but he didn't listen. He didn't trust any bank as they were always getting robbed. He felt that if it were in a city other than where they lived, they couldn't be there to protect it. It turned out to be a bad decision. A decision that haunted him each time the subject came up.

It was no use worrying over though, the brothers did not quarrel about it and made due just fine. When Sam Colt died in '62 their 5% of sales commission went with him. They lost all leverage with the company as soon as that bastard Eli Root took over. It seemed that the old man would not let the past die, despite how many years had passed. Sales continued to do well so they made out fine enough, choosing to continue their banking down south in Fort Scott Kansas. There was a military garrison there and the President of the bank, Mr. Tuchscherer seemed an honest enough man.

Chapter 8 – the Free State Hotel
Lawrence Kansas, April 1856

There were many times over the past 10 years that Finnegan questioned the world's sanity and it became most apparent in April of '56.

Finn had intended to read a book and enjoy a smoke this night but his thoughts seemed to be fixed on that fateful month back in '56. It was such a rough patch in their family's history that the mere thought of it brought back such intense feelings of sorrow as well as equally intense feelings of affection and humor.

Business was booming but at what a cost.

The Gabriel Crew had been split between Fort Scott KS and Lawrence KS as Doc Cooper hoped to capitalize on the tension between Missouri and Kansas. It was a tough time then, often referred to by the papers as "Bleeding Kansas." It was bloody indeed. To be honest, they could not even keep pace with the orders for revolvers and rifles. Finn recalled the day in Lawrence when Sheriff Samuel Jones was shot. It was April 23rd, 1856. They had just finished up paperwork on a large sale to Federal Marshal J. B. Donaldson the day prior. After wiring the order back to Hartford CT, the Gabriel Crew set to celebrating.

The men decided to celebrate in their usual method, consisting of pints and whiskey. They strolled into the Blue Bonnet Tavern with an ominous gait and an aura of confidence. What started out as a tense atmosphere quickly changed to that of jubilation as Finnegan declared that he would be treating everyone to a round on him. The tavern erupted with the sounds of elated cheering drunkards.

Declan merely shook his head. He would never understand the need to buy others drinks. He was more comfortable with "convincing" others to pay for his own. Why would he stoop to buying them one? It seemed illogical and stupid to him. He would celebrate in his own manner and scanned the tavern for a pretty face. When he realized that there were none to be had; he decided he would be forced to drink one pretty.

"Barkeep; bring me a bottle o' Bourbon and the skinny girl in the corner" smirked Declan. He was going to celebrate his way and she would help. He just needed a little bit of those fine Kentucky optical enhancers.

As the night came to a close, the headaches intensified as if in tuned with the sunrise. Most of the crew had gone back to the hotel but Finnegan decided to walk the quiet streets. It was the only time he could appreciate the town of Lawrence. All of this "free state" and "pro slavery" non -sense drove him crazy. If it were not for the need of firearms to kill each other, he would have lost his mind. He often felt guilt arming the stupid but they always seemed to come up with the cash and therefore had a right to bear arms. He also had a right to eat so the endeavor seemed a tolerable one. Regardless of his personal opinion on a given subject, he generally found both sides to be filled with stupid people and therefore found it rather easy to be neutral.

The county sheriff, Sherriff Samuel Jones was a wretched man and the two did not see eye to eye. The Federal Agent Donaldson didn't seem to mind to whom they sold firearms, why should Sherriff Jones? He was always cussing the Gabriel Crew and it took everything Finnegan had to keep Declan from sticking him like a pig.

The serene tranquility of that morning was suddenly

disrupted by the sound of a gunshot. Finnegan instinctively squatted and scanned the streets looking toward the direction of the shot. He saw a group of settlers standing over a man lying on the ground.

Finnegan drew his sidearm and ran over to the crowd of citizens standing over the Sherriff. "What's goin' on here?"

"Sheriff was trying to arrest us simply because we're Free State settlers. When we said that were our position, he began to arrest us" replied a thin man in his 70's. "My names James Tolbert and I take full responsibility. Leave my family out of this."

"Grandpa!" a small child pleaded.

"Go on now; get to the Free State Hotel"

Finnegan noticed that during the commotion and discussion of who was to assume responsibility, Sheriff Jones scooted off behind the nearby building.

"I'll kill all ya'll son's a bitches! You too Finnegan O'Sullivan; and your pansy brother Declan!"

"Now you've gone and dun it." answered Finn. "A stupid threat like that is about the only thing that can wake me brudder up from a Bourbon slumber. I'd be surprised if he wasn't standin' behind yer back in two seconds ya fool."

Before Finnegan and Sheriff Jones could continue their conversation of colorful insults and threats, more citizens gathered and headed to the Sheriff. The hollering and commotion were so loud and so dusty that he barely noticed Sheriff Jones as he took off out of town. The crowd erupted in cheers and celebration and Finnegan marveled at just how naive these people were.

Finnegan knew better. Sheriff Jones had a propensity towards violence, one that equaled Declan but he also had a monstrous pride to boot. He knew it was only a matter of time before Jones would be back with help and they would have to be ready. It looked as though the town was going to need some more guns and the ones that Agent Donaldson ordered would have to get here a little quicker.

Finn went to the telegraph office and wrote out the following message for Hartford.

Urgent!

BREAK

Expedite order for federal marshal J.B. Donaldson.

BREAK

Deliver ASAP.

BREAK

More orders sure to follow.

BREAK

Jobber Finnegan; Gabriel Crew

The telegraph operator assured him that it would go out today but Finnegan insisted on waiting until it did. He was not about to miss out on a good sale and the publicity that agent Donaldson would give when he defended the city with Colt's firearms. After a short while the message was sent and Finn was on his way.

No sooner did he step out onto the porch when Doc Cooper rushed up to him.

"What in tarnation happened here? Heard the Sheriff got himself shot by a one eyed old lady."

"Sometin' like dat Doc" laughed Finn. "Just sent a wire to Mr. Colt asking fer him ta expedite yesterday's order and dat more are sure ta follow."

"Good thinking son, although I think that we may need to think about relocating the crew down south to Fort Scott. We can still conduct our business here but keep the crew down there." said Doc.

"Yer just worried about Agatha, aren't ya?" Finn jested. He was amused by the softer side of Doc.

"You leave her out of this. You've got a little one to think about and if we're not all careful, yer brother will up and kill all these fools. Either that or we'll all end up dead. Do ya want that for your little girl?" Doc chastised Finn and he was right, he was worried about Agatha. He was worried about them all. He could feel something bad was coming.

Federal Agent J.B. Donaldson was a peculiar man. Finn guessed him to be mid-50's. He was kind of jittery; most assumed that came with his profession. He had sandy brown hair that was always hanging in his eyes and a bushy mustache. He dressed much like a lawman, all in black but with a yellow ascot. He had not one, but two gold pocket watches which Finnegan thought was just plain arrogant. He carried a Walker Colt Model 1847 and a pocket model .31 cal in a holster on the side of his boot.

When you spoke to Donaldson, he spoke very fast and jittery. He appeared nervous, like he'd had too much coffee. He rarely made eye contact, usually scanning the area all around. It was somewhat exhausting to be honest but he seemed like an honest man and had been true to his word.

"Sure am obliged that you managed to get these revolvers here in such a short time. I have a bad feeling that we'll be needin' them soon. If the rumors are true, Sheriff Jones is gathering a large posse with the intent of causing trouble for the town" stated Donaldson. "I've wired Washington asking for help but I don't think that we'll be getting any soon."

"Don't worry Sir, this hotel is built to withstand anything. Those boys are in for a rude awakening if they come looking for trouble" one of the Agent's men stated. He seemed quite sure of himself. One thing that Finnegan had learned the short time he'd been here is that you can't put anything past these people. The Kansas territory wasn't the most hospitable, especially to those ill-prepared. Folks had to choose sides real quick, whether to be "Free state" types or "Slave state" types and both sides were equally intimidating.

"That may be true son but we'll be staying in the Governor's house. Governor Robinson was kind enough to let us borrow the place as our head quarters."

The crew of officers chuckled at the statement. Their confidence was soon to dissipate as word arrived that Sheriff Jones was on his way with a nearly 800 man armed posse, armed with Colt firearms no-less. Finnegan was now starting to get nervous and thinking about how best to protect Priscilla. Upon return to their rooms at the hotel, he demanded that Mrs. Agatha take little Priscilla to the Jefferson's farm about 20 miles west of Lawrence. Naturally she protested but agreed once she had the details. He reassured her that he had no doubt that she would be handy in a gun fight but nothing was more important than his little girl's safety.

Doc Cooper decided to send most of the crew with Mrs. Agatha and the girl as he did not want his men involved in someone else's quarrel. In fact, the only reason he stayed was to add a fast draw to Finnegan's defense.

"Doc, go wit da others. I intend to stay and hope to smooth tings over here. Everyone is simply being unreasonable and tanks to us, they are all armed to da gills. I can't have things here end badly" Finn stated.

"You shut up now. I am the Agent here and this is my operation. No one, not even Mrs. Agatha Foggybottom tells me what to do. If we can settle this peacefully, we can continue to sell guns to both sides. If not, you Sir are gonna need my help."

Doc was a smart man but Finnegan knew they were playing with fire. Finn just wanted to look Sheriff Jones in the eyes and let him know that he had nothing to do with the troubles. He didn't want anyone to think that he was running from the Sheriff's threats either. Even though he knew his pride would be the death of him, he knew that it wouldn't be now.

Declan was there, leaning against the wall chewing on a cigar. He looked like quite the gunslinger. Even though he was only 17 years old he was tough as nails.

"What about yer little brudder?"

"What, ya tink I'm gonna miss a good fight?"

Finn laughed out loud. He knew that his brother would always have his back and it was a reassuring feeling. He was also glad that Declan was on his side.

The crew settled in for a long night, not knowing when the next day would bring. All he knew for sure was that he had Doc Cooper and his Declan on his side. He felt quite confident that they would prevail.

Chapter 9 – A cannon?
Lawrence Kansas, April 1856

One thing that Finnegan loved most about America was breakfast. It had been a while since he had left Ireland but he still remembered Potato Farl. Back then, during the famine, food was scarce so to get a Potato Farl was a real treat. Now, he sat down to an enormous breakfast that would make any “fry up” back home pale in comparison. His love of the American breakfast was becoming evident and his brother Declan took every opportunity to tease his growing waistline. He didn’t care though, it was good and this day in particular might be his last.

“Care fer a shot of whiskey Mr. O’Sullivan?” asked the barkeep.

“Don’t mind if I do Joe, much obliged. Mother always said that a shot helped to settle a big meal like dis. Besides, may need it to calm me nerves. Today should be interestin.”

After breakfast, Finn went and took position in the Free State Hotel. Around 10 am, Sheriff Jones and his posse of nearly 800 arrived at the outskirts of town looking for a fight. Finnegan went to the top floor of the hotel to speak to Declan.

“Look o’er der, a large number of dem is by Mount Oread and it looks as if dey have a cannon.”

“A cannon?” Finnegan looked over at Bobby Smithers. “Go and fetch Doc Cooper, tell him what we seen here. Tell him ‘bout dat cannon. Den go over and tell Agent Donaldson, and be quick ‘bout it. ”

Guns were one thing but cannons were another thing altogether. No point in that unless you mean to destroy the whole town. The two brothers noticed that Sheriff Jones was entering the town with hundreds of his posse. It looked as though most routes out of the city were blocked by his men.

“Well little brudder, time to do some a dat smooth Irish talkin.”

“You talk, I’ll fight” smirked Declan.

“Let’s go see what der intentions are” Finn insisted.

By the time that Finnegan and Declan got to the front of the hotel, they noticed a few things. First, Agent Donaldson was nowhere to be found. It would seem that he and his troops had left the city with their tails tucked between their legs. This scenario was not good because if it did come down to a fight, Finn kind of wanted a few more numbers on his side.

The posse was led by Sheriff Jones. He carried a blood red flag with the saying "Southern-rights" on it. Next to him sat a toothless man holding the US flag.

Sheriff Jones had dispatched men to destroy the printing presses. Finn could see the men throwing equipment into the river and lighting the building on fire. The whole posse was heading towards the Free State Hotel. On the opposite side of Massachusetts Street Finn could see a cannon. A loud boom shook the earth causing the brothers to flinch as a large lead ball flew by the building, missing it entirely.

Finnegan, Declan and Doc Cooper rushed over to Sheriff Jones and initiated parlay.

"I'll give you credit you Mic Bastards, you got gumption. Tell me why I shouldn't just shoot you here in the streets?" asked Sheriff Jones.

"Sheriff Jones, I realize dat your here for revenge on the man that shot you. Surely there is a way to resolve this without innocent folks getting' hurt" pleaded Finnegan.

"It's more than that. Kansas is a Pro-slavery territory

and will enter the Union as such. I'll have no more printing presses spreading their "Free-state" filth nor will I allow that hotel to remain where it is. It is clearly a fortress for the abolitionists and it comes down today!"

The sheriff's men cheered and followed up with some rather threatening glares. They were clearly not here to debate. He could see that there would be no talking him out of it. Instead, he decided to negotiate surrender.

"Let me get da folks outta da hotel and to a safe place."

"You got five minutes boy!"

Finnegan ran into the hotel to herd the few remaining people out. It was not the optimal outcome but he would take it.

"Get moving people, they likely ain't smart enough ta tell time so get a move on!"

His commands were abruptly drowned out by a cannon ball crashing into the front of the hotel. He screamed at the people to hurry up and get out while Sheriff Jones continued to have his cannon fire on the building. It was a chaotic mess as men, women and children frantically rushed to get out. Thankfully, Sheriff Jones and his men did not shoot at the people fleeing for their lives. Finnegan watched from across the street with the others. The Sheriff's men seemed more interested in destroying that stupid hotel than anything else. He figured that it was just as well considering the alternative. All in all, they shot nearly 50 shots at the hotel but caused very little damage. After detonating two barrels of gun powder the hotel still remained standing, like a solitary fortress hanging on for dear life. Finally frustrated, Jones's men lit the hotel from the inside setting it ablaze.

Even at the site of the charred remains of what was once a symbol of freedom, they generally considered it a good day as only one person was actually hurt. Finnegan guessed it also meant that both sides were still alive and in need of weapons.

All in all, the posse destroyed the hotel, two printing presses and looted most of the homes. As soon as they were out of sight, Finn hopped on a horse and rode to check on Priscilla. One question remained though; where the hell did that coward, Federal Agent J.B. Donaldson get to?

Chapter 10 – Plasma for you, plasma for me
Lawrence Kansas, January 1865

Finnegan's thoughts drifted back to the present. His little girl sat there, still intently drawing on her pad of paper. His thoughts returned to their discussion on plasma and he began to ponder the technical description she gave. Unfortunately, it was as if she was talking underwater and he couldn't quite make out what she was saying.

"So plasma ya say? Could we really make a gun out of it?"

"Sure, but it would really, really hurt someone!" stated Priscilla.

Declan laughed. "Those make da best kinds kiddo."

"Perhaps we should try buildin' me little girl's invention. If it did work then we could be as rich as Sam Colt's widow."

"It looks simple enough to fabricate. Little one, what are those globes on the top ta be made of? Glass? It's tough to find a glassmaker these days." Declan thought, and as he did so, the door swung open and in burst Ms. Agatha Foggybottom.

"Wake up you lazy bums! Get off your duff's and help

me out." The outburst nearly stopped Finnegan's heart. Things quickly turned to laughter at what happened next.

Declan had been standing near the door to begin with. He was naturally kind of jumpy and had moved over to the side of the door as it opened. No sooner than she finished her second sentence, Declan had his knife drawn and moving for her neck. He had no intent on actually cutting her but he did wish to scare her.

In case you haven't been paying attention to this point, Ms. Agatha Foggybottom is no ordinary lady of 1865. No Sir! Perhaps she anticipated Declan's move or was simply quicker than he was. None-the-less, as his knife moved in position so did her notorious meat cleaver. As he moved in, she gestured towards, well, his Confederate region. The look on his face went from a grin to that of a child caught in the act of misbehaving. He did not expect to have a meat cleaver inches away from making his life a whole lot less … pleasurable. Ms. Foggybottom's facial expression turned even spryer as she looked her would-be-victim in the eyes.

"You Sir are too slow! Good news is that from what I hear, you don't have much to lose."

"Oh Dear God, you are sometin' else Ms. Foggybottom. Please do not cut me brudder. I'm gonna need him to help me wit Priscilla's newest idea. Seems we could be going into business for ourselves soon. If dis turns out like I suspect, we could be lookin' at a ton o' money."

The meat cleaver made its way back onto the back of Ms. Foggybottom's belt and her expression turned to one of pure pride.

"That's my little jelly sandwich! Smart as a whip this one, must be that good Gypsy blood. Lord knows she didn't get it from the likes of you two!" she proclaimed.

She had been caring for Priscilla since she was a little baby and generally regarded her as her own. She would have in fact taken her from these two goofball's years ago but she admired Finnegan's devotion to his daughter. He also paid her handsomely and equally as important; on time. This trait was not prevalent among men of this day and age.

She actually liked Declan too but it was so much fun to tease him. Declan never missed a chance to insult Agatha despite his general disdain for small talk. She imagined that this was what it was like to have a little brother, an annoying little brother. She also enjoyed the fact that she could get under his skin at will while everyone else was terrified of him. It made it easier for her to have her way around others. It was always the same thing, 'Don't mess with her, or you'll be wishin you'd picked a fight with Declan. Heard she can not only outshoot him but once beat him in a fist fight! That's why he doesn't talk too much, she won't let him!"

She loved how rumors became reality. They didn't have to have an ounce of truth, only be somewhat believable. Usually, the more extreme the rumor the more people wanted to believe it. What made it more amusing was when she herself created a good rumor only to hear it come back to her a few days later.

So far she was rumored to have been the one to sack Lawrence Kansas back in '56 and that she once derailed a locomotive simply because George Pullman owed her money. She was even rumored to have saved the Plymouth Congregational Church in '63.

This rumor was however true. It seemed like such a long time ago but alas it was not even two years passed.

Agatha got a little choked up as she recalled the events of that day.

As the story goes, when Quantrill and his men descended upon the city of Lawrence in '63, amidst the murder, looting and burning of the city, his men came upon a large group of citizens taking refuge in the church. They were unable to enter the church because on the door step stood Ms. Agatha Foggybottom. She stood there all alone with an Indian tomahawk in one hand and her giant meat cleaver in the other. She had both of her Colt revolvers on her shoulder harness but much preferred to wield the blades. It made a far greater impression to other would-be-attackers. Any man that dared to approach was quickly and soundly cut down in his tracks. William Quantrill himself came over and threatened to shoot her on the spot if she did not 'get the hell out of the way'.

Now, as the story goes, she spit in his face and then knocked out a tooth with a right hook. Then she cut off his big toe with that meat cleaver and spit on him again. This rumor was entertaining indeed but the truth of the matter is... oh wait, did I forgot to mention that this rumor is true?

Truth of the matter is that she knew William Quantrill personally and he wanted no part in a fight with Ms. Agatha. He likely imagined just what she might do to him and indubitably knew where that meat cleaver would end up. At best, he could only hope for it to be lodged in his skull but the truth was, it was more likely to have been lodged somewhere less pleasant. Either way, the story goes on to state that William Quantrill ordered his men to leave the church alone and continue on with the rest of the city.

Agatha grinned. She had bested many a man in her day, usually with her reputation alone. As she looked at Declan she was brought back to that day in front of the church. She could see him now, all bound up like a calf laying in the corner of that church cursing her six ways to Sunday. She had saved his life for sure and he knew that but it angered him none the less. He and his brother, along with Priscilla managed to escape that horrible day with their lives when so many others did not. Her gaze traced the large scar under his right eye. That, well, that is another story.

"You alright Ms. Foggybottom?" asked Finnegan.

"Yeah, I am fine. Just remembering' how I saved your ass in '63."

"Indeed you did. I dare say there'd have been 202 victims instead of 200 that day." There was a sudden silence as the group thought of the fallen friends that day.

"We all miss Doc luv; all of us."

Declan decided to break the tension with a bit of humor. "Don't feed her ego brudder. She's likely to make up a story about how she saved the Pope's life during her many trips to Italy!"

"You've been to Italy Ms. Agatha?" asked Priscilla.

"You betcha kiddo, go every year for Christmas!"

The room erupted into laughter as they no doubt would hear all about it next week from Mr. Peebly the grocer. Ah how the town would talk and they wondered what embellishments would be added.

Declan headed out to the porch with full intention of sitting down and enjoying a glass or two (or three) of bourbon and a good smoke.

"Don't forget to…"

"Yeah, yeah, yeah, yap yap yap!" retorted Declan. He had no intention of doing anything for Agatha, or anyone else for that matter. He had a date with some bourbon and that was that.

Agatha smiled, well, smirked actually, and sat down next to her little 'jelly sandwich'.

"What's this little one?"

"It's a plasma generator. I think 'Eve' is appropriate."

"A what? Eve?"

"Plasma is an ionized gas; a gas into which sufficient energy is provided to free electrons from atoms or molecules and to allow both species; ions and electrons, to coexist. Plasmas are the most common state of matter in the universe actually. They are very common. Plasma is a gas that has been energized to the point that some of the electrons break free from, but travel with, their nucleus. Gases can become plasmas in several ways, but all include pumping the gas with energy. A spark in a gas will create plasma. A hot gas passing through a big spark will turn the gas stream into plasma that can be useful. We could make a plasma torch for example to cut metals. Or, we can use this generator to produce plasma and then discharge it kind of like lightning. Daddy thinks that he can make a gun from it but I think that is just plain mean."

Finnegan and Agatha looked at each other, and then back at the little ten year old that sat before them. She had already gone back to doodling on her pad of paper. Declan poked his head back in from the porch and looked at both of them.

“What da hell did she just say?”

“More talk about dis plasma business” replied Finnegan.

“Don’t worry about the why Daddy, just make it like I draw it and you’ll have your gun. When you are rich, can I have a pony?”

Declan burst into laughter. “You damn sure can kiddo, if he doesn’t buy one fer ya, I will.”

“Uncle Declan, you are not nice to say swear words. Ms. Agatha’s gonna wash your mouth out with soap. Ms. Agatha, tell him!”

Agatha grinned at Declan.

“Sorry ‘bout dat little one.” Declan stated. His eagerness to please her invoked curiosity in the ten year old. She was starting to realize that they really, really wanted her idea. Perhaps she could use this to her advantage.

"Daddy, I have a proposal. I'll make you a deal. I'll design your gun but you have to do something for me."

"You can have a pony, you don't need to bribe me luv."

"Na, it's not that Daddy, I want you to eat like me, like a vegetarian."

Finnegan stopped in mid thought, 'vegetarian' seemed like cruel and unusual punishment. He tolerated his daughter's desire to not eat meat but now at the mere thought of it, he began to get nauseous. He was very partial to a good rare steak, or large chunk of smoked bacon or a fried pork chop. As he began to drool at the thought of all the meat products that he would be expected to give up, he was interrupted by Declan.

"Yeah Daddy, no more meat!" Declan teased.

"You too Uncle Declan! The deal is for both of you."

"F.." he began but was quickly interrupted by Agatha.

"Sounds like a fair deal to me, as long as I'll be sharing in on this wealth too" Agatha stated. "You two could stand to eat better and my bean stews are quite delicious as well as good for you."

"I feel a fart coming on just tinkin 'bout yer bean

stews" Declan teased.

"Alright, let me tink on this one. Isn't there some other deal you'd like to make?"

He felt as though he was starving already, just at the thought of it. He knew that this could be the big break that they all needed and that they could change weaponry forever. In fact, this could be the beginning of a whole new era of weaponry. He just did not want to give up eating meat. It was just … unnatural, cruel even! He debated on giving her his own ultimatum, one that involved a good spanking.

"You have your terms Sir. I shall await your answer and we shall speak of it tomorrow in detail. Good night Father, good night Uncle, good night Ms. Agatha" proclaimed Priscilla.

The young lady held her head high as she left the room. Her posture straightened and for the first time, her father could see a young woman as she walked away. She triumphantly left the room and went to bed. Finnegan wasn't sure but he thought he saw a small smirk on her face as she left.

In one way, he was tremendously proud. In another

way, he was painfully hungry.

Chapter 11 – I am starving!
Lawrence Kansas, February 1865

Ms. Agatha Foggybottom loved her job. She had been with the O'Sullivans for more than a decade now and one thing was certain, life was never boring.

She peaked around the corner and watched a dodgy Declan O'Sullivan sneak off to the Blue Bonnet Tavern. She knew that he was looking for something to eat and it would certainly be a plate full of meat. Priscilla's new rule was the best thing ever. She had attempted to torture her employers in numerous ways: practical jokes, ground chili peppers in the food, greasing the outhouse seat. This rule however, was proving to be her favorite as it provided her a constant supply of entertainment. Both Declan and Finnegan were becoming desperate and sneakier by the day. Priscilla had asked her to keep an eye on them and she took this task with abject pleasure.

Declan slipped into the tavern and she followed moments behind him. As she entered, she kept to the walls of the dimly lit room. The grey wood planked walls seemed to suck the color right out of the room. Light shone in from the high narrow windows casting beams of light acting as spotlights. One such spotlight shone on the back of Declan. In his ravenous state, he never noticed Agatha lurking in the shadows like a lioness ready to pounce. He shook and nervously looked around much the way old men do who've gone without a drink for some time. As he ordered a large portion of bacon and gravy smothered pork chops with fried potatoes, Agatha waited patiently. She wanted to wait for the food to arrive, wishing to catch him at the height of his anticipation.

Declan watched the waiter bring the steaming plate of food from the kitchen. The bacon seemed to glow a heavenly red and stood out amongst all the dreary grey of the room. The smell of it caused him to sit on the edge of his seat with anticipation. However, just as he was about to stuff his mouth with a fork full of bacon, a voice boomed out louder than any firearm he'd ever shot.

"Don't you dare Declan O'Sullivan. You made a deal and I am here to make sure you keep it!" blurted out a grinning Agatha.

Declan's head sunk down low and he looked as though someone had shot his favorite dog. As he turned his head towards her, other diners cleared a path. It was as if they anticipated guns a blazing and bullets a flying. Some went left, others went right. The only real problem was no one knew just which way to go as both were equally dangerous.

"Why don't ya mind yer business WOMAN!!!"

You could see the desperation in his face and it was almost enough for Agatha to leave him be … almost. Declan knew this new plasma design was truly a modern marvel and he acquiesced. He quietly pushed the plate away from him and walked out of the Blue Bonnet Tavern in humbled silence.

The dull thud of his footsteps echoed as he approached the door. He slowly leaned forward and opened the door with a dreadfully slow manner. Once opened, an incoming patron tipped his hat greeting Declan with a cheerful 'How are you today Sir?'

Declan reached back, almost comically so, and punched the poor fellow square between the eyes. The man fell to the wooden planked porch with a crashing thud. His cane stood, as if balancing on its own. The man's top hat slowly rolled down the stairs almost bouncing on its journey. All the patrons inside the tavern, to include Ms. Foggybottom, cringed. She may have even felt a tad guilty.

"SHITE; me day is complete SHITE ya twit!" Declan looked around and then walked off out of sight, fists clenched in a rage. Agatha thought it best to leave him be and tend to the bewildered man who was starting to slowly come to.

"Wha….wha..what happened? Owwwww, dear God in Heaven, why does my head hurt so?" question the bewildered man.

"You walked into the door you klutz! You should be more careful next time." Agatha stifled a laugh over her bold-faced lie.

"Hmmm, guess you are right. Ohhhh … my knees are a bit wobbly."

Agatha helped him to a table and brought him Declan's plate of food.

"Oh, did I already order? Was it quick or have I been waiting long? I can't seem to remember." he was still clearly dazed and confused.

"Just eat your food deary and watch out where you're

walking next time." Agatha tried to console him and hoped that the food would provide a bit of distraction for his unfortunate mishap.

Agatha then left for home. While it was only a short distance to walk, it seemed like an eternity as she dreaded the potential conflict between Declan and herself. Hopefully he would not be too upset with her for while she genuinely enjoyed making him suffer, she did not wish to push her luck.

Chapter 12 – The Senator
Lexington Kentucky, January 1865

Gideon Tinkersmith was your average 10 year old boy, well, for the most part at least. He was very smart and creative, often times choosing to tinker in his father's workshop instead of playing with the other children his age. While he constructed all sorts of inventions they were usually little more than simple wooden toys.

Gideon's father, Senator Flavious Tinkersmith, simply did not understand the boy. He thought that he was weak and wished that he would be out with the other boys. He was worried that his only son would continue down this path towards becoming a pansy of a man.

Life was hard and the world needed strong leaders. He had intended on leaving a legacy for his son but instead he feared it would all be for nothing. Gideon would need to be strong and prepared to handle the family business, and things were not looking good at this point. The South would not win the war and everything he and the others of the Confederacy had struggled for now seemed lost. He worried how they would survive. Thankfully the family cattle business was fairly stable and still generating a modest income.

He looked through the doorway at his son, sitting at a workbench scribbling on a piece of paper.

"What are you doing boy?"

"I had an idea Father. I think that we can use it to make the cows bigger."

"Why would we want to do that?"

"If they are bigger, then there would be more meat to sell, right?"

"True, but you can't make them bigger unless they grow bigger."

"Plasma energy. By using plasma energy, I think I can stimulate proteins to create a peptide hormone. It should stimulate growth in the animal resulting in a significantly larger size and a more rapid and dramatic growth."

The Senator looked at his son with an all too familiar feeling of disgust. He honestly did not believe that his son was capable of creating larger cows and debated on whipping him right then and there for wasting his time. There were far too many other constructive things that he could be doing at this moment than sitting there scribbling on a piece of parchment talking like a little madman.

"Gideon, I can't begin to tell you how disappointed I am. Why, you are sitting here wasting time with silly notions that aren't even possible. You should be out doing your chores or something productive!"

"But Pa…, Father, this will work, I know it will! Trust me!"

"Like all the other little wooden toys here? They work dandy, don't they?"

"That's different Father, this is the real thing."

"I suppose that you'll be in need of supplies and equipment, correct?" The Senator was condescending at this point. He had no patience for his son's nonsense.

"Father, I will need things, yes. But think about it, if we could increase our product by as much as 100% then our profit will be proportionally equal. We may even be able to make a version that works on vegetables. We could end world hunger!"

"I don't care about world hunger. I care about our family's survival and prosperity."

"Our prosperity will benefit from this, I swear!"

As he resisted the temptation to begin yelling he

considered Doc Young. Doc Young was a veterinarian in his employment. He had hired Dr. Young when he fled the North at the outbreak of the war. He recalled the Doctor's primary interest was in biology, or, something of the sort.

"I'll have Doc Young come talk to you about this, to see if there is anything of substance here."

"That would be great Father. So … you aren't mad at me?"

"Depends on what Doc Young says. If what you say is true, then we stand to make a handsome profit. If the South falls, and it looks like it will, we will at least have some leverage towards our family's survival."

The Senator left without as much as a goodbye. Gideon was not surprised; his father was not the type of man to show emotions. Well, not an emotion that was positive at least. His anger was legendary so Gideon continued to work. He was not going to let this deter him.

The Senator was tired and had resolved to sit in his office and enjoy a bit of peace and quiet. He had planned on reading some more of his book and on enjoying a good pipe. He packed his pipe and slowly looked up as his sanctuary was disrupted by a frantic Doc Young. The

Senator could feel his blood pressure rise and the massive vein on his forehead protrude as his face reddened with anger.

"Dear God Senator, your son is a genius!"

"What are you going on about you old loon?"

"Plasma Sir, plasma! Gideon is truly on to something here. It … it appears the possibilities are endless!" Doc was frantic and as giddy as a young girl.

"You think the boy is on to something? Do you think that you can make it work?"

"Absolutely, I believe that we can have some results in as little as two weeks."

The Senator was stunned. He thought that Doc Young would tell him that Gideon was a stupid boy and wasting more of his precious time. He thought for sure that this was another one of his childish inventions. He now began to allow himself to feel a little pride for the bugger. Perhaps Gideon would amount to something after all.

He decided that he would humor the boy and take a gamble that it might pay off.

He instructed Doc Young to begin and to his handyman to start stocking the workshop with whatever young Gideon needed. He could now smell the money and he could see the time dwindling away. He had just been presented an opportunity and he would capitalize on it.

Chapter 13 – "Bloody Bill"
Lawrence Kansas, February 1865

Declan sat on the porch gazing into the night's sky. He often sat there enjoying a smoke and a glass of fine bourbon. Well, occasionally it was fine, more often than not it was mediocre. Regardless, it was strong and did the trick. He'd rock his chair back and forth listening to the soft thud of the back of the chair as it hit the house. He would get a chuckle as he guessed just how many thuds it would take for his neurotic older brother to come out and demand that he stop. Ten he thought, no, tonight it will be eighteen. Finnegan was exceptionally excited as construction of the first plasma gun was nearly complete. They'd be testing it out by the end of the week.

Thud - eleven, thud - twelve, thud – thirteen, thud – fourteen, thud – fifteen, thud – sixtee…

The porch door swung open. "Would ya stop it already?!?! Christ almighty, you're drivin' me mad out der with yer constant thumping." Finnegan looked less uptight as he usually did. He must be getting closer to finishing that gun, Declan thought.

"Sorry, didn't realize I was doin' it." Declan grinned and chuckled quietly to himself. His brother was so predictable. He loved the big lug but boy was he neurotic.

Declan looked back out into the night sky and gazed at the stars that littered the heavens. He often pondered it all and if there was some other guy like him looking back in this direction.

Immersed in thought, his tranquility was disturbed by an insect as it landed on his face. As he wiped it away, he stopped to run his finger down the shiny scar below his right eye. It was a painful scar, not physically but rather the memories it invoked. It was however a manly scar; one that he felt made him look tougher. He liked how it added more mystery to his persona. As he traced its shiny red surface, he thought of the man that gave it to him. He remembered that day as if it were yesterday. That day nearly two years ago when so many people died. The day that irritating woman, Agatha Foggybottom saved his life.

Lawrence Kansas, August 1863

It was Friday, August 21st of 1863. The day started out like so many before and so many afterwards in Lawrence Kansas. It was hot and dry and he didn't want to be there. He could smell breakfast cooking over at the Blue Bonnet Tavern. The smell of bacon and fried potatoes lingered in the air and seemed to travel about as if an apparition of temptation determined to torture him. It was occasionally interrupted by the sweet scent of maple syrup, pancakes and coffee. Everything seemed to be more intense this morning, except Declan's impatience. He was relaxed, optimistic even.

Priscilla was with Agatha and they were headed to go the church to discuss something with the preacher. He seemed to remember her joking about praying for forgiveness for him or something silly like that.

Finnegan would be down in Fort Scott today and tomorrow negotiating a deal with the US Army garrison there. He had taken most of the jobbers with him however Doc stayed back. Declan thought that was odd but Doc had been talking a lot lately of retiring and opening a shoe store of all things.

As he headed over to the Blue Bonnet he gazed over at the Plymouth Congregational Church. In the doorway his vision focused in on Agatha. She was pointing at him and waving frantically. Declan squinted his eyes focusing on the frantic woman's gestures. A sick feeling came over him as he realized that she was pointing to something behind him. He whirled around expecting the worst.

Declan, and the whole town for that matter, were caught completely by surprise that morning when nearly 500 revenge-crazed men descended upon Lawrence Kansas. They rode hard and fast and were shooting every male citizen they came across. There was no warning, no provocation, no threats; just cold blooded murder. Every male citizen was a target, even little boys. The men were taking people from their homes and simply shooting them in the streets.

Declan needed to get to the women. He could not protect them from here but it was a good stretch to get to the church. Declan chose to head to the left side of the street and take cover in the bank. Bullets whizzed through the air in what seemed like a swarm of bees. It was a miracle that he was not hit. As he burst through the front door of the bank his mind thought of two things: the girls in the church and their money here in the bank. He wondered if he could make it safely to the church. There were just so many men in the street and they were shooting everyone in sight. Bodies had already begun to litter the roads and small rivers of blood began to pool and clot on the dusty roads.

As Declan pondered his options the front window of the bank shattered from the impact of a bullet. Large glass shards fell to the floor as residents in the bank screamed in fear. Declan only had his one sidearm on him, he was not prepared for this at all. He counted his ammunition and realized that he may have to go out big as he only had about 30 rounds. They were lining his belt plus the six in his revolver. The way he figured it, he'd take out as many as he could and then get to work with his knife. That bear jaw grip and steel blade had proven to be quite useful over the years. Now it would have to do more than just scare people. He looked through the broken glass just to see swarms of lawless men in a hellish chaos of murder.

Declan was startled by a group of men that began to kick the front door of the bank. It was a heavy oak door that normally had iron bars providing additional protection. In his haste to enter the bank, Declan had forgotten to close it so all that stood between a good fight and he was that door. Even though the windows were broken they still had their iron bars. This was keeping the marauders from entering. Declan saw an arm stick through the window with a revolver and it began to fire blindly into the crown of huddled and terrified people.

Declan grabbed his knife and as he 'dis-armed' the man he yelled through the window: "Tanks for the gun jack-ass!" At least he now had two revolvers. He looked down at the twisted hand, its fingers bloody and gnarled in pain, its owner screaming in agony on the other side of the wall. Despite his predicament he was forced to chuckle. The irony of it amused him. 'I should have said tanks fer da hand', he thought.

'Now where the hell is Doc', Declan thought to himself. It was about to get real hairy in there and he could use Doc's speed and skills. The door looked as though it would splinter apart at any moment. As the men outside screamed and yelled with a renewed vigor, one in particular screamed louder than the others. Declan found this amusing and scoffed as he threw the dismembered hand out the window.

"I thought you might be in need of a hand but it looks like you got that covered!" Doc joked as he approached Declan near the door. He hurried towards Declan from the rear of the bank.

The two laughed out loud with a hearty, deep bellied laugh. They got to their feet and stood left and right of the doorway. When it gave way, it seemed to fly forward as if they'd used dynamite. The two remained patient as they waited for the men to enter before letting loose with their coveted Colt revolvers. They did not want to waste bullets so each round had to count.

As Declan fired his last round he looked over at Doc. He too was out. They both unsheathed their knives and prepared for what Declan liked to call 'a Stitch and Bitch'. He called it this because by the time he was finished with these boys, they'd have to stitch them all back together in order to bury them. If only Finnegan was here. He had no intention of dying today however if one of these guys got lucky, he at least wanted to have his brother around. It was likely for the better though as he knew his brother well and Finnegan would not stand by and let innocent people get hurt. He probably would have been one of the first to die. Declan pictured him standing in the middle of the road to challenge their head man.

Through the smoke and mound of bodies, a man strolled in taking long strides to step over the dead. He looked to be in his mid twenties but his eyes suggested he'd lived a long, hard and violent life. He had a mangy beard and shoulder length wavy hair. His eyes were intensely blue and he stared at Doc and Declan like a hungry wolf.

"My names William T. Anderson but my friends call me Bloody Bill. You two are gonna need a priest 'cause I's about to send you to yer maker" the arrogant man boasted. He scanned over the two and stopped at Declan.

"YOU! Yer that son of a bitch I told to stay away from Josephine!"

"Shit." Declan knew exactly what he was talking about. Josephine was Bill's little sister. She was very cute but only 14. That was an acceptable age for some but Declan thought the girl a bit too stupid and timid for his tastes. He preferred a stronger woman, one with gumption and spunk. In fact, he had only really spoken to the girl a few times as they passed through. It wasn't long after that that Josephine and the others were arrested by General Ewing for giving aid to Quantrill's raiders.

It was a shame how they died. It must have been horrible as the third floor of their makeshift prison collapsed. He could understand how Bill and the others would be outraged however all of what happened in Kansas City. It did not happen here and Declan certainly had nothing to do with it.

"I did as you asked and I had nothing to do with her arrest or death. You should be going after General Ewing." As Declan stated this, he felt surprisingly calm.

"Yer Jayhawker trash and you'll die like all the men of this town. Fer my sister Josephine, fer Charity McCorkle Kerr, fer Susan Crawford Vandever, fer Armenia Crawford Selvey, and most importantly … fer Osceola"

Declan turned his knife in his hand so that the blade pointed down instead of up. It ran the length of his right arm and he prepared. He planned to fake with his left arm to distract Bill while his right hand could then follow up with a slashing blow to the throat. Seemed like a good enough plan. At least he'd take out this lunatic. He had definitely earned the nickname 'Bloody Bill' and had shot more than a few unarmed men in his day, most of whom in the back.

Bloody Bill must have expected the attack so when it came he brought his own knife straight up like an uppercut. He almost got his target. Luckily it only grazed Declan up the right side of his face leaving a huge gash from the cheek up to the eye. Blood poured everywhere and pain radiated throughout Declan's body.

As Doc rushed forward to Declan's aid, he caught a bullet in the chest from Bloody Bill. Declan was on his knees somewhat dazed by the blow and his vision was completely blurred by the blood. He heard the gun shot followed by the thud of Doc hitting the floor. Doc never once yelled or cried out in pain, he merely gave out one last insult and a request prior to departing this world.

"Your day is coming Bill. Pray that God help you 'cause the Devil's surely waiting."

Doc placed his hand on Declan's arm. "Tell Agatha that I am sorry. I am sure it would have been a beautiful wedding and I'd have done my best to make her happy."

Wedding? Declan was surprised, he knew that Doc was sweet on her but had no idea they intended to marry. 'Oh God, the girls are in the church!' He didn't have time to spend one more thought as Bill's second round pierced his shoulder. As Declan dropped face first onto the floor he cursed Bill Anderson and he cursed this town. Lawrence Kansas had been his least favorite town and now it looked as though he'd be stuck here forever.

Bill instructed his men to loot the bank. They shot every man in there and told the women to get out as they were going to burn the building to the ground.

As the men left, the smoke filled the lobby of the bank and the flames in the back climbed the ceiling. Declan's eyes opened and he coughed. He gathered himself and slowly got to his feet. As he stepped out of the burning bank, he grabbed his knife and he put Doc's lifeless body over his shoulder. The pain shot down his back thanks to the bullet wound but he did not care. He would not leave Doc here. As he walked out into the street and headed across the street to the church he hoped for a miracle. The streets were filled with chaos and Declan's vision was blurred. Thick clouds of smoke filled the air. The smell of gun powder and the taste of blood in his mouth made him cough. Quantrill's men were shooting the male citizens as the women folk pleaded and begged for their lives. Young children ran in terror and the raiders shot with reckless abandon. Declan continued to walk, each step felt as though someone was stabbing him in the chest but he had to get to the girls. He had to protect them. He'd rather die than let something happen to Priscilla.

The smoke and chaos acted as cover for Declan and he finally got to the church. Agatha screamed as she opened the front door to let them in.

"Doc! NO!"

It only took Agatha a moment and then she regained her composure. She looked at one of the women helping Declan.

"Get them over to that pew and hog tie Declan. You heard me; hog tie him and then see to his wounds. Put Doc over by the altar. Priscilla, sit with your uncle and keep him calm. DO IT NOW!"

Agatha did not intend on letting Declan get into any more trouble. She figured that he was too stubborn to die. She was going to protect this church and the refugees hiding inside, especially Priscilla. She'd die before she let anything happen to that little girl. Hers or not; that little girl was everything to her.

Shortly before heading outside, she tended to Declan's wound and reassured him that this was necessary. Naturally he cussed her. Agatha could see the look in his eyes; he really didn't want to die in this town. She then took a long look at Doc and used the tragic image of her love as her inspiration. She loved that man and now he was gone too. "Some fool is gonna be pork chops in a minute!"

Ms. Agatha Foggybottom walked towards the front door of the church. The light shone through the windows which were thankfully high. The light illuminated the smoke that thinly filled the room. She could hear the chaos outside and prepared to face it. As she stepped out of the front door it was almost quiet. She could hear the locks behind her and the heavy beam slide into place. This was it; she was not getting back in there easily nor was she going to let anyone else in. She clutched her tomahawk in her left hand and her trusty meat cleaver in her right. She had pistols but would save that for when she had no other choice. She was going to kill someone and it was going to be painful, not quick like a bullet. No Sir, she wanted to hear these boys scream. Somebody was going to pay God damn it and she wanted it to hurt.

One such fool stepped forward as the crowd of raiders approached the church. Agatha feinted with the tomahawk and then lodged the meat cleaver deep into the side of the man's neck. He screamed alright, so loud and high pitched that one of his fellow men shot him just to shut him up. William Quantrill stepped through the crowd and ordered her to step aside or he'd shoot her on the spot.

"I got my little girl in there and ain't no one gonna lay a finger on her or any of these women held up here. You want to destroy this town go ahead, just leave the church and women or you got to go through me first!"

Quantrill knew Agatha and he could see in her eyes that she was not about to back down. Agatha was a good woman and had even delivered two of his children. He knew the piss and vinegar this woman possessed and he did not have the heart to shoot her.

"I don't know about you boys but this one seems like she can take all of us out. Why just look at old Jimmy here, nearly cut his head clean off! You gotta admire that kinda spit in a woman. Leave the church but burn everything else. Do not harm the women folk. Our quarrel is with their cowardly men, not them. These Jayhawkers won't be making any raids into Missouri any time soon; unless they send her of course."

"I want the man that shot Doc Cooper! NOW!" screamed Agatha. Tears began to well up in her eyes. Her cheeks were flustered and red and her heart ached for vengeance.

"Now Agatha, that would be Bloody Bill and I am quite sure that you don't want to go down that road." Quantrill's voice was calm and soothing, he even sounded concerned for her.

"Bill will get his day, mark my words. That bastard will beg me to kill him before I am done!"

"That may be darlin' but it ain't gonna happen today. Go on, git back in that church and tend to yer women folk."

As the crowd of men continued on, William Quantrill gave one last glance to Ms. Agatha. He tipped his hat and walked away. She stood there for nearly an hour as the massacre continued. She had an unobstructed view of the horrors that unfolded that day. When all was said and done, 200 male residents were murdered and many of the women had been raped. No one wanted to admit that of course but the truth was there and she had to witness most of it.

"Damn fools, every one of dem!" cursed Declan as he looked back at the stars. His vision slowly came back into focus as his thoughts returned to this quiet starry night. That day in Lawrence Kansas was one that he'd never forget, a horror deeply seared into his soul. She had saved him alright and he didn't even mind that she teased and reminded him of it frequently. She had earned it. He had only lost a bit of his pride while she had lost so much more.

Chapter 14 – When cows go wild
Lexington Kentucky, February 1865

Senator Flavious Tinkersmith never had much faith in his son. This however changed after his conversation with Doc Young. As he sat, making an honest attempt to enjoy his breakfast, he was interrupted by the normally quiet man.

"Senator, Senator! This is truly amazing! We've managed to build the machine your son described and it works! It actually works!"

"Slow down Doctor."

"It generates a light and then small amounts of lighting shoot out. Gideon focused it on his little jar and in no time, the cells actually increased in mass! We had to borrow an old Jackson Lister from the university to see it but it actually showed the cells growing! I've never seen anything like this. Your son's invention may actually be the scientific breakthrough of the century!"

The Doctor was almost frantic. "It WILL be the scientific breakthrough of the century!"

"You already said that Doctor. Do try and maintain your composure. When do we test it on the cattle? Never mind, that wasn't a question. You'll begin testing immediately. I want only one tested, can't be damaging the herd."

"I'd like to take one of the cows and seclude it from the others. We can begin administering the hormone today" answered Doc.

The Senator began to actually get a little excited. Who would have thought that his son had it in him? He was his son after all and therefore had to be good for something. He gave instructions that he be notified before they began.

Shortly before lunch, Doc Young was ready. He stood there, wide eyed and almost giddy as a school girl. Senator Flavious was still a bit skeptical yet hoped for the best. Doc Young had a large syringe that looked as though it contained syrup-like fluid. After looking at the Senator for approval, he injected the cow with the growth hormone. They all leaned forward as if expecting some dramatic, immediate change. Naturally nothing happened, nothing at all.

"Father, we will have to administer these shots twice a day and may see results within the next couple of months" stated young Gideon.

"Months!?!"

"Yes Sir. It will take time for the cow to show results, maybe even a year."

This was not the news that the Senator wanted to hear. It was now February of '65 and the end of the Confederacy was very close. He knew that he would not be able to rely on his political influence once that chapter closed and he needed something to sustain his family. His cattle industry was all he had to rely on. This was their future.

"Double the dose and frequency and get me results sooner than that!"

Gideon and Doc Young agreed to do so even though they suspected it to be a bad idea. None the less, they had orders and orders were one thing that you did not disobey when dealing with Senator Flavious Tinkersmith.

Several days went by and they noticed no size difference in the cow. They did however notice that the cow displayed increasingly aggressive behavior starting the fourth week. It seemed to be going insane. Doc Young desperately wanted to believe that there was a rational explanation but he knew that something else was happening here; something terribly wrong.

By the end of the fourth week though, the cow was out of control. It rammed the fence and charged at anything in sight. Its eyes were completely red and it made the most God-awful sounds. It bit at the fence and tried to kick its way out of the enclosure. By the end of the day Doc felt it best to shoot the cow before it got out of control. The Senator agreed and promptly notified Doc that this was coming out of his salary.

Gideon inspected the cow's flesh and brain under the Lister microscope. Even though the cow was dead, the cells were still active and incredibly aggressive towards the others. It seemed as though the proteins were going through some sort of change and corrupting other, similar proteins. He noted that the cow's brain had deteriorated into a sponge-like matter in many areas. Clearly the growth hormone did not work as intended and had caused a different reaction altogether.

When he showed Doc his findings Gideon became alarmed. Doc seemed to be forming his own ideas and plans with this new information. He stated several times that this could really help the South, but how? As Doc left the workshop and headed for the main house, Gideon developed a sick feeling in his stomach. He began to wonder what he had created and what Doc Young intended on releasing into the world.

"Senator, I think that we may have something altogether different here. I'd like to run some more tests. I will require another cow … and a human subject."

Senator Tinkersmith did not like the idea of losing another cow but he had a human subject in mind. "What will happen to the human?"

"It is likely that he will end up much like the cow. If that is the case then we will have succeeded."

"What are you going on about Doc?"

"It took nearly four weeks before the cow showed alarming symptoms. I think that given that time, we can have it transported via railway to locations in the North. They will likely be slaughtered before the symptoms become evident. If my suspicion is right then whoever eats the meat will suffer a similar affliction. We could cripple, maybe even destroy the North altogether with this, this disease."

"Only one problem you fool, the North doesn't buy

beef from me."

"Not yet but when the war is over they will need to re-establish trade and the nation's economy. That is when we can strike."

This idea seemed like a good one and Senator Tinkersmith gave the go ahead to test another cow. "Take young Bobby Talbot as your human test subject. In fact, give him the meat from both cows. We need to know if there is a shelf life. That little son of a bitch won't be eyeing my daughter any longer."

Doc Young took another dose of the hormone and secluded a second cow. The hormone was injected and they began to wait for symptoms. Meanwhile, Bobby Talbot sat down to a nice steak dinner. He had never seen such a large cut. He thought that the Senator may not be such a bad guy after all. Perhaps he would even entertain his intentions to marry his daughter Lucy. As he finished off the enormous steak, he sat back and even considered gloating a bit. He doubted very seriously that any of the other hands had received such a treat. Little did he know how true this was.

The door to the servant kitchen opened and in walked

Doc Young with two large men. They looked like they were up to no good and it made Bobby instantly nervous.

"The Senator offered. I … I didn't do anything wrong … I swear." His voice trembled with fear.

"I know Bobby but you're gonna have to come with us. We don't know how long this will gestate in you and we can't have you running wild on the estate. You're going to have to wait in the back barn until we know what happens to you."

"Wha…*what* happens to me? What did you do? I don't understand!" He looked at the empty plate and suddenly knew that this was all too good to be true. He'd been set up, poisoned with whatever made that cow go crazy. Before he could begin to throw up, one of the men wacked him over the back of the head. As he lost consciousness he thought about Lucy. He wondered if he'd ever see her again as the pain consumed him and his vision faded to black.

When Bobby awoke he was in a room that had a small pile of straw and little else. He quickly scanned the walls looking for a window but found nothing. He looked at the floor hoping to see wooden planks that he could remove or break through but only saw concrete. He knew this place, he was in the old abandoned grain silo and there was only one door. He frantically banged on it but no one answered. He screamed as loud as he could but knew that no one would come for him. They were on the old part of the farm and aside from the harvesting months, no one ever came around this part. Sadly enough, it was months away from harvest time. He knew that he was pretty much screwed.

"You behave yourself down there and I'll lower two meals a day so you won't starve" a voice echoed down from above. It was Doc and he was lowering a bucket from above. Bobby was hungry but did not trust to eat. The bucket only contained bread and a jug of water. This was not what he considered a meal.

"Doc, please let me out of here. I didn't do anything wrong, I swear!" He was afraid and his voice showed it. It cracked and changed pitch as he pleaded for his freedom.

"You did something for the Senator to volunteer you for this experiment. Either way I don't care, I must see what this growth hormone does to the human body. You may be the key to saving the South. Think of it as a great service to your country. At least your life will finally have purpose and meaning" Doc joked.

"Purpose and meaning my ass…" Bobby slumped down on the pile of hay and attempted to figure out his options. Quite frankly, there didn't seem to be many.

Chapter 15 – A shocking revelation
Lawrence Kansas, March 1865

The gun was coming along very nicely. Finnegan was quite pleased with himself. He figured that it would be ready for testing by the end of the week. It was an odd looking contraption, certainly not like anything that ever came out of Sam Colt's factories. It had a long cylindrical shape affixed to a carved wooden handle. The end had five arms that formed a shape similar to that of a closed rose. Along the main shaft, two more support shafts ran parallel and held the three plasma containers. When filled, they were quite the sight to see with their blue and purple sparks constantly moving as if searching for a way out. The globes were surrounded by magnets that became charged by way of the plasma energy. This in turn caused the plasma globes or containers to charge themselves. In theory, the gun would never run out of energy. It was itself, a mini-reactor.

Finnegan pondered about the discharge of the energy and what an acceptable amount would be needed to be effective but yet not completely deplete the globes. Priscilla was sitting next to him grinning ear to ear.

She looked angelic with her rosy, freckled cheeks. Her smile revealed her dimples and emphasized her fine features. She would indeed be a beautiful woman one day and Finnegan prayed that he could delay this day for as long as possible. Her hair was shoulder length and wavy. Its strawberry blonde hue made him think of the beautiful sunsets that Kansas had.

"What?" She looked nervous now as if some hideous flaw had been noticed.

"I am just immensely proud of ya kiddo."

"What was my momma like?"

Finn was not expecting that one. It took him completely by surprise. After composing himself, he did his best to answer and discuss the delicate subject. Priscilla was a tough girl normally but nothing prepared a young woman for the kind of pain that came from losing one's mother.

"I told ya love, she was young like me and her father wouldn't allow her to keep ya. It turned out great fer me though. Otherwise I'd never had the opportunity to have ya all fer me'self. [pausing] ... She was a beautiful woman, olive skin and dark wavy hair. Her eyes were a golden brown and when she looked at you, well, you were unable to look away."

"Did you love her?"

"Aye, I did but her place was with her people and dey don't fancy outsiders. She was Romany, a gypsy and dey was traveling trew Hartford. We only had a short time together … well, ya get da idea."

"Jimmy Peebly says that I am really Declan's daughter on account of my red hair."

Finnegan laughed out loud. He had heard this before, especially while working at the factory in Hartford. It was true, both he and Esmeralda had dark hair but it was not uncommon that red hair sprouts up in families, just like peppermint. Finnegan's parents were both redheads and his father faced similar jesting when they had a dark haired baby Finnegan.

"No love, ya be me daughter 100%. In fact ya look just like yer Grandmuther. She died during the famine along wit yer Grandfather." Finnegan was getting lost in painful memories and attempted to change the subject.

"I am confused on the discharge part o' dis weapon. I can't figure out the ratio of discharge per storage. I'd hate to make a gun dat fires twice and then has to be brought back here to be 'refueled'."

"Well, you'll have to make a dial that controls the amount of electromagnetic energy produced. There should be a setting for standby that produces only the max capacity of what the globes can handle. I think that if the dial can adjust to 5 times the amount, then it can handle charging and shooting at the same time and it won't be depleting the plasma energy too fast. You'll just have to be careful to set it properly as 5x will cause the globes to explode without discharging."

"How can we increase the amount generated 5 times?"

"It's really constantly at 5x, the dial is just an attenuator that attenuates it down to a level that can be contained."

He smiled with pride and kissed his girl on the head. "I'm off to the workshop luv."

It took some time for Finnegan to make the necessary changes to the function of the gun. He often times had to get Priscilla to tell him how to make something as he truly did not understand the technology that he was building. It was a daunting task yet exhilarating at the same time.

Once the gun was finished, Finn decided to give her a name. He thought long and hard on it and decided to go with 'Tintreach'. He didn't remember a lot of Gaelic but as he recalled, this meant lightning. It seemed a fitting name for something that he hoped was destined to "shock" the world. This technology was going to make them rich beyond their wildest dreams.

Finnegan went back into the house and informed everyone that they were now ready for the first test. He had set up a firing range in the middle of a corn field and was desperate to try out 'Tintreach'.

"Dat's a stupid name." teased Declan.

"Tanks brudder knew I could count on ya fer support" replied Finnegan.

The crew left the house and walked towards the corn field. The level of anticipation was extremely high. They could not help but wonder how effective it would be. It was unclear if it would simply make their hair stand on end or if it would really disable a man.

"I am just sayin', it's a stupid name. It should be sometin' English and more intimidating. Sometin' like "Da Annihilator!"

"And ya tink my name is stupid? Da Annihilator? Piss off" retorted Finnegan.

The two men laughed, they truly didn't care what it was called, only that it would work as expected and make them lots of money.

The range was simply a clearing in the corn field. In the middle of the clearing stood a scare crow and it was wearing a grey Confederate hat.

"Allow me to introduce you to Jefferson" stated Finnegan. "Let's see what Tintreach can do, shall we?" said Finnegan.

"Everyone put on yer goggles, don't want anyone blinded by me daughter's genius" warned Finnegan. The pun was wretched but they all laughed regardless.

Finn seemed a bit apprehensive and Priscilla could have sworn that he closed his eyes when he pulled that trigger. It was hard to say for sure because when he pulled that trigger, well, all hell broke loose, literally.

Finnegan held the gun tightly. He knew that when he finally fired it that the effect would be powerful, he just did not know how powerful. It was a two step process to fire the gun.

First, you adjusted the attenuation dial up to 5x. He estimated that the gun could handle 5x for about 5 minutes before the globes containing the plasma energy would become unstable. He hoped so at least. It was the first time that they had really discharged Tintreach. Prior tests were with one plasma ball, at 1x and he nearly caught his workshop on fire.

“This is gonna be amazing! Can you smell dat?” asked Declan.

“Smell what?”

“Money brudder, we’re gonna be rich!”

“Let’s just hope that it works little brudder.”

Finnegan felt that the gun had charged enough. The sound of it was intimidating. It made a sound like something mean was winding up. The squeal got higher pitched as it did so and gave one the impression that they were holding a stick of dynamite.

“Stand back everyone!”

This warning was really quite unnecessary. Finn did not need to warn the others. If he could have seen himself, he would have noticed that everyone was hiding behind him as if to dodge a barrage of bullets. They eagerly peered around him though, to see what would happen.

The second step of the process was to simply squeeze the trigger and let loose. This task seemed quite easy and Finnegan let loose.

What happened next was quite impressive and very comical. Surprisingly enough to Finnegan, there was no recoil like firing a conventional weapon. There was however, a LOT of light.

From the five tips of Tintreach, bolts of lightning erupted forward to poor old Jefferson. Once it hit the scarecrow the lightning splintered out in every direction igniting corn. The corn smoked and exploded shooting fluffy white popped corn in every direction. Thousands of kernels popped and shot in every direction. Bill on the other hand was a smoldering pile of ash with little left that was recognizable. Before Finnegan stopped, he was lying on his back looking up at the sky.

He snapped to and looked around. There stood the others, laughing hysterically at him. Had they a mirror, they'd be laughing at themselves as well.

They all looked quite ridiculous as their faces were blackened; their hair was standing out on end as they all rubbed their eyes and popcorn was everywhere.

"I'd say dat was a success. Old Jefferson der is little more dan a pile of dust" Declan joked.

"I'd say you just invented one hell of a popcorn machine!" Agatha added.

"I think we need to work on da concentration of da blast, and get stronger protective goggles" said Finnegan.

The crew took a great deal of pleasure with their accomplishment, with the exception of one. Priscilla looked very concerned. She was thinking about Jefferson the scarecrow and imagining some poor young man that was sent off to fight. How many people would meet their maker this way? How many people would Tintreach take away from their homes and families?

"Father, I know you are happy but do you think that we are doing the right thing? What if bad men get a hold of this? What will we do then?"

"Don't ya worry 'bout it little lady. We are gonna make a couple of other models and variations, and then go to Washington. I think Mr. Lincoln is gonna put these to good use. Just think we could end the war single-handedly!"

"And get rich!" Declan chimed in.

"Yes, and get rich in the process. Now I've got ta get back in da lab and start working on da corrections and other models."

Priscilla didn't buy it. She knew that she was young and not very wise in the ways of the world but she figured that was a good thing. One thing that she did know was that they acted more like little kids than little kids did. At least little kids were cute. She knew that her father and uncle meant well but she also thought that the same "big kids" that bullied others would eventually get their hands on these weapons and then their problems would become even more complicated.

Finnegan knew that his daughter was right; you can never curb the wrong folks from using technology to further their own aspirations. He also believed that anything that is invented by one will be invented by others. He wanted to be the first so at least he'd have an income to help him deal with their pending moral issues.

Declan just wanted to get paid and to eat a good meal; one with meat.

Miss Agatha Foggybottom was so proud of her little

'jelly sandwich'. She didn't care much for the moral debate. It was her experience that men would fight with anything, sticks, knives, plasma and even cooking pots. She just knew that she was with good people that she loved … and soon she'd be asking for a raise.

Chapter 16 – The War's over!
Lawrence Kansas, April 15th 1865

Finnegan sat back in his chair. He marveled at his second creation. It resembled the Gatling guns the North used but rather spun at a variable rate. Rather than shoot a projectile, it discharged a concentrated plasma blast. The blast did not splinter out like Tintreach. It rather resembled a beam of light. It went quite a distance, approximately 50 meters and then lost effectiveness the farther it traveled. The result on the targets were quite impressive though and because it fired from a rotating set of barrels, each barrel could go through it's needed process of cooling and receiving another magnetic charge.

He was experimenting with the plasma containment units as he no longer wanted to use the glass globes. These were breakable and posed a danger to the wielder of the weapon and everyone around.

The new gun would need a name and Finnegan resorted to his previous method of finding one.

"Hmmmm, what ta use?" he thought.

One word did not summarize the function and so he

was stuck. He thought about the gun and how it would completely obliterate anything that it was pointed at. He thought of enemy soldiers leaving this world to meet their maker.

"Hmmm, … leaving, … good bye..." pondered Finnegan.

Perhaps he would use Slán. It literally meant "safe" or "health." Back home in Ireland, they would use it to wish someone a safe trip and healthy return.

This phrase seemed fitting to Finnegan, to wish someone a safe trip as he sent them to meet their maker. It seemed respectful in a way, and gentleman like. Respectful as one could get when disposing of another's life. At least this way he was still showing them some dignity.

Suddenly the door to the workshop burst open. Through the door rushed a very excited Declan O'Sullivan.

"Brudder! It's over, the War is over!"

"What do ya mean over?"

"General Lee surrendered a week ago at Appomattox Court House" Declan reported.

Finnegan sat back and slumped into his chair. He was torn. On one hand he was elated that the war was now over however he now wondered how likely the President would be to purchase their weapons.

"Loose the long face brudder. They'll still want o'er guns. Everyone will want o'er guns and I am willin' ta bet dat they'll pay extra for exclusive rights. So they'll keep the upper-hand."

He was right, no matter the severity of the need; they would always need new and improved weapons. He breathed a sigh of relief as he thought of it.

"Check her out. I made da adjustments to the barrels like ya suggested."

"Oh Jeezus! Dat is definitely my kinda gun!"

Both Declan and Finnegan were quite pleased with themselves. Declan had designed and built most of this one with Finnegan working primarily on the plasma tanks and discharge unit. It was a beauty as far as weapons go and both men were anxious to test it out now that it was finished.

……………………..

Meanwhile, in Lexington Kentucky, the testing on the second cow was not going as planned. For some reason there was no change to the cow and it remained as docile as always.

"I don't understand; why is this not working? Are you sure you made the hormone the same as the other strand?" asked a frustrated Doc Young.

Gideon nodded his head but kept quiet.

Doc Young began to suspect the boy was up to something. He had noticed a lack of excitement after the effect the last injection had on the first cow. He was quiet and did not seem to be in it any longer.

"If your father finds out that you are sabotaging these tests, you know what he'll do to you, right? Now tell me why this is not working."

"I will not let you or my father, use this as a weapon to hurt innocent people" Gideon said as he stood a little taller.

Before Doc Young could respond, Lucy burst into the makeshift laboratory. She was out of breath and seemed frantic.

~ Between breaths ~ "Doc….Father wants ….. to see

you… right now! ….There is ….a man… here from the government.”

A man from the government? He was nervous as he pondered which government they were talking about. Doc left the workshop in a hurry and stopped in the doorway before leaving.

“You better work on this hormone and fast. I’ll be reporting to your father and I am not taking the blame for this. God only knows what he will do if you disobey him.”

“What’s he talking about?” asked Lucy.

“I won’t do it I tell you, I won’t do it. This hormone does not work like I thought and instead of letting me do tests to fix it. I have to reproduce something that turned a simple cow into a monster. It was horrific Lucy. God only knows what they’ll do with it. Father is, well … you know … not always kind.” Gideon pleaded his case to his older sister but knew that she would take his side. She always took his side. She was always a Daddy’s girl.

“I would do as you are told Gideon. You are right, Father is not always nice and that is precisely why you should obey him. I wouldn’t put it past him to do something hurtful and mean if you don’t” said Lucy.

"What is the man here for?"

"No idea, Father just told me to come and get Doc immediately."

Gideon knew that he would have little hope of blatantly disobeying his Father. He knew that he was capable of anything and he really didn't want to get on his bad side. These past few weeks were amazing as his Father actually paid him a good deal of respect. He also knew that if this hormone, the virus really, was used like he suspected; the world could change forever and countless people would die.

Gideon decided to go to the house and see if he could find out why Federal agents were at their home. He entered the house through the slave's entrance, an action that his Father despised.

"Only the slaves and staff enter through that door and you Sir are neither!" his father would often say.

Gideon did not care though. It was the quickest way to get in the house and the best chance he had at not being noticed. He rushed through two hallways until he came to his father's office door. Inside he heard two men speaking with his father and Doc Young.

The two men were not from the North but rather from Virginia. They worked for Jefferson Davis and were here to break the news of the Confederate surrender of General Lee. They also proceeded to inform him that President Lincoln had been shot just the day before.

"This is fantastic!" shouted Senator Tinkersmith. "Hope is not lost gentlemen. I have news of my own and you must take it to President Davis. We may still have a way to pull through this dark time and rise again."

Before Gideon could hear any more, he was startled by the door opening and his irate father's angry words:

"Boy! Get to the workshop and continue your work, NOW!" Flavious screamed.

Gideon rushed down the hallway and towards the workshop. It was killing him to not know what they were planning. He had to figure out a way to find out what was going on.

As the agents left the main house, Gideon found himself increasingly nervous. The two men seemed elated as they rushed to their horses and took off out of sight. He could only imagine what news they brought the Confederate President. He also knew that his father would be in the workshop any moment. Unfortunately, he was right.

The door opened slowly and in walked his father. He was quiet and seemed to be relishing the moment, choosing his words carefully and deliberately.

"Son, I know what you are doing and I can assure you, you WILL create another batch of hormones and you WILL conduct the test according to Doc Young's instructions. I will NOT tolerate anything less than your complete cooperation. Have I made myself perfectly clear?"

"Ye … yes… yes Sir." Gideon was terrified and knew that he had no other choice but to comply.

Three days later more men arrived, this time from the Union President. The traitor Andrew Johnson had become President after Lincoln was assassinated. Johnson was a southerner like them but was considered a traitor for siding with the north and accepting Lincoln's nomination as Vice President. Gideon had heard his father many times ranting and raving about Johnson. He wondered what news and perhaps terms the agents were bringing.

"So let me get this straight, your President Johnson..."

"YOUR President Johnson Sir. The war is over and the Confederacy is no longer" corrected the agent.

"Absolutely… my apologies. OUR President Johnson would like to place an order for cattle?" questioned Senator Tinkersmith.

"That is correct Sir. The President wishes to put this awful war behind us and get the country moving forward. He is also offering that you retain your position in the US Senate and remain a Senator for Kentucky; a very generous offer."

"Generous indeed, surely the Republicans will not tolerate this though."

"Congress does not reconvene until fall. A lot can happen by then" replied the agent. "President Johnson intends on getting as much done as possible before then."

This news was very good indeed. If Flavious was going to proceed with his plans, he would let the North help deliver their own death sentence.

"Gentlemen, please tell President Johnson that I graciously accept his offer. I can have cattle on the train headed for Washington by the end of the week."

Senator Flavious Tinkersmith now had the final piece

to his horrific plan: a target and a damn good one at that. He pictured those Yankee politicians sitting down to their dinner tables to celebrate. They'd be serving up their own death sentence.

It was almost too easy.

Chapter 17 – A bad night at the theatre
Washington DC, April 14th 1865

When President Lincoln woke on April 14, he was in a very good mood. Robert E. Lee had surrendered several days before to General Grant and now he awaited word from North Carolina on the surrender of Joseph E. Johnston. The morning papers announced that the he and his wife would be attending the comedy, *Our American Cousin*, at Ford's Theater later that evening.

At his cabinet meeting, the president met with Grant and his Cabinet. At the end of the meeting, General Grant gave his regrets that he and his wife could no longer attend the play. Secretary of War Edwin Stanton pleaded with the president not to go out at night, fearful that some rebel might try to shoot him in the streets. It was a common fear the past few weeks however Lincoln did not buy it. He felt that the American people were fed up with this war and that they would finally be able to celebrate as a nation, rather than as the winning side and the losing side. He did not want to hide behind body guards and soldiers. He was a people's man and that was how he would conduct his day to day business.

President Lincoln told his wife about the Grants and that perhaps it was best to skip the show tonight. She was very determined to see it however and really wanted to be able to celebrate the good news about Lee's surrender. She pleaded with him to maintain their announced plans and asked Major Henry Rathbone and his fiancée, Clara Harris, to join them instead.

After an afternoon carriage ride and dinner, Mary complained of a headache and considered not going after all. Lincoln commented that he was feeling a bit tired himself but needed a laugh and was intent on going with or without her. Now it was she who relented. He made a quick stop by the War Department with his body guard, William Crook only to hear that there was no news from North Carolina.

As they returned to pick up Mary, Crook practically begged President Lincoln not to go to the theater. Lincoln was rather annoyed but knew the man was just doing his job. How sad it was to constantly worry. He had spent the past five years worrying and now was the time for a break. It was a time to celebrate and finally relax. Crook asked if he could go along as an extra guard. Lincoln rejected both suggestions, shrugging off Crook's fears of assassination. Lincoln knew that a guard would be posted outside their state box at the theater and that should be sufficient.

Due to her headache, Mary was a little late getting ready. Lincoln looked at her fiddling with her outfit. He chuckled to himself and thought about how many married couples were doing just this. They arrived after the play had started and the two couples swept up the stairs and into their seats.

The box door was closed, yet not locked. The box was guarded by police officer John Parker. This was probably not the best plan as John Parker was a notorious drinker. As one might expect from a drunkard, Parker left his post in the hallway during the second act and went across the street for a drink.

Just blocks away, President Lincoln's bodyguard William Crook paced the living room of his house. He could not shake the feeling that something bad was going to happen. He felt that his place was by the President but President Lincoln was very adamant that he stay home. He did not want to disobey a direct order but he also did not want to see anything happen to this man. This man had persevered during our country's darkest hour and somehow kept an entire nation together. William regarded him as the most patriotic American this country had ever produced.

"Damn the order, I am going to the theatre" barked William.

"Dear, you've been given an order, and the night off. Why can't you enjoy it with your family?" asked his wife.

"I can't explain it love, I have to get there right now. Something is wrong, dreadfully wrong." William bolted out the front door of his house and ran in a full sprint towards Ford Theatre. His heart pounded and the thundering beats resonated throughout his head. It was not due to the run but rather the fear that welled up in his stomach, the fear that something bad was about to happen. He feared that he may already be too late.

As William Crook rounded the corner he was stopped dead in his tracks by a blinding blue-ish light. He heard a crackling sound similar to lighting and then a deep thud. Before him stood an odd looking gentleman who wore a peculiar copper backpack. William could not be certain but it appeared that the backpack was spinning.

"Who the hell are you?" demanded Crook.

"Lord Wesley Chamberlain and you must be William Crook, correct?" His accent was a very posh English accent. William thought he sounded like a butler and wondered why an Englishman was in Washington.

"Out of the way you, I've got to get to the theatre."

"Yes, we haven't a moment to spare" answered Lord Chamberlain. "The president is in grave danger and unless we stop it, all will be ruined!"

While William would rather have spent more time questioning this fellow, he felt it more urgent to get to Ford's Theatre. He wondered how the man knew something was about to happen.

It was the third act, the President and Mrs. Lincoln drew closer together, holding hands and enjoying the play. Lincoln was glad that he had decided to come after all. It was indeed a funny play and he felt so much better already. He looked over to Mary and thought what a lucky man he was to have her in his life. It was true, she did spend too much money on unnecessary items and parties but truth be told, he did not mind all that much. All of their work had culminated to this point and much like the joy found in this play, so would his beloved country find again in their daily lives.

Behind them, the door opened and a man slithered into the box like a thief. His entrance went unnoticed until he pointed a Derringer at the back of President Lincoln's head. Without remorse or hesitation he pulled the trigger. Mary saw the man out of the corner of her eye but could not react quickly enough. The shot was loud and rang in her ears causing all of what transpired to be a muted ringing sound. She reached out to her slumping husband and began shrieking. Now wielding a dagger, the man yelled, "Sic Semper Tyrannis!" ("Thus always to tyrants") and slashed Major Rathbone's arm clean open to the bone. As he leapt from the box he caught his spur in a flag which caused him to crash upon the stage breaking his left shin in the fall. Rathbone yelled for someone to stop him as he escaped out the back stage door.

Major Rathbone looked at the President. He was mortified at the sight. Here sat his hero, his personal hero to which he had the pleasure of serving these past few years. He sat there, hunched over, bleeding out of the side of his head.

"Help me get him out of here!" he yelled to one of the officers that entered into the booth. "We need to get him somewhere safe … and fetch the surgeons!"

An unconscious Lincoln was carried across the street to the Petersen House and into the bedroom of the War Department clerk. The bullet had entered behind the left ear and ripped a path through the left side of his brain, mortally wounding him.

"Oh dear God! We're too late, something has happened!" exclaimed William Crook. He could not tell what, but something horrible had definitely happened. There was a large crowd in the street and people were openly crying.

"What has happened here?" demanded William Crook, nearly screaming.

"I fear we are too late my friend" answered Lord Chamberlain. "It seems my calculations were off … again. Perhaps a quantum fluctuation has caused me to arrive 10 minutes too late. This cannot be happening again. Every time I try the scenario or time changes."

"You: do not go anywhere. Johnson!" William Crook

searched for one of his men in the crowd. "Johnson, make sure this man does not go anywhere! I want to speak to him. If his backpack lights up or he so much looks as though he will run, shoot him in the face!" William Crook knew that something was wrong here and that the Englishman was somehow involved. He had to get to the President first though. He had to see him. He had to apologize for not being there.

Lord Wesley Chamberlain decided that he would have to make a run for it. He could not be certain if he had been late or that the children's inventions were to blame. Either way, he needed to get somewhere private so that he could activate the "Portable Hadron Collider" or PHC. It made quite a bit of noise and light and could cause problems, more than he had already created so far.

"I have my orders Sir and will not hesitate to execute you should you try to leave my sight" Johnson stated. His calm delivery left Lord Chamberlain little doubt of his seriousness.

"I did not want to do this young man but you leave me no choice." Lord Chamberlain had a round disc in the palm of his hand and it began to light up. All of a sudden there was a flash of light and Wesley Chamberlain was no longer standing in the street.

"What the.... witchcraft? How am I gonna explain this to the boss?"

The President had been carried across the street from the theater to the house of a Mr. Peterson. William Crook entered by ascending a flight of steps above the basement and passing through a long hall to the rear, where the President lay extended on a bed, breathing heavily. Several surgeons were present, at least six. Among them Crook observed was Doctor Hall. He inquired of Doctor Hall, the true condition of the President.

"The President is dead to all intents, although he might live three hours or more." answered the doctor.

This giant of a man lay extended diagonally across the bed, which was not long enough for him. His slow, full respiration lifted the clothes with each breath that he took. His features were calm and striking.

Senator Sumner was there, when William Crook entered. Soon after, he was joined by Speaker Colfax, Mr. Secretary McCulloch, and the other members of the cabinet, with the exception of Mr. Seward. A double guard was stationed at the door and on the sidewalk to suppress the crowd, which was of course highly excited and anxious. The room was small and overcrowded. The surgeons and members of the cabinet were as many as should have been in the room, but there were many more, and the hall and other rooms in the front or main house were full as well.

A door which opened upon a porch or gallery, and also the windows, were kept open for fresh air. The night was dark, cloudy, and damp, and about six it began to rain. William Crook remained in the room until then without sitting or leaving it, when, there being a vacant chair which some one left at the foot of the bed, he occupied it for nearly two hours, listening to the heavy groans and witnessing the wasting life of the great man who lay expiring before him.

He began to pray. Suddenly his prayers for a miracle were interrupted by a flash of light. There stood the stranger from the street. He looked at William with a disparaging look.

“Do not be alarmed, I am going to fix this. We cannot afford to lose such a great man” said Lord Wesley

Chamberlain.

He placed his hand on the president and a bright white light filled the room.

William Crook leapt toward the stranger and the President. When the light dissipated, William noticed that he was in what looked like a hospital, only like none that he'd ever seen before. There were lights everywhere and machines, the likes he had never seen.

"What the hell is going on here? Where are we and what are you doing to the President?" screamed William Crook, reaching for his sidearm.

"I am fixing the world! Now sit down and shut up or I'll send you to the Dark Ages Sir!"

The sight of the President, lying on the table, completely limp and helpless turned William's stomach. If this stranger could in fact save him then he figured he better shut up and pray for the best. If he failed, well, he prayed that this would not happen. There would be time for questions later. For now, all his thoughts and prayers were directed towards the life of Abraham Lincoln.

Chapter 18 – That's one crazy town!
Lawrence Kansas, June 1865

"It's time we start to Washington" Finnegan stated to his family.

Both weapons were finished, Tintreach and Slán, and they were ready to demonstrate the incredible power to the US government in hopes of a lucrative contract. While the war had been over for nearly two months now, they figured that governments would always need weaponry to maintain strength, authority and relevance. These two weapons could change the course of modern warfare and he hoped, would be powerful enough to actually deter armed conflicts. That's what he told himself at least. He chose to focus on optimism and it was now time to hit the road.

Leaving Kansas would be difficult. While it held a tremendous amount of painful memories, it was his home. Even a broken home remains your home and is therefore difficult to abandon.

"I ain't gonna miss dis shite dump one stinkin' bit" exclaimed Declan. "Good riddance I say."

"Maybe I'll meet a nice gentleman and I'll be able to leave you blaggards!" Agatha jested.

"Wha..?" began Declan.

"It is an unprincipled contemptible man or an untrustworthy person. It describes you perfectly" retorted Agatha.

"Dat pretty much sums you up little brudder" Finnegan chimed in now.

"Me knows wha a blaggard is ya git" said Declan.

"As long as you take me with you miss Agatha. I don't know how long I'd last with these two without you." Priscilla was now getting into it.

The mood of the group was light and cheerful. They seemed to be brimming with optimism at their new prospects in life. Finnegan had already sold the house and workshop earlier that day and purchased a wagon and two horses for the trip. He had put in for a leave of absence with Colt firearms but knew that it would not last. They did not have time for part time agents and the longer he was away, the less likely a job would be there waiting for him. It was all or nothing now and this would have to work, there simply was no other option.

"We should all get some rest. We'll finish packing tanight and den head out tamorrow mornin." said Finnegan.

"Yes Pa!" jested Declan and Agatha at the same time.

Later that night, as the crew headed off to bed, Finnegan took Priscilla by the hand and asked her to sit with him. He was immensely proud of his daughter. He often found himself wondering how she would get along with her mother. It wasn't right how they separated and he would love to have his little girl meet her mum.

"Are ya excited ta be leavin' town?" asked Finn.

"I guess so. Guess it doesn't really matter so much for me as I don't have any friends here. All the girls here are too dumb to talk to and they think I'm weird" answered Priscilla.

"You are right der, dey ain't smart enough fer ya so dey avoid talkin' to ya. Makes dem remember how simple dey are. I was tinkin', maybe after we are dun in Washington, we could take a little trip to Connecticut. Perhaps we'll find yer mum's people and you could finally meet her. Would ya like dat?" asked Finnegan.

He knew that it was a touchy subject for Priscilla and

he didn't want to get her riled up but he did want her to know that it was OK to want to meet her mother. To be honest, he wanted to see her again as well. So much time had passed but he found himself thinking of her often. In the past 10 years, he hadn't really committed to any woman. He had seen a few over the years but never anything serious and he tried to keep that part of his life private and hidden from his daughter. This was of course impossible in a small town like Lawrence but he did his best.

"I'd like that very much Pa. I'd like to meet her. I always wonder what she looks like, if I look like her and if she will like me."

"She's gonna love ya sweetheart. I bet there isn't a day that goes by where she doesn't tink about ya. Now give yer old man a hug and get off ta bed."

"Night Daddy."

"Night love, see ya tammara morn."

Finnegan watched as she walked off to her room. For a split second he worried if Esmeralda would in fact be happy to see her, or if they could even find her. He figured that once she spent a little time talking to Priscilla she'd be as proud and happy as he was so that worry left his thoughts nearly as quick as it came. The real problem would be finding her. He figured that it shouldn't be too hard tracking gypsies. Everyone kept an eye out for them for different reasons but everyone knew when they were coming, where they were, and where they were off to.

"There will be time enough to worry 'bout that after Washington" Finnegan said to himself.

The following morning the crew packed their things and said their goodbyes. Declan desperately wanted to stop by the Blue Bonnet Tavern and have a plate of fried pork. It had been months now, an eternity it seemed, since he had eaten meat. He was getting used to it but he often found himself drooling, fantasizing even, about a juicy steak or a plate of bacon. He had given his word and would stick to it, he just had to figure out a way to change Priscilla's mind.

It didn't take long to have the house packed, the workshop on the other hand, well that was a different story. Finnegan found himself staring at the clutter of tools, tubing, hoses, gauges and parts that he had taken comfort in over the past few years. He only had so much room on the cart and if things went as planned, he would be buying a factory soon enough. He had to make sure that he had the bare essentials to work on the guns if need be so he packed a crate with a few of his trusty standards.

That morning was a hot one. It was well into the 90's by 7 am when they left. Finnegan wanted to leave earlier but getting this gaggle of people together was not an easy task. Declan had celebrated the night before and was not easily woken up. He in fact looked as though he'd only gotten to bed a few hours before getting up. He smelled of bourbon, tobacco and cheap perfume.

There were times where Finn envied the carefree nature of his brother. This trip however, was not one of those times. They were heading through Missouri and there were sure to be run-ins with former Confederates not too happy with them. He had to make sure that they were not recognized for not only were they Lawrence survivors of '63, they were also part of the group that took out Bloody Bill and his boys. That was another story however, one for Agatha to tell.

Finnegan decided to travel due east, towards St. Louis. Even though this meant he would be going right through the heart of the South, he figured this was the best route. Surely people were just happy that the War was finally over and that they could go on with their lives. He figured that it would take about 5 days, maybe six. He did not want to go at breakneck speed. He preferred to rather enjoy the trip. It would be long enough without making it unbearable by the pace.

The first day was surprisingly calm. The four of them had been traveling through Missouri without incident or confrontation. Finnegan figured it was a sign of the coming years and that people were happy that the war was over. Perhaps they no longer cared or were too weary to do anything about it.

As they got closer to Columbia Missouri however, they noticed that something was wrong. The town seemed abandoned, like a ghost town. There were no people out and about, no merchants, and no soldiers. Most of the homes had been sloppily boarded up with wooden planks covering the windows and doors. Some of the homes were burnt to the ground with little more than ashen timbers sprouting out of the ground like scorched trees. Had it had been destroyed near the end of the war? Finnegan had heard reports of Atlanta being destroyed by General Sherman a year ago. Perhaps Columbia had suffered a similar fate. It was hard to imagine though as this didn't really seem like a city of any significance.

As the sun began to set and darkness crept towards them, the family began to get a very uneasy feeling. It was as if some unseen presence was watching them and waiting for a good time to pounce.

"We'll need ta find somewhere ta stay tonight and it doesn't look like anyone's here ta protest our selection" Declan stated.

"Look for something easy to defend, without windows" stated Priscilla. "I got a bad feeling about this place."

Suddenly, Agatha saw movement out of the corner of her eye. It looked like a boy running the length of a roof top. There seemed to be other movement, much like cockroaches scurrying about. Everywhere she looked; it seemed as if every shadow was alive and waiting to pounce on them.

"This place is not abandoned, they are simply hiding" stated Agatha.

"Yeah, we got ta get in shelter before we find out who they are hiding from" Finnegan said.

"Or what" added Declan.

"Let's not scare Priscilla" warned Finnegan.

"Priscilla? Hell, I am scared!" stated Declan.

Finnegan spotted what looked like a small fortress with a large cast iron blacksmith sign above the door. They headed the wagon over in that direction. The darkness was gaining ground over the sunlight and their uneasy feeling was only moments away from being panic. Declan jumped off the wagon with Slán in hand.

"Ya better get yer popcorn maker charged an' ready. I have a feeling like we're gonna get ta test it for real this time" warned Declan.

Finnegan worried that he was right. He gave the reins to Ms. Foggybottom and jumped down off the wagon.

"Daddy, I am scared" stated Priscilla.

"Don't worry little one, just keep quiet" answered Finn in a whisper.

As Declan opened the massive wooden doors to the blacksmith shop a woman appeared with a rifle and fired a blast in their direction. Finn and Declan pointed their weapons at the woman, fearing she was shooting at them. Just before returning fire, Finnegan looked behind him and saw the woman's actual target. On the ground, lay a man wailing and moaning in agony. The man was covered in blood. It was hard to tell if that was his own blood as a result of the rifle shot or someone else's. He noticed that the man's eyes were blood red and his face was scrunched as if in intense pain.

"Ya'll better get inside before more of them come" warned the woman.

"More of *them*?" asked Declan.

"Yeah, more of the Loons. Don't dally about, get your sorry butts inside … now!" she commanded.

Declan always admired a strong woman but this one, she was something different all together. There was something about a gun wielding beautiful woman that he really, really admired.

As Finn and the gang got the cart inside about a dozen crazed individuals appeared about two blocks up. They were wailing and howling with rage. Their eyes were blood red and their clothes were torn and tattered with apparent signs of their vicious nature. Finnegan decided it was time for a little test of Tintreach. He probably could have gotten in the doors safe and sound but he wasn't sure if they'd get the doors closed and secured in time and quite frankly, he was itching to try her out. These people, or Loons as the lady had called them, seemed beyond reason and in need of some "enlightening." He chuckled at the thought of the pun as he turned the dial knob to 5x. It was as if time slowed with each click of the dial. As he got closer to 5x the weapon began to hum and resonate a high pitched sound that built up. Tintreach was buzzing and Finnegan's heart rate increased. His pulse thundered in his chest as the anticipation grew with each passing second.

A sudden rush of fear engulfed him as the group of Loons charged him. They were very fast and moving with extreme purpose. As they came within 10 feet of Finnegan he heard his brother yell.

"Get yer arse in here ya fool or blast those idiots to kingdom come!"

There was a moment where Finnegan hesitated. He knew what the outcome would be, that they stood no chance of survival. Old Bob the scarecrow had proven that however this was human life, however inhuman it seemed.

"Fook dis" Finnegan stated and he pulled the trigger. He had remembered to pull down his goggles thankfully because the blast was bright, intensely bright. It lit the darkening streets much like lightning during a storm. He aimed for the center of the group knowing that the blast would splinter out left and right arching throughout the crowd. He hoped that it would take out all of them for if it didn't, they would surely be upon him in seconds.

Finnegan's face was lit by the intense blue light of Tintreach. His goggles looked as though they glowed and his face grimaced. A combination of fear and the disgust of taking so many lives. He had taken life before but this seemed different and this weapon, his creation, seemed God-like. It was an overwhelming feeling as the discharge destroyed all of the Loons with just the one blast. The plasma blast hit the first man and splintered left and right as well as up and down. The entire group froze in smoldering tracks, several catching fire.

Finnegan could hardly believe the awesome power he had just wielded. With one shot he had taken out a dozen attackers. As the elation of his success peaked, he was also overcome by the thought that he had just sent a dozen people to their makers. He scanned the charred bodies and noticed that one was a young child of 9 or 10. He was horrified at what could turn a child into something that vicious and at the horror that he had just killed one.

"Get in here Daddy, now!"

As Finnegan backed in through the doorway he noticed that more were on the way.

"What the hell was that?" demanded the young woman.

"We are inventors and gunsmiths Ma'am. We're on our way ta Washington" Declan stated, obviously trying to impress the young woman.

"I mean what the hell kinda gun is that?" asked the frantic woman.

Finnegan didn't pay her much mind as he rushed to secure the doors. The woman had obviously prepared her defenses well as the doors were heavy oak doors re-enforced with iron bars on the inside and three large beams that slid down into place making an impregnable barrier.

"Nice door ma'am" noted Finnegan.

"You need it these days; the streets are becoming crazier by the day around here. The Loons are spreading and it is harder to get out and about without running into them."

"What is wrong with them?" asked Priscilla.

"No one knows.... It started four days ago with Mr. Peabody. He went mad and killed his whole family. The sheriff apprehended him and hung him the same day. The next thing we knew, Sheriff Scott went mad as well. After that, we all just barricaded ourselves in not sure what to do. Not all have survived and you are lucky I opened the doors when I did."

"What is your name love?" asked Agatha.

"Victoria Aschenbecher. My father and mother emigrated here from Prussia when I was a couple of years old. My father was the town blacksmith" answered Victoria. There was pain in her voice and she stared off into the distance for a moment before collecting herself.

"I assume they have perished?" asked Declan.

"Yes, thankfully before all of this happened. I don't know how my mother would have fared to see everyone sick like this."

"Sick? Yes, so do you know why you haven't been affected?" asked Agatha. Her nurse profession was now kicking in and she became increasingly paranoid for the safety of young Priscilla and the others. Her maternal instincts became apparent as she clutched young Priscilla closer towards her.

There was loud banging on the doors and Priscilla screamed with fear. The howling outside the walls seemed… in-human.

"Is der another way in? Do we need ta cover any other entrances?" shouted a panicked Finnegan.

"No, this is the only entrance and the walls are too high for them to climb" answered Victoria.

"Can you take Priscilla and Ms. Agatha inside please?" pleaded Finnegan.

"Come this way, I have some bread. It's not much."

Finnegan stood there next to Declan and weighed their options. Thankfully this room was large enough for the cart, two horses and all of them. It was the blacksmith's workshop apparently but everything had been moved to the sides. The ceiling was a good 15 feet tall and the walls were brick, painted white and without windows. A large ventilation opening caught Finnegan's eye as he surveyed the room and the ceiling. It made Finn nervous. Surely these 'Loons' could climb and it was only a matter of time before he might be firing Tintreach indoors. He shuttered at the thought.

"At least your little toy der is good for more dan makin' popcorn." joked Declan. He was always good for a tension breaking jest. Finnegan laughed but as he did so, he was reminded of the young boy that now lay dead in the street thanks to him. It was a sobering thought and one that mortified him.

"Don't let it get ya brudder. Whatever dis illness is, it does not discriminate, nor should we. If we're going ta survive, we may need ta be a bit rough around da edges if ya know what I mean."

He knew his brother spoke the truth. Whatever this disease was, if they were to survive it, they would have to put moral issues aside and not hesitate. Suddenly Tintreach started to make a buzzing sound and Finnegan remembered the dial. He quickly turned it down to 1x and nervously waited for a sign that it was stable.

"Dat was a close one brudder. Why don't ya get some

sleep. I'll take the first watch. You come relieve me in 6 hours" said Declan.

"Yeah, me nerves are a bit shite at da moment" replied Finnegan.

"Nice work on da guns. I tink we definitely got somethin' here."

"Your guns just as much as mine brudder" stated Finn.

Finnegan went through a hallway and entered a large room the others had congregated in. It was very simple but very cozy at the same time. It reminded him of the old country. The furniture was all hand made by an obviously skilled craftsman. On the floor lay a very large area rug which was quite rare. Agatha and Priscilla had already claimed spots and were settling in for a bit of sleep. Priscilla laid there with a blank stare, slowly tearing off small chunks of the dark piece of bread.

Finnegan laid down next to his sweet daughter and kissed her on the forehead. "Good night my luv, sleep tight. We'll figure all of this out in da mornin'".

As Finnegan drifted off to sleep, his thoughts and dreams were consumed by that little boy. Priscilla laid there next to him and gently brushed his hair with her hand.

"Don't worry Daddy, we'll be OK" she said attempting to comfort her father.

"I hope so little one, I hope so" answered her father as he drifted off to sleep.

Chapter 19 - Bobby Talbot, cowhand extraordinaire
Lexington Kentucky, June 1865

Doc Young hid in the root cellar. He had taken a weapon, as much ammunition as he could put in his satchel and an armful of bread. He knew better than to grab any meat. He barricaded himself in the cellar early and prepared to wait things out. He had taken Lucy down just before and so he sat in the dark, damp and musty cellar alone. He stared at Lucy, who lay catatonic and lifeless on a canning table. Glass jars lay broken on the floor, an accident from earlier when clearing off the table to make room for Lucy.

It was a horrific sight on the plantation. It was unimaginable how the disease had spread this rapidly. He thought he had contained the virus by containing Bobby Talbot in the old silo. He had, that is, until Lucy went to see him.

"Stupid girl" he snapped at the lifeless young woman. "You've never been able do as instructed. Good thing that the Senator and Gideon left when they did."

He debated on killing the girl, just to make sure that

she wasn't infected. All signs pointed to the fact that she was not. All of the others displayed clear signs within 30 minutes of being bitten yet Lucy had been bitten nearly two days ago.

Two long days ago one of the slaves had brought Lucy to the main house. She had gone to see Bobby and inadvertently let him loose, getting bitten in the process. As more and more of the staff and slaves became affected, it was apparent that the disease was transmitted via saliva or blood. Why Lucy was not affected was a mystery and the only reason she was down here in the cellar. He intended to conduct tests to find out why she was not affected like the others. Unfortunately he would have to improvise considerably as he did not have the time to bring many testing supplies and equipment.

The Senator had already left for Richmond two days prior with Gideon so he had no idea of what had befallen his household, or his daughter. Doc Young blamed him for all of this anyways. True this was his idea but the Senator's impatience had pushed them past logical, controlled testing, and shoved them into a path of reckless abandon that was common of lunatics rather than scientists.

There was pounding now on the door. He could hear them on the other side, wailing and screaming in pain. They knew he was down there and there was nothing he could do but hope the door held. He grabbed the gun and held it close to his pounding chest as he cowered in the corner.

Suddenly the scene above seemed to change a bit as they appeared to be distracted by something. He could hear rustling and a lot of loud, dull thumping sounds. He detected movement above him to the left. A man shouted and a series of gun shots followed. There were a few thuds which Doc presumed to be the Loons falling to the floor. Then he heard a man yell orders to others. He was saved! Thank God he was saved!

The elation that Doc felt came to an abrupt end as he noticed Lucy was no longer lying on the table. He quickly scanned the dark room, looking for any sign of the girl.

"L.....Lucy? Lucy girl, are you ....there?" a terror stricken Doc Young asked.

"What's a matter Doc, you aren't happy with your creation?" a cold and sinister reply whispered from the opposite corner. It was too dark to see her and the shelves that contained all of the mason jars blocked a direct view.

"Oh … th … thank God you are alright dear. I was so worried about you. I brought you down here to protect you from the horrors above, from the monsters. Men are here now and I think that we are saved" said Doc.

"You should not use the word safe when referring to yourself Doctor Young" replied Lucy. Her voice was not normal and sounded raspy. She barely spoke at an audible level.

Doc watched as she slowly walked towards him. Her head was hung low as if she was staring at the floor. Her body looked stiff and rigid as she tilted her head to the side creating a popping sound as one's knuckles often do. She looked down at Doc and the dimly lit room revealed her blood red eyes. This was remarkable, he thought. She was the only one that seemed to be able to control herself; the only one capable of rational thought and speech. All the others reacted like stark raving lunatics, killing everything in sight, sometimes even each other. 'I must have time to study her' thought Doc.

"Down here! Help, you must save me! Please hurry!"

screamed Doc Young.

Lucy calmly cocked her head to the side and looked up at the ceiling above. “They cannot help you coward. You shall die here in this cellar by the very creature you have created.”

He let loose a whimper and then a scream as she rushed towards him. In a blur of motion she grabbed and flung him at the stone wall, a distance of nearly 20 feet! Doc Young was not a big man, weighing a mere 120lbs however she had thrown him across the room like a pillow. Lucy gazed upon her own hands with surprise and admired the detached arm she now held in her hands. She was strong, so much more than before and she had to get out of here. Those men above would soon come for her now that Doc had begun to scream like a stuck pig. She rushed to the terrified man and snapped his neck like a twig. The movement was so quick and effortless that she nearly severed it. She wished that she had more time to make him suffer but this would have to suffice.

She scanned the basement and searched for a way out. Above her on the north wall a small rectangular window was near ground level. It would be a squeeze but she had no other choice as the men above had already begun to shoot at the door attempting to break through.

As Lucy squeezed through the tiny window her skin seemed to soak in the warm sun. She began to run and headed towards the wood line as fast as she could. She was focused, more acutely than ever before, and thought of nothing but finding Bobby. As she ran she remarked at her own speed. She was easily running as fast as a horse. The movement was effortless and she was overcome by the strength and power she now possessed. As she leapt over a stack of hay barrels Lucy heard Bobby speaking. It startled her for she did not hear his voice with her ears but in her head. He was calling her name yet she heard no actual sound. Was she now mad as well? 'Where are you Bobby?' she thought and as she thought of him he responded. 'I am over here by the silo, please hurry' thought Bobby.

Lucy covered a distance that was surely two miles in what seemed only a couple of minutes. It was remarkable. As Lucy reached the silo she was greeted by her love. While neither was certain exactly what was happening, they were at least relieved to be together, even if it be in this state.

They held each other in their arms and found comfort for the first time in a very long time. Lucy felt safe now that she was with Bobby. She was very worried about her father and Gideon but for the moment, she thought of little else than Bobby.

“I am so hungry I could eat a cow” remarked Lucy.

“Careful love, that’s what got us in this trouble to begin with” responded Bobby.

Chapter 20 – A new and improved President
Geneva Switzerland, April 2023

"Are you ready to go back Mr. President?" asked Sir Wesley Chamberlain.

Lincoln looked at his left arm in disgust. He was appalled with the monstrosity that it now was. He looked in the mirror in front of him and nearly recoiled at the sight. He did want to go back, to see Mary but he was afraid. He was afraid of her reaction, afraid of what she would think of him. He feared the general reaction of people, if they would reject him as their President.

"Mr. President, it was either this or your death and you've seen what your death does to the United States and the rest of the world. You've seen what will happen and why I had to do this." reasoned Sir Wesley.

~ sighs ~ "I know. I just can't help but think that THAT was meant to be and that THIS is not. The American people will not want a monster as their leader. I look like a monster."

"No Sir. What is important is what you can now do for the country. We are introducing a new technology that will better all of humanity. This will be your legacy. As for your prosthetics, you won't be alone. Think of all the survivors of the War that will now have new limbs, who will be able to walk again." Sir Wesley Chamberlain was doing his best to convince the President of his plan. They had had this discussion many times over the past few weeks and he was slowly starting to push Lincoln towards the idea.

"I don't know Wesley, it just isn't natural. It doesn't seem like something that God would want. It reminds me of a story I once read."

> *"I saw the pale student of unhallowed arts kneeling beside the thing he had put together. I saw the hideous phantasm of a man stretched out, and then, on the working of some powerful engine, show signs of life, and stir with an uneasy, half vital motion. Frightful must it be; for supremely frightful would be the effect of any human endeavor to mock the stupendous mechanism of the Creator of the world." ~Mary Shelley - Frankenstein*

"Sir, if God did not want this then why did he provide

me with the ingenuity to create all of this, to travel back in time to save you?" he pleaded.

"Perhaps it is but the cruel temptation of the Devil instead of the work of the Lord" responded Lincoln.

The three men sat in a secret room that Wesley had built in the basement of his own home. He had taken every precaution to build every square meter of it himself and it had taken nearly ten years to do so. It was quite plain with white walls and shiny white tile flooring. No artwork hung on the walls, only large screens and boards where Wesley made drawings and notes. Lincoln was sitting on a table that looked like a cross between a hospital bed and an ornately cushioned couch. The reddish brown leather covering was surprisingly comfortable. Wesley had gone through great effort to hide this room to include the power its machinery consumed. He was essentially tapping power from all of his neighbors so that his projects and testing would not raise any alarms. Wesley could not have anyone know, especially members of the Empire. If the Emperor found out, Wesley knew he would be tortured. He knew he would have to watch his family be tortured and murdered. He was painfully aware that his invention would be used to wreak further havoc on mankind. The damage the Emperor could do with it was unfathomable.

The world was not as it should be but working at CERN did provide Sir Wesley the environment he required to conduct his research. Officially he was working on emerging energy sources; unofficially he was perfecting time travel via his latest invention, the Portable Hadron Collider, or *PHC* for short. It was a relatively old technology but the scientists there never really achieved the same results that Wesley had. While they worked on weapons, he focused on Quantum Foam and Tiny Wormholes perfecting theories on time travel. Well, perfecting was perhaps an overstatement. One thing he had learned to be definitive; there was no such thing as "perfect" time travel. No matter how hard he tried, or how many times he tried, some things were just destined to happen regardless of his actions to change them. While he did not want to believe in destiny, he had experienced constant evidence that some things could not be changed. This time however, would have to be one of the exceptions.

Sir Wesley thought of the past 158 years and how mankind had spiraled onto the brink of total destruction. He knew that it was entirely possible that any day now it could all come to a crashing end. He hadn't slept in nearly 13 days and the virtual sleep sessions were no longer doing the trick. If he could just get President Lincoln to accept his new condition, deliver him back to April 1865, then the world could possibly take on her new course. The Emperor may never come to power and the British Empire would actually be that; British.

"Not the work of the Devil Mr. President, I cannot undo what has transpired. We can only move forward and hope for the best" stated Sir Wesley.

"So … please allow me a moment to comprehend" began Lincoln.

"You introduced technology that was nearly 100 years too early and it caused this world that we or YOU now live in? You are responsible for all of this? You inserted technology into the minds of children?"

"Not inserted Sir, downloaded. It's kind of like reading a book and afterwards having the ability to not only remember it but to comprehend every aspect of it. I believed that, if introduced in the proper environment; that of an innocent child, it could grow into something pure. I thought that it might be nourished and grow into a concept for good, one that might help people. I did not factor in the influence of parents in the 19th century. I forgot how things used to be and how different your society was from ours. Our children are independent as of the age of 5, aside from their automated attendants."

He had attempted to better mankind with the introduction of this revolutionary change in technology but the children's environments had been a factor that he had not given enough thought to. Their parents had taken his intent and twisted it for their own personal gains and desires. Rather than seeing the potential for good in the knowledge, they only saw the potential for profit and power.

"Answer the question Wesley; humor me."

"Yes Sir. It was not my intent but it did set the unfortunate course that brought us to this point. I think that by bringing you back and restoring a good and honest leader to guide the world that we can change that course for the better" responded Sir Wesley.

"How do you know that this won't make it worse?"

Wesley sighed. It was a valid question and a valid concern. Creating a utopia was becoming a theoretical impossibility but perhaps one where science guided men instead of war was obtainable.

"I do not believe that we should undo the technological changes that I've introduced. I do believe that by having you there to lead them that we can steer things back on course" said Wesley. "This world [gesturing around] is our alternative and I can assure you Sir, this is a horror."

Lincoln thought about it. He had already made up his mind to go back. He knew that there was chance of working and he desperately wanted to see Mary again. He missed her immensely but could not shake the fear that she would still reject him. He was still himself on the inside but the outside however, well, that was permanently altered.

"With all this technology, why couldn't we have disguised my modifications?" asked Lincoln.

"Sir, we have to keep in mind the resources we will have at our disposal in 1865. I fear that I have one more trip before I perish. The radiation poisoning will not allow me to make another and my body is deteriorating at the molecular level. If I didn't use the resources available then, you would not be able to sustain the bionics. You would perish sooner than the time we need to complete our mission."

"Everyone has to die Wesley, only God can defy death."

Wesley knew history's version of this man but the past several weeks he had gotten to know the real Abraham Lincoln and it only strengthened his resolve that he was the perfect leader for such a daunting task. He truly loved mankind and his honest and idealistic view and hope for the world was what they would need to rely on in order to pull through their troubled future. If there ever was an honest politician, Abraham Lincoln was him.

"Yes Sir, and sometimes God blesses us with the gift of time, time to accomplish great things. Sometimes we get a second chance. I believe that is the foundation of your religious beliefs, is it not?"

William Crook sat patiently by his President's side. He did not speak for he knew that this decision was an impossible one for the President. He knew that he was not smart enough to influence him one way or another. He also knew that what Sir Wesley stated was true. This man, as odd as he now looked, was his personal hero and the hero of thousands, if not millions of their fellow Americans. He knew that if anyone could do it, to unite the country…again, he could do it.

"What do you think Mr. Crook?" asked Lincoln.

"I … I don't know what the right answer is Sir. I just know that I will be there with you regardless of what you choose. You have my support and my loyalty, until the end."

"William, you are a good and honest man. You give me hope that I can do this and that America is capable of what lies ahead. Wesley; prepare us for the trip."

Lord Wesley Chamberlain was elated. He was truly optimistic that this would work. It would have to. He was also torn as he knew that this trip would likely be his last. While he had perfected the process of time travel, he had not been able to mitigate the side effects of the radiation poisoning. If he only had more time to work on this, he thought, and then he would figure that part out too. 'More time' he thought as he laughed to himself. Time was the one thing that this whole experiment did not truly grasp.

Wesley prepared his outfit. He loved the late 19th century fashion. He loved the elegant and formal nature of it and it made him feel like the English Lord that he was, not the slave to the Emperor that he had become, the slaves they had all become. It was ironic that Abraham Lincoln's legacy was not only to end slavery in his day but to rescue future generations from the slavery of Emperor Myamoto Musashi.

"Gentlemen, let's see if we can't save the world" stated an optimistic Lord Wesley Chamberlain.

They joined hands and prepared for the journey. Wesley pressed the activation switch that hung from his PHC and … nothing happened.

"How peculiar is this! The PHC is running perfectly, yet, nothing is happening" stated a perplexed Wesley.

Suddenly there was a pounding on the main door and the three fearfully looked in its direction.

"By order of the Emperor, I command you to open this door immediately!" a muffled voice on the other side shouted.

"It's the Imperial Guard, oh dear God! They are probably using an Electromagnetic Field to lock us in!"

Wesley was now in a panic. If he did not get them out of there immediately they would lose everything and he would never get President Lincoln back. He knew that the Emperor's men would confiscate the PHC and then he would have the power of time travel without any of the moral restrictions that Sir Wesley had. Even with his good intentions, he may have yet again led the world to ruin. He started to get the shakes as his stomach twisted and turned. What could he do now?

From behind the door Wesley heard a terrifyingly familiar voice, the voice of Emperor Myamoto Musashi. What could have brought the Emperor here himself? Surely this was beneath him. The only think that made sense was if he knew about the PHC.

"Oh dear God, he knows of the PHC. But how could this be?" said Wesley

"Lord Chamberlain. Open this door now; I shall only give you one chance to obey my order. If you do not, we will begin the interrogations on your family and friends at once."

“It doesn’t make sense; he could vaporize the door in a second if he wanted to. There is no real way for it to restrict him.” said Wesley.

“Perhaps he wants your rucksack and is worried that it will be damaged” said William Crook.

“Noooooooo, it’s to keep the EMF in place. If he uses a disintegrator to destroy the door then he will have to first lower the EMF. We will have to force him to break through the door. This will give us little more than a second or two to activate the PHC and get out of here” exclaimed Wesley.

“But what about your family?” asked Lincoln. “Surely you do not intend to leave them here to deal with this horror, not on my account.”

“If I get out of here Sir then this whole ordeal will have been avoided. Don’t you see, we have to get you home, it’s the only hope we have to ensure that this reality does not come to pass.”

“LORD CHAMBERLAIN! Open this DOOR!” screamed the irate Emperor. He had cut men’s heads off before at the mere thought of their disobedience and could not fathom being so blatantly disobeyed.

“Drop the shield and open this door” commanded the Emperor.

Wesley, William and Lincoln clutched each other’s hands with anticipation. A bead of sweat slowly trickled down President Lincoln’s forehead as they waited for their window of opportunity. They knew that they had a narrow sliver of time and that they would only have one shot at success. As they heard the Emperor screaming on the other side of the door Wesley clutched the trigger switch in his hand. He held his breath as the door bent inwards and then splintered into a billion particles of dust and tiny slivers of wood.

As the door vanished from sight the Emperor and his Imperial Guard rushed into the room as Wesley hit the trigger. A crackling of electricity and a blinding blue light filled the room as the men disappeared from sight. A bewildered Imperial Guard stood there, unsure of what to do next.

Chapter 21 – Just what I expected
Charleston West Virginia, June 1865

The caravan of wagons and armed men reached the outskirts of Charleston West Virginia and Gideon leaned over the edge of his wagon to throw up; again. He had been feeling ill due to the hot weather for the past few days. He could see his father's disdain for this sort of weakness and therefore chose to sit in the back of the main wagon. It hurt Gideon deeply that he could never be viewed by his father in a positive light. It seemed that no matter what he did, it would never be acceptable. The one exception was of course the virus. Gideon became sick at the idea that this would be his legacy in this world. He was too young to have ruined his life and hoped that he could figure a way out of all of this, a way to stop his father.

"Why are we not on a train Maxwell?" asked the distraught young man.

"Sir, the trains are monitored by the Yankees and any travel we could hope for to Richmond would be surely intercepted. We need to get to Jefferson Davis before it's too late." answered the gentle old man. He looked at the boy as if he was his own son. He was a good boy and deserved more than the cruel old codger that they all worked for. Even this poor young man, barely 10 years old, could enjoy a moment's peace. Maxwell took great pride in looking after the boy.

His train of thought was disrupted, abruptly, by the sounds of yelling and gun fire at the rear of the caravan. Gideon stood up and looked back. His knees wobbling, he maintained his balance. Maxwell stood as quick as he could but his old bones rarely cooperated these days. With a groan and some popping sounds, he managed to get to his feet. He saw people running at the rear of the caravan and they appeared to be leaping like madmen, hurling themselves at the soldiers with reckless abandon. The members of the Senator's party opened fire on their attackers but as each attacker fell, another would take out the gunman. It was a horrific sight to see. The attackers were not using weapons but rather bit and clawed their way through these seasoned fighters. The attackers seemed like raving lunatics, like ……

"Oh dear God, they have the disease!" screamed

Gideon. "But how could that be possible?" There had only been one shipment of cattle and it was to the North, to Boston. The virus should have exposed itself by now but it should be affecting areas days north of Charleston.

Gideon watched in horror as his "creation" ravaged a small army of men. The wagon jerked forward causing him to topple forwards and fall to the ground. The chaos around him was deafening. Men were fighting for their lives, firing their guns into the horde of attacking lunatics. Their screams seemed acutely louder than the muskets firing but the worst of it was the howling and screaming of the infected. They frantically grabbed and tore at the living, biting and tearing the flesh from their bodies.

Gideon stood and attempted to get back on the wagon only to notice that it was speeding off down the road. With each moment the distance between him and escape grew farther. He saw his father at the reins, whipping frantically at the horses. His father even looked over his shoulder twice and Gideon could have sworn that he noticed a cruel smile.

He had to get away but to where? The infected were swarming the convoy and working their way towards

Gideon's location. He knew he had little time, perhaps a minute or two. Scanning the area around him, he decided to hide in a nearby tree. Gideon ran and leapt to a low hanging branch. As he kicked his feet over the branch in an attempt to bring himself up he could hear one of the infected approaching. He looked into the man's eyes. They were opened to the point of bulging and were blood red. His face was twisted and gnarled as if in excruciating pain. He had narrowed down on Gideon and unless the boy was quick, it would be the end for him.

Gideon's hands were cut and bleeding as he clawed his way to get up on the low branch. His heart pounded in his chest and in the back of his throat. He desperately wanted to scream but no sound escaped his mouth. Desperately he pulled himself up and just as his feet cleared the first branch; the infected brushed by narrowly missing him. Gideon did not stop to breathe or assess his safety, he just kept climbing. He climbed higher and higher until he noticed that the branches were starting to bend and curve with his own weight. It was only now that he really noticed just how high he had climbed. As Gideon looked down scanning the area beneath him in a panic, he looked for anyone who might be climbing after him.

Surprisingly no one pursued. He noticed that at the base of the tree, perhaps 50 feet below, the infected had all but killed everyone on the ground. He noticed that in the absence of victims the infected turned on each other. Gideon found this interesting because it meant that the virus would eventually kill itself assuming that the healthy could protect and isolate themselves long enough for the virus to run its course. He also noticed that they did not attempt to climb the tree and come after him. It was a simple logical thing to do, climb the tree and kill him. It appeared that the infected lacked the basic ability to reason or problem resolution.

Gideon sat in the tree, clinging to the branches around him. He watched the horror below him unfold and then he thought about his father. He thought about how that coward took off and left him there to die. Even through his anger and hatred, Gideon still wondered if he had made it out alive. He was still his father and he loved him, even if the bastard did not deserve his affection or to live.

Gideon was getting tired now and it had been several hours since he saw the last infected on the ground below.

He had every reason to believe that they were not intelligent enough to be hiding and waiting for him. He had seen how they had turned on each other until most were dead. The remaining seemed to form a pack and head east. He wondered why some attacked each other and why some did not. Why had they formed a pack? What was it that drove them? Food, violence, anger? Even though he saw no one below, he had no intention of getting out of that tree. At least here he was safe. It was however getting more and more difficult to keep himself in the tree so he decided to tie his shirt sleeves and belt around the tree so that if he slept, he would not fall from safety.

As Gideon drifted off to sleep, his thoughts clung to his dear sister Lucy. He wondered how she fared and if the virus had made its way back to its birthplace. He wondered if the world would ever return to normal or if he had destroyed things forever.

Try as he might, he could not blame his father for everything. He should have been stronger, he should have simply said no. It was too late for that now, perhaps too late for all of them.

Chapter 22 – On the road again
Columbia Missouri, June 1865

It was late and Finnegan was tired. He hadn't slept much, in fact the only peace he had was his sweet daughter attempting to comfort him. It was as if he was the child and she the parent. He thought it terribly sweet and he wondered what effect this would all have on her. Would she be emotionally scared? Would all of this leave her cold and bitter? They had seen some pretty horrific things in their day but this was unlike anything anyone had ever seen. Finn felt as though he'd only slept a half an hour or so but knew it was time to relieve Declan.

He arose quietly so as not to wake Priscilla and the others walked towards the outer workshop area where Declan stood guard. As he got closer though, he heard voices. It was faint but he could tell that Declan was speaking with someone.

As he inched closer, being extremely careful to not alert them that he was there, Finnegan noticed that Declan was speaking with Victoria. They seemed to be deep in conversation and quite enthralled with each other. Finnegan decided that he would go back to bed and not disturb the two. He was not sure he had ever seen Declan really having a conversation with a woman. This surprise was a wonderful one in such a dark and disturbing time. 'Perhaps there is hope fer me brother yet' thought Finnegan.

As Finnegan turned to head back to bed his foot caught on a box of steel rods causing it to topple over on the stone flooring. The noise was loud enough to wake the entire city. As Finnegan cringed and froze in his spot, he could hear the screaming and moaning of the desperate Loons outside increase. Now the loons were pounding on the door and walls once again.

"Smooth move ya moron. I am heading ta bed, tanks for relieving me and wakin' da whole fookin' neighborhood" smirked Declan.

"Sorry bout that", stated an embarrassed Finnegan.

Finn headed to the workshop room to stand guard. There was a burlap sack of grain lying on the floor next to the wall. Seemed like a good enough place to sit. He leaned his back against the wall and listened to the commotion outside. He laid Tintreach across his lap and looked at their creation. She was a beauty of a weapon, like something from another world. The glowing globes gently lit the room as their purple and blue sparks danced within their glass confines. He ran his finger over one and watched as the little bolts of lightning were drawn to his finger. They looked much as he felt, yearning to get out of their imprisoned state.

Finnegan looked up at the ceiling in a moment of panic. He could swear that he heard movement on the roof again. It was faint though and surely not that of a loon. It was soft and careful. Clearly the loons were not capable of subtleties and grace. He figured it was someone hiding on the roof but could not figure a way to get up there and check without heading outside and that was NOT going to happen.

'Oh well' he thought, if they came down through the vent he would light them up like Bob the scarecrow. Meanwhile, the horrible sounds outside the door and walls were enough to make one go mad. It was incessant. The others had placed raw cotton in their ears so they could sleep but Finnegan did not want to miss anything so he left his out.

The night dragged on for what seemed like an eternity.

When day finally broke, the others woke. Finnegan could hear the rustling of bodies getting to their feet. He could hear the sounds of a stiff night's sleep releasing the weary travelers.

Finnegan's lovely daughter was the first to make her way over to the exhausted sentry.

"How are we going to get out of here Daddy?" asked Priscilla.

"Not sure sweetheart, … I'm just not sure" answered Finnegan. "Victoria, how did this all get started? What happened here?"

"I am not entirely sure to be honest. Mr. Peabody was the first in town to show signs. He killed his whole family and must have infected the Sheriff before they hung him." answered Victoria.

"What did Mr. Peabody do for a living?" asked Declan.

"He's the town butcher, why do you ask?" inquired Victoria.

"It may help us determine just what is going on…"

"And what to avoid" interrupted Agatha.

The group was startled to hear a child's voice speak

down from the ceiling vent. His voice, while young and child-like had an aura of confidence and toughness that surprised them all.

"It's the meat" spoke the young man.

Finnegan quickly raised his gun towards the vent and ordered the young man to come down where they could see him. "Show me your eyes!" yelled Finn. He had noticed that all those infected had blood red eyes and if the boy had so much as pink eye, he might get annihilated.

The young man lowered a rope and repelled down towards the floor. He opened his eyes wide and with a fair amount of sarcasm stated; "The name's Jonathan Stone. I may be young but I've killed more loons than you all combined and I did it without the help of some fancy weapon."

The young man made quite an impression. He stood less than 5' tall. He wore a dirty white shirt that looked to be about three sizes too large for him. He had a brown wool vest with a sheriff badge pinned on it. His pistol belt had two pistols and over his shoulder he had a sawed-off shotgun and a satchel which looked to be bulging with extra ammunition. His face was dirty which only made his big blue eyes look more intense as he stared at Finnegan. He wore a beat up old bowler hat with a set of goggles on them.

"That's quite an arsenal ya got der, I'm impressed" stated Declan.

"I've been surviving the best I can."

"Where is your family, are they…"

"Dead?" interrupted Stone, "Yes, they were killed by our neighbors one night. They just came over in the middle of the night and…." He seemed to be getting choked up.

"It's OK big fella, ya don't need to tell us more. You can travel with us if ya like." Finnegan offered. "You are obviously one tough young man and we can use all da help we can get."

"We're heading east, to Washington. Which way did you come from?" asked Declan.

"Kingdom City" came the somewhat disappointed reply.

"Let me guess, that's east of here?" asked Finnegan.

"Yes, I spent the last two days to get to here and now I get to go back? Wonderful!" answered Stone.

“So how did you survive?” asked Agatha.

“The Loons won’t climb, they’re too stupid. I happen to be a good climber so it worked out well for me” he replied.

“Why won’t they climb?”

“Don’t know for sure but they also have a real short attention span, kinda like my brother Joseph. He is alwa….” Stone stopped himself. It was obvious that this was a tough subject to relive.

“It’s OK son” said Agatha. She grabbed him and held him close. You could tell it had been a long time since the boy had been shown any degree of affection. His tough demeanor melted away and he quietly wept into the embrace of the equally tough Agatha Foggybottom. No one really spoke; they all seemed to be entranced in the moment and accepting the newest addition to their ragtag outfit.

“A very important man once gave me some words of advice. He said that the big man upstairs wouldn’t give us anything that we couldn’t handle. He just wished that he didn’t trust us so darn much!” said Finn.

The group let loose a reluctant bit of laughter. Agatha

revealed a smile, even if only a half one as she looked over to Finnegan."

"Doc Cooper was a great man" she said.

"Aye, dat he was" responded Declan.

"So, on to how we get out of here. I am tinkin' dat we open da doors and let ol' Tintreach show some more a' what she can do" said Finnegan.

It was quiet outside and it appeared that they may have a window of opportunity to get out of there without much resistance. The crew got their things together and Victoria packed a few boxes onto the cart. As she lay one down it made an awful thump.

"Jezzes, what ya got in der?" asked Declan.

"A few tools and essentials, I can't do my job without them. What if the wagon breaks down or you need to work on yer guns?" said Victoria.

Jonathan Stone scaled the rope as quick as a monkey and before they knew it, he was on the roof. "I'll check things out and see what things look like."

"You be careful up there!" warned Agatha. She had already taken a liking to the boy and felt the need to mother him.

"So does this mean I have a little brother now?" asked Priscilla with a smirk.

"You hush! Brother, nephew, cousin; call him what you will but that boy is a part of this family now. The poor wretched thing" replied Agatha.

It was as if a lost puppy had seen its way into the heart of rough and tough Agatha Foggybottom. It seemed to be going around though. Priscilla noticed that Declan was unusually quiet and very attentive at helping Victoria. She had never seen her uncle act this way around a woman. He was usually rude and callous and joked about 'drinking 'em pretty'. Now, her uncle was trying to be helpful and was even … polite. This was an interesting morning for sure. Victoria seemed to enjoy the attention but was playing a little hard to get. Priscilla got the impression that she was equally interested in Declan.

"Who'd of thought it possible?" said Priscilla softly.

"Aye, it's a friggin miracle if ya ask me" answered her father somewhat under his breath.

About an hour later, everyone was prepared and the cart was loaded and ready to go. Stone peered in through the ceiling vent and announced that all was clear.

Finnegan asked the boy “Ya don’t see any o’ dem at all?”

“Nothing Sir”

“Well, let’s all keep our eyes open and alert. Just ‘cause we got dees here weapons don’t mean dat we can stop ‘em all should dis be a trap.” Finnegan warned.

“Don’t shite yer britches brudder, I gotcha covered” Declan boasted.

Priscilla looked over to Ms. Agatha and laughed. She was quite amused at the behavior of her uncle. He was actually attempting to show off and impress Victoria.

“Alright, I am gonna open the door, we’ll round the corner and then Declan and I will mount the wagon and get the hell out of here. Declan, cover me while I open da doors.”

As Finnegan removed the heavy beams that helped secure the doors, then the iron bars, his anticipation grew until a lump formed in his throat making it difficult to breathe. As the heavy wooden doors opened, he could see the disgusting evidence of the scratching on the doors. It appeared that the Loons had scratched at the doors until their fingers bled. Finn reached forward to something small, coin-like, and white. As he removed it from the door he noticed that it was a fingernail. He dropped it in disgust and wiped his hand on his trousers. It was apparent that insanity and pure aggression drove the Loon's actions. Finn feared what lay ahead and wondered if they should just bunker up at the blacksmith shop.

"Let's get going, this town gives me the creeps!" whispered Priscilla.

Looking out into the street, Finnegan could see that the coast did in fact seem clear. There were signs that the Loons had been there but none that they still roamed the streets. As the crew left the workshop and veered left everyone breathed a sigh of relief. It was perhaps a mile until they would be free of the city but they all seemed to wonder what lay beyond the town limits. The Loons seemed relentless in their pursuit to attack anything alive and had perhaps moved out of the town into the woods. The thought made Finnegan very nervous as this was the direction they were headed.

Declan and Finnegan climbed up into the wagon and kept their weapons at the ready. Jonathan Stone followed along the rooftops and seemed reluctant to leave the relative safety of his aerial position. Nearly half way out of town he finally came down and boarded the lonely wagon heading eastward into the unknown.

Chapter 23 – Ladies and Gentlemen, the President of the United States Washington DC, June 1865

Mr. Peterson sat in his living room and attempted to enjoy the evening. It had been nearly two months since the President had disappeared from his home. He feared the worst but all agreed that he must be dead. The memories of that night kept him sleeping on an old sofa that was far too soft. He sank into it each night and woke each morning with a horribly stiff back and neck. 'It doesn't matter' he thought, he was not going to sleep back in that bed ever again. The President had died there and it was just too much for him.

Even at work things were different. He was now shunned by the other clerks at the War Department. It was as if they didn't want his bad luck to rub off on them so they avoided him altogether, which considering they all worked in a large room resembling a horse stall, was extremely awkward.

He had a wonderful glass goblet that his mother had given him years ago and tonight it was filled with Brandy. He sat back in the sofa and packed his pipe. Tonight he would ensure he got a good night's sleep, even if it meant a throbbing head the next morning.

The pipe was a lovely cherry wood, carved into a classic form. He had purchased it some time ago in a tobacco shop on 5th street. He packed the whiskey flavored tobacco and grabbed a match. He struck the match and placed it over his pipe, illuminating his face with a warm orange glow of the flame. Behind him the entire room became illuminated with bright blue flashes. Mr. Peterson dropped the pipe in his lap nearly burning himself. He was mortified. Up the stairs and around the corner, in what appeared to be coming from his bedroom, there was another extremely large flash of light and then a boom. He could hear steps now in his room and men speaking. At first he thought it was a burglary and perhaps the men had climbed in through the window but now he heard them cheering. He certainly did not have anything worth stealing so he felt comfortable ruling out thieves.

Mr. Peterson timidly walked over to the cabinet where he kept his musket. He removed it from the cabinet; his hands trembled as he loaded it. Powder spilled on the floor, going unnoticed as he kept his eyes on the stairway.

He clumsily placed the patch and then the lead ball, ramming it down the barrel with the long wooden rod. Lastly he placed the copper firing cap and cocked the hammer back. He felt somewhat safer now that he was armed and he inched forwards little by little, almost too afraid to walk. Each step he took seemed to get louder and louder and as he began his ascent up the stairs, each one creaked louder than the previous. He held the musket tightly in his hands as they began to shake again. His whole body in fact began to shake. As he cleared the landing and began the second flight of stairs the bedroom door opened. He raised the musket and almost fired until he saw him.

"M....Mr...........President?" asked the horrified man.

"Good day Mr. Peterson. Please do not be alarmed, I may look quite peculiar but I assure you, I am the same old me. Do forgive the intrusion, this sort of travel is quite new to me and I am afraid not a very exact science" said Lincoln as he glanced over at Lord Wesley.

"M, M... Mr President, they said you were ... you were dead." stated the frightened Mr. Peterson.

"Nearly so my good man, nearly so. Thankfully we were able to help" answered Lord Wesley Chamberlain. He clutched his stomach and leaned forward somewhat as if in pain. A moan escaped him.

"We need to get to the White House and call a cabinet meeting" blurted out Mr. Crook. "I apologize Sir, what should we do?"

"I think that is a splendid idea Mr. Crook. I should like to see Mary as well but perhaps in the proper environment. Mr. Crook, please run along and ask Mary to join us. Then get Vice President Johnson to assemble the cabinet." Lincoln was nervous. He had endured challenging times like the best of them but this was different. He was about to "return from the dead" looking like some abomination of man and machine. He was quite the vision, the poster child of sorts for the Industrial Revolution.

Mr. Peterson stood there, with clutched musket in hand, mouth wide open. He even had a bit of drool dribbling down the side of his cheek.

Noticing a possible accident just waiting to happen, Mr. Cook carefully removed the weapon from his hands and placed his right hand over Mr. Peterson's shoulder. He led him back down the stairs and onto the couch.

"It's alright man, we are about to embark on a whole new world and you have contributed splendidly!" said Wesley with encouragement.

"But the President ... is he alright?" asked the timid man.

"He is fine, better than fine actually. He's quite the technological advancement if I do say so myself." Wesley was quite proud of himself. Things were going better than he thought. Now he hoped that Mary would be as accepting.

"Whoa, perhaps it would be best if I took a seat as well." Wesley was beginning to feel quite ill and the pain in his head caused him to feel very nauseous. He wondered if this was it.

Mr. Crook was now running out the front door on his mission. He had no idea how he would make Mrs. Lincoln understand but he had to try. He did not know if he should make her aware that her husband was alive or if he should leave it a mystery. She was a no nonsense kind of woman who was very strong willed and opinionated so he chose to go with the truth and hope for the best.

As he ran down the streets to the White House he became very worried. He had a sick feeling in his stomach, much like the one that he had the night of the shooting. He ran faster and faster until he could feel his pulse thundering in his chest. Then, suddenly, off in the distance, he saw a familiar flash of light and a thundering boom. He hoped that it was Lord Wesley heading back to the future, or simply thunder but that feeling in his gut told him otherwise. As Mr. Crook sprinted down F Street, he passed the five blocks westward and then approached the Department of the Treasury. The night watchman yelled at him asking where he was going in such a hurry. William stopped and hunched over, nearly out of breath.

"Sir, I didn't recognize you. Where the hell have you been? You've been missing for almost two months!" inquired the police officer.

"Never mind that, you have to get Vice President Johnson and …"

"You mean President Johnson?" corrected the officer.

He was right. As far as they knew Lincoln was dead and Johnson would now be President. "Yes, forgive me. Get General Grant rather and tell him that we must meet in the White House as soon as possible. I have news that is a matter of grave importance to the nation!"

"Aye Sir. I'm on it" answered the enthusiastic officer. He blew his whistle and moments later two more officers exited the building and came to his aide. He barked orders but Mr. Crook could not hear as he had already begun to circle the north end of the building to cross the field and then he came upon the east side of the White House.

As William Crook came closer to the White House, he saw police officers running towards him. They were yelling for him to stop and he complied.

"I need to speak with the President, immediately!" shouted William.

"Sir, we all thought you were dead. Where have you been?" asked one of the officers.

"I'll clear all of that up as soon as I speak to the President. It is extremely urgent."

"President Johnson has retired for the evening. I am not sure it's a good idea to wake him" warned another officer.

"Again, it is a matter of the utmost urgency. I insist!" pleaded William.

William Crook was more than just the body guard of President Lincoln. He had spent a good many of years on the Washington DC police department before the war. He had served in the Union army and he knew just about everyone of the local law enforcement. He was a very well regarded and respected man and so it was not surprising that the young officer abided his request and entered the White House to wake the President.

William entered and sat in a waiting room to speak with President Johnson. He wondered if he would be happy to hear President Lincoln was alive. He hoped that he would be. He also wondered where Mrs. Lincoln was.

"This inconvenience had better be worth it Mr. Crook. I do not appreciate being disturbed so late in the evening" stated an irritated President Johnson, obviously having gotten out of bed moments earlier. His hair was a mess and he was tying up a heavy bathing robe to hide his pajamas.

"Sir, the … the President is alive. He'll be here any moment." said William.

"Alive? How can that be? Wha…."

"It is a long story Sir, one best explained by President

Lincoln."

As he said that, President Johnson flopped down in a nearby chair. He seemed to look as if someone had punched him in the stomach. William really hoped that he would be happy at the news but it did not appear that this was the case.

"Is everything alright Sir?" asked William.

"Yes. Smith; … assemble the cabinet and be quick about it!" ordered Johnson.

Mr. Smith left the room in a hurry. William could hear commotion in the hallway just beyond the confines of the awkwardly quiet room. They all acted as though the ghost of Washington himself had just entered. As Abraham Lincoln entered the room with his usual graceful gait he took long strides. His head was held high but he had a nervous smile on his face. He came to a stop in front of Vice-President Johnson who was still sitting in his chair. Johnson simply sat there. His jaw hung low and his mouth was wide open. He was clearly in shock, and for good reason. Here stood a man that was considered by all to be dead. Even though he disappeared, it was widely agreed by all the physicians that he could not have survived the abduction. Yet, here he stood and looking more than peculiar.

Lincoln was a very tall man standing at 6'4". He wore his favorite black trousers, white shirt with suspenders and a black knee length coat. His left arm however was anything but ordinary. He had brass and copper pipes that ran the length of his arm with gauges and hoses. The main copper pipe had holes in it and a wondrous blue light escaped through them. On his back, he wore a rucksack that appeared to be an engine of sorts. It was an odd contraption made of wood, brass and copper. Tubing connected the rucksack to the arm and had what appeared to be a smoke stack exiting the top of it. On top of his head, Lincoln wore a tall black top hat with a gauge, tubing and copper pipes protruding from the side. It appeared to be more of a fixture to his head rather than a hat.

"Andrew, I realize that I look a bit shocking. Do forgive me if I have startled you. I've been away for a short time and thanks to some modern marvels of science; I've been given a second chance to continue the work we started. I trust that we've apprehended the culprit that shot me?" inquired Lincoln.

"Yes……. Ah yes sir. Boston Corbit, a young soldier tracked him down and shot him almost two weeks after you were ….. well, shot. He was disobeying orders. He was ... they were all instructed to bring him here alive" Vice President Andrew Johnson stated.

"Just as well I suppose. I trust that Mary was unharmed. Is she around, I should like very much to see her and the boys" asked Lincoln.

"Sir, they left for Chicago two days ago. Mrs. Lincoln was quite distraught and wished to be with her friends in Illinois." Johnson seemed as if there was more he wished to say but was holding back.

"Thank you my friend. Perhaps we should retire to my office and await the arrival of the Cabinet" suggested Lincoln.

The two men walked silently to the Oval Office, both seemed as though they wished to say something but neither spoke. Upon entering the office Lincoln sat at the head of the large mahogany table. Johnson sat to his right, as proper protocol would dictate.

"Mr. President, I am afraid you've returned at yet

another difficult time for the Nation. I've heard some disturbing news regarding the South. Our agents inform us that Senator Flavious Tinkersmith of Kentucky has joined with Gen Johnston in Richmond and are planning to march on Washington."

"What of General Sherman? Is he not in that area?"

"Yes Sir but he is farther south, closer to Raleigh. That's not all I am afraid" Johnson sounded very grim at the moment. His tone caused Lincoln great concern.

"Go on; what else?"

"Lincoln, we've been receiving reports of a sickness that is rapidly spreading throughout the country. It seems to make those infected completely insane and extremely violent. Men have been killing their entire families, entire towns have been decimated." Johnson was almost ill as he delivered the grim news. He rested his head in the palm of his hand and gently rubbed his temples.

"I see. What do the doctors think of this? Is there an inoculation or some sort of treatment?" asked Lincoln.

"I am afraid not. We don't even know what is causing it. It seems to have started near St. Louis but we cannot be certain."

The two were interrupted by the sounds of baffled politicians approaching the office. Lincoln could hear the confusion as they neared. One in particular was recognizable immediately. A loud and boisterous man bellowed out orders and demanded answers.

"How can this be? How can the President have survived that wound and what the hell do you mean he looks like a machine?"

The door burst open and in walked Edwin Stanton, Secretary of War. He was a rather tall man with a large protruding belly. The buttons of his waistcoat were nearly bursting. His beard was long and scraggly. It almost appeared that he was disappointed to see the President.

"Oh Dear God! ….. Mr. President ... Wha….what happened to you? Where have you been?"

"Secretary Stanton, it is a pleasure to see you again. We do have a lot to go over and I'd prefer to go into detail when the other members of the cabinet have arrived. How have you been?" Lincoln attempted to redirect the conversation.

"Fine Sir, … just fine."

Edwin Stanton took his seat but continued to stare at

Lincoln intensely. He was well known for being quite brusque, even intensely rude. Lincoln could not help but dislike this man. He could not shake the suspicion that Edwin Stanton was involved in John Wilkes Booth's plan. Lincoln naturally had nothing to support this but his gut feelings were usually quite accurate. He knew Stanton had no love for the South but he had butted heads with this man on many occasions regarding how this war should be fought. He figured at some point tonight, he'd have to find out if Stanton had plans to leave town.

Not long later, the cabinet was assembled and Lincoln addressed them. He left out the details of his trip to the future but rather went into detail about the technology that he would be introducing to the country. He spoke of his plans to usher in a new revolution which had America at the helm. He informed them about how it had saved his life and while it left his appearance somewhat odd looking, he was still alive and able to lead this wave of change. Not all of the members of the cabinet were thrilled with this but Lincoln expected some degree of fear and hesitation. He hoped that being at the head of this revolution would be enough to gain support. He was pleased to hear John Usher, his Secretary of the Interior, state the possibility of helping all the war veterans who had lost limbs during the war. This was the kind of forward thinking that he was hoping to foster.

"Gentlemen, we have two major issues to deal with before we can plan for the future. I am told that Senator Flavious Tinkersmith has met up with Gen Johnston in Richmond and is planning on marching their 30,000 force on Washington."

"Oh dear God, we must evacuate the city!" a panic stricken member spoke.

"Gentlemen, we did not get to this point by running away from difficult matters. If we do not defend the capitol, countless people will be harmed or killed and many of our national treasures will be destroyed. I have no doubt that Senator Tinkersmith intends on destroying the city."

"Sadly enough, this is only half of our problem. I've also been told that there is a sickness that is spreading throughout our great nation. I'm dispatching a medical team and a company of soldiers west to assess the situation and to work on identifying the virus as well as to develop a cure. All we really know at this point is that when infected, the individual becomes uncontrollably violent."

"As for General Johnston and Senator Tinkersmith, we will meet them head on and end this once and for all. General Grant and his army are prepared, battle hardened and eager to close this tragic chapter of our history."

"Gentlemen…" General Grant interrupted. "My army still controls Richmond. I've moved them north to Fredericksburg a month ago so we are in position to head them off before they even get close to Washington. I will be joining my soldiers tomorrow morning."

"And I'll be joining them as well" added Lincoln.

"Sir, I must protest, we lost you once before and cannot afford to lose you again" said John Usher.

"I think that it's a great idea and will motivate the men to fight. Surely seeing the President on the battlefield can do nothing but help" stated Stanton.

Lincoln had no doubt that what he meant to say was that it would be great if he were to perish in the battle.

"Gentlemen, we hold this great nation's destiny in our hands and a new era is but a few courageous acts away.

We have one greater test of the will of the people and of this government and I for one will do all that is humanly possible to ensure our success."

"I wish you all a good night. I must ready for our trip tomorrow."

Lincoln looked around the room at the bewildered faces that stared back at him. How many times had he rallied them, and the nation, in the face of great adversity he wondered? How many more times would he be asked to do the same? He hoped and prayed that their victory would be swift and with minimal casualties although history had proven to be different. He feared that the reality was something entirely more horrific.

Chapter 24 – Lucy and Bobby
Lexington Kentucky, June 1865

Lucy had decided to find her father. She knew that he was heading east to Richmond and she desperately wanted to confront him about Bobby. She had always cowered before him, her entire life, but now things were different. Now she had power, she had strength and she was going to make him pay for what he had done to Bobby; to all of them. So many people were dead now and it was all because of his sick and twisted ambition. She also needed to find Gideon. Her poor little brother would be an easy target for any Loon. It may already be too late but she had to try and find the little guy. He would likely be the one smart enough to fix all of this.

She was curious as to why she and Bobby were different than the others and why they could communicate with their thoughts. She thought to herself; only two people could really answer that and one was dead. 'All the more reason to find the second' she thought.

Bobby didn't really care where they went but he did relish the idea of making the Senator pay. Even though he was infected, he felt like a million dollars. He felt like he could do anything and the fact that he was finally together with Lucy made him almost grateful to the Senator. 'I am gonna kill him regardless but maybe I'll thank him before I rip his head off' he laughed to himself.

Lucy punched him in the arm. He would have to get used to having her listening inside his head.

"Sorry but you know that he deserves it and besides, I've heard your thoughts as well."

"We have to find Gideon. I have to save my little brother."

Lucy and Bobby headed east down the road that they knew the Senator would have taken. They left early morning, not knowing what to expect along the way. They found that by jogging, they could make a pretty good pace. For all intents and purposes, they were making good time and both were impressed with how easy this all was.

"I feel like I could run clear to the coast...."

Bobby's boast was interrupted by the sound of wailing and moaning. They both froze in fear and prepared to fight. They knew what that sound was and they knew that they would have to fight. They could hear the commotion getting closer and started to see the sadistic images of their infected brethren. They were a terrible sight with blood stained clothing that had been torn and tattered from various struggles. Their blood red eyes searched for some poor soul to destroy and feed on. Their mouths were open and gasping as if in excruciating pain and they were getting closer.

"What are we going to do?" asked Lucy.

"We fight my dear, we fight. We're already infected so we don't have to worry about that. I say we find out how tough we actually are."

As the rabid crowd of Loons descended upon Bobby and Lucy they seemed to hurl themselves wildly at them ripping and clawing frantically. Lucy did what she could but there were just too many of them. She reeled back in pain as she felt teeth tear into her shoulder tearing her flesh. The pain was excruciating and she felt the warm blood run down her back.

"Stop!" she yelled.

No sooner than she said it, the loons paused, as if obedient children listening to their parent. Bobby looked over at Lucy who was now bleeding significantly from her shoulder.

'What did you do?' he asked.

'I don't know' she thought.

Lucy thought to herself, 'sit down' and watched as the mass of loons all sat down.

'Holy cow Lucy, do you realize what this means?'

'Yes, I think so. It means we now have an army.'

'Stand up', and the loons stood up. They obeyed every command that the two thought. They had their own lunatic army.

'My father doesn't stand a chance' thought Lucy.

As the motley crew set out on the road again Lucy thought about her brother. She looked around at the group to see if she recognized anyone. One of the loons looked like a soldier that worked for her father. She tried and tried to communicate with the loon but got nothing back but darkness, pain and suffering.

Lucy was becoming tired and concerned about her shoulder. The loon that bit her did one hell of a job and she was in considerable pain. She would just have to tough it out she thought to herself. Bobby had bandaged it the best he could and it wasn't bleeding any longer. It was simply a terrible amount of pain rendering the arm utterly useless.

Lucy and the group had been running for nearly two hours when off in the distance she thought she heard music. Looking over at Bobby, he confirmed that he heard it as well. They instructed the group of loons to wait in the tree line as they proceeded over towards the sound.

It appeared to be a circus tent. It was only supported on one side with the rest leaning over or laying on the ground. It appeared to have been on fire at one point and there were a considerable number of dead bodies lying around. Lucy scanned the area and noticed a small man sitting in a chair turning the handle of a music box. He was a very small man, Lucy figured he was around three and half feet tall. He was definitely infected but didn't display the same behavior that the others did. Perhaps he was like them?

'Who are you?' Lucy thought to the man.

His face perked up and he looked over in her direction.

'Can you hear me?' the man thought.

'Yes … we both can' answered Bobby.

'Oh thank God, I thought I was the only one that

hadn't totally lost it.

'Can you control the others, like we can?' asked Lucy.

'Only enough to make them stay away from me' came the reply.

Bobby thought about their "posse" and ordered them to come over.

'That is amazing, you can actually control them?' the man asked. 'The name is Harlesden Chessington, ring master of what used to be the Hatton Cross Circus. You can call me Harley for short.'

Both Bobby and Lucy snickered.

'Wow, I had no idea you had so many of them with you' said Harley.

'We don't, we have jus....' Lucy stopped mid sentence. She could hardly believe her eyes. They had left roughly 40 loons in the wood line but there must be hundreds now, perhaps more. Bobby decided to do a quick test. He thought the following commands:

'Stop, sit down, jump up'.

The group did as he commanded and Bobby breathed a sigh of relief. As long as they were able to control the loons he felt they would be fine.

As Bobby, Lucy, Harley and nearly a thousand loons continued their walk eastward to confront Senator Tinkersmith, Lucy could still only think of her brother.

'How about a piggy back ride? You know I can't walk as fast as you giraffes' protested Harley.

Lucy selected a sturdy loon and instructed him to carry Harley. She was starting to get a headache and was becoming more and more confused. She found it harder to concentrate.

The group, this "Loon army", was moving quite fast. Nearly two days later they approached Charleston West Virginia. For some reason Lucy felt her brother was near. She wondered if he had been infected and was like her but could not 'talk' to him like she could with Bobby and Harley. As the army funneled their way through a heavily wooded pass Bobby spotted evidence of an attack.

'Aren't these your father's wagons?' he asked Lucy.

'Don't know, could be. I never really paid attention to things like that.' Then she spotted something shiny near a tree. She ran over to investigate and noticed a bent set of brass binoculars. These she did remember. She had been punished several times as a child for playing with her father's binoculars. She wondered how many times she wished to own these and now they lay here on the ground, destroyed with spots of blood on them. Lucy picked up the once cherished item and wondered about her father. This was definitely his caravan. Although she wished him dead, she suddenly felt a pain inside.

Her head hurt as the strain of controlling this many loons pressed her to the brink of exhaustion. Her powers over them seemed to increase daily but it was more symbiotic than control. She was becoming a part of them and they a part of her. It was one big beast of a creature with her and Bobby at the helm. She was starting to have images flood into her head as she began seeing what they saw. Fighting off the barrage of thousands of images made her head feel as though it would explode. The overwhelming urge of the mass to kill made it rather difficult as well. Focusing that rage was nearly impossible and starting to take a toll on Bobby as well. Harley hadn't displayed any signs that he could exert control yet so it either took time to develop or they were the only two that could do it.

She could not shake the feeling that Gideon was near.

As she held the binoculars in her hands she started to see images of him in a tree. Was that it? Was Gideon in a tree somewhere hiding from them?

Lucy thought to the loons, 'Look up'. She hoped that she would see him somewhere and would find him unharmed.

As Gideon looked down at the mass of loons he was overwhelmed with exhaustion and fear. He attempted to count them but there were just too many. He figured that there must be thousands of them. He had been in that tree for nearly three days. He'd only come down once a day to scavenge for food and then retreat to the safety of his high perch. All he could do was sit and wait for them to leave. He hoped and prayed that they would move on.

One thing that stood out though was how passive they were. To this point, he had observed the loons to be completely out of control. When there was nothing living to kill, they would turn on each other. This group however, seemed disciplined. They still howled and moaned in the horrific manner that he was used to but they hadn't attacked anything, not yet at least.

Gideon thought that he was losing his mind. One of

them, a girl, looked just like Lucy. He knew that this could not be for if it was, then she was infected and he had lost all that he loved. No, that was definitely not her. He hoped and prayed so at least.

Lucy looked up in the tree and noticed the boy. She knew immediately that it was Gideon. Her intense desire to hold her brother incited frenzy amongst the Loons and they too wanted to get their hands on him. The army of Loons swarmed the tree and began shaking it causing it to rock and sway back and forth. Gideon held on for dear life and was thankful for his makeshift harness. He was too weak to hold on however and started to slide down the tree, despite the belt. He clawed at the tree, desperately trying to maintain the safety of his perch.

'STOP' thought Lucy. She could not however stop them as they rocked the tree back and forth. She watched in horror as the poor boy held on for dear life. His body flinging about in that tree. She knew that he did not have much time before he would come crashing down to a rabid army of Loons.

'Bobby, help me! We have to command them to stop!'

Bobby thought for a second and then Harley chimed

in, ‘Order them to attack that cabin over there!’

Both Bobby and Lucy concentrated on the command and the army of loons swarmed the abandoned log cabin. It was a good size log cabin that had obviously been burned and ravaged some time earlier. The windows were broken out and black soot marked above the windows and door. Part of the roof was gone entirely and the rest reduced to charred timbers. As the loons moved towards the cabin Gideon slipped free of the makeshift harness. His small body bounced between tree limbs and branches as he fell and went limp before she managed to catch him. The poor boy was unconscious and did not look well. His poor little face was bruised and he looked half starved to death.

‘Concentrate Bobby; keep them over there away from Gideon.’

The loons no longer cared about their orders and began slowly walking back towards Lucy and Bobby. She could feel their hunger and their rage. They were struggling to get to them as if walking upstream. She knew that she and Bobby would not be able to hold them back much longer. It appeared that as long as there were no normal people around they were controllable but as soon as fresh blood was available, they might be unstoppable.

'We have to bite him, we have to infect him. It's the only way to save him. He'll likely be just like us' thought Harley.

'NO! I have to protect him!'

'Lucy, we don't have a choice. If they get to him, he won't survive the attack. We have to do it to save him!'

She feared he was right. Try like she might, they could not hold off the thousands of Loons hell bent on getting to her brother. She leaned down and bit him on the shoulder. Gideon screamed out in pain and the Loons echoed his cries. The deafening sounds of anguish and Hell filled the forest air.

Lucy cried as she saw her brother drift off into a coma. She knew that it was too late; he was now one of them. She could only hope that he would end up like her and Bobby and not like the mindless creatures that surrounded them. The wave of blood thirsty loons weakened and they stood there, staring at them, no longer pushing forwards to attack. She held her little brother close and hoped for the best.

Her thoughts now turned to rage at the thought of her father leaving poor Gideon here to fend for himself. Now she had focus and so did the loon army. They let their heads back and howled in rage and she could feel the collective's anger and determination towards finding Senator Tinkersmith. Nothing would stop them, she would kill them all. The rage had engulfed the Loon army and they now searched for a target. The bloodlust was unstoppable and the ground below seemed to reverberate and rumble. The Hell that had been unleashed on Earth now had focus.

The sound of the Loon army could be heard for what seemed like miles. It was a most horrific sound; thousands of Loons moaning and howling in unison. The dull thump of their feet as they jogged eastward seemed louder than the heartbeats of the terrified residents just one town over. They prayed that the army would pass them by for survival did not seem possible should their paths cross.

It did not seem that anyone in this world would survive.

Chapter 25 – The Cricket
St. Louis Missouri, June 1865

Finnegan and Declan were quite pleased with themselves. They had encountered a great number of Loons along the way and their weapons had proven to be invaluable. Every single time they were called upon to defend the wagon they performed remarkably. Declan attempted to keep count of the Loons he had killed but gave up after the third day.

"I tell ya brudder, dis be the finest firearm ever created and yer popcorn maker ain't so bad either" jested Declan.

"Aye, dey be provin' der worth. Just have to hope an pray dat dey hold up."

"Ah, did ya have to go an jinx it?"

"Will you two shut the hell up? Just 'cause you got them guns don't mean that we are invincible. We still have a long way to go to get to Washington and we have no idea the state that it is in" chastised Agatha. She was worried about the group and in her experience; nothing threatened the safety of the group like stupid men strutting their stuff like peacocks.

"Agatha is right; we'll be in St. Louis soon and have ta stay prepared."

Finnegan knew she was right but she didn't have to make them feel like little children all the time. He'd have given her a hard time but figured it was better to take his chances with the Loons than to mess about pissing off Agatha.

Declan looked over at his brother and grinned. Finn could tell he was about to say something smart and thought it might be a good idea to get out of her way. If Declan wanted to get his tail whooped then so be it. Agatha did not seem to be in the jesting kind of mood.

"Why Agatha, what do ya …." Declan was interrupted by the all too familiar sound of howling Loons. Their wailing and moaning was only slightly louder than the commotion they made while running through the forest.

Oddly enough, the Loons were coming up from behind, as if they were chasing them. This observation gave Finn some hope that they might not have made it to St Louis yet and if they could kill them all here, they may end up saving the city.

"Dey be commin' up kinda fast brudder, you got yer

popcorn maker ready?"

Finnegan adjusted the dial to 5x and prepared to let Heaven and Hell rain down on these poor unfortunate creatures. Both of the men donned their goggles and prepared for a fight as the children huddled under the protective wings of Ms. Agatha Foggybottom. She held her two Colt revolvers tightly in her hands, drawn and ready. Her trusty meat cleaver was tucked into her belt behind her back.

"We have to get up in the trees Ms. Foggybottom" said Stone. "They won't climb and we'll be safe there."

"We don't have time and my behind ain't getting up in no tree, not in this lifetime at least" Agatha proclaimed. There was a tree with some low hanging branches about 20' away. "Can you get to that one quick enough?"

"Yes Ma'am"

"What about you Priscilla?"

"I .... I... think so" answered the young girl.

"Then get to it!" ordered Agatha.

The two hopped off the wagon and ran as fast as they could to the tree. You could tell that Jonathan Stone was quite familiar with this part of their current situation but

Priscilla was not. Stone was in the branch quicker than a squirrel but when he looked behind him he noticed that Priscilla was having trouble. Her dress was making it increasingly difficult to climb the tree and kept getting in her way.

Declan and Finnegan had already started to open fire on the Loons. Finnegan guessed that there must be at least several hundred of them. He noticed by their clothing that they were not from the city but rather from a small farming community. He always hated this part. Even though it was clearly a matter of survival, he still hated to shoot the little ones. It could just as easily be his Priscilla running after them. As Finnegan depressed the trigger the all too familiar crackling sound of plasma being released flooded his ear drums. The light was a beautiful bluish-white with the edges fading off into an intense purple. As the bolt of plasma hit the center of the group, it did as it always did; and split and splintered out to everything near it. They dropped like smoldering flies.

Over to his right he could see Declan. He almost had to laugh at the sight. Clearly Declan did not share his hesitation or remorse when firing upon the Loons. There he stood, with Slán held at his right side, its barrels spinning furiously as short blasts of plasma bolts fired into the crowd. Declan had a half chewed cigar hanging out the side of his mouth and his top hat was cocked to the side. His goggles reflected the bright blue light and despite the cigar, he still managed to laugh hysterically, even howling at times. He was clearly enjoying this way too much. The occasional obscenity flew by the cigar towards the Loons; who fell to the ground quicker than they could run.

Finnegan looked over to his left and noticed Priscilla attempting to climb into a tree. He panicked and yelled at Ms. Foggybottom, "Dear God woman, help her!"

Ms. Foggybottom ran towards the girl with pistols drawn. He didn't figure her to attempt to climb the tree so she must be going to help fend off the Loons and guard the children. She was definitely going to need help. Twelve shots would not last her long with this many Loons.

"Declan, we need to work our way over to that tree!" shouted Finn.

"Just don't shoot me in da arse while ya be running like a girl!" he shouted back with a grin on his face.

The two men traversed the 30 or so feet with Victoria right behind Declan. She stood there with her shotgun but didn't fire. She was the backup should Declan's gun stop working and she held precious ammo. Her left hand was on his left shoulder and you could see that she was bursting with pride. Declan would occasionally look over his left shoulder and kiss her hand, then bellow an wolf-like howl of excitement. They were definitely a match made in heaven. Well, one of the two locations at least.

The attacking Loons were nearly decimated by the time that they reached the tree. Their numbers had surely been reduced to perhaps a hundred. Finnegan noticed that Priscilla was now at a safe height in the tree and even appeared to be yelling curses at the Loons. It appeared that young Stone was aiming his shotgun at approaching Loons. In what appeared to be a heroic attempt to protect Ms. Foggybottom, Stone un-wisely fired his shotgun from his position in the tree branch. While it seemed like a good idea at the time, it proved to be a poor choice. The recoil of the shotgun sent him flying through the air backwards, about 10' into the bushes. He had fired the gun before but usually was able to brace himself to absorb the recoil.

Agatha gazed in horror as Stone flew by, almost in slow motion, until he crashed into bushes. She gave one last glance at Priscilla to make sure she was secure before she rushed over to Stone's location.

"Stay put little one! I gotta get Jonathan" screamed a frantic Agatha.

Finnegan and Declan stood there with their backs to the tree so they were unable to see that Priscilla had jumped from the relative safety of the tree limb to pursue Agatha down the hill towards Jonathan.

As Agatha approached the unconscious young boy her heart pounded. She feared the worse and panic overcame her. Tears streamed down her cheeks and she sobbed uncontrollably, a most unusual behavior for the rough and tough woman. She didn't care though, this boy was very important to her, almost as important as Priscilla. She could hear Finn and Declan still firing their weapons at the Loons but she figured that she would only have moments before her position was discovered. She knew she had to grab the boy and get back to the tree as quickly as possible.

As Agatha grabbed Stone and slung him over her shoulder her vision came into focus and was horrified to see several Loons within twenty feet of her. As she opened her mouth to scream a blinding bolt of light took off the head of the closest Loon. Then another blast and another until the small group of straggler Loons had fallen. Agatha could barely move, overwhelmed by the shock of how close she came to death. She looked for Declan to thank him but saw only Priscilla.

Priscilla stood there with a look on her face somewhere between amusement, excitement and fear. She was holding a very small gun barely bigger than her coin purse. Priscilla looked at Agatha and gave a smile that resembled her uncle. It was more of a smirk really.

"Not bad if I do say so myself" came the girl's modest boast.

"Indeed. Where the hell did you get that gun?"

"I think we should get to Pa and uncle Declan. We can talk later."

Agatha was dumbfounded.

Shortly thereafter all of the remaining Loons lay in smoldering piles of ashen waste. Declan walked about ready to finish off any that had managed to survive. He walked through the piles of what used to be a sleepy farming community but thanks to this virus, were smoldering piles of deranged lunatics. Despite what his brother thought, he did not enjoy killing them. He just got one hell of an adrenaline rush during the excitement of saving Finn's ass all the time. He was amused and prepared to tease his brother.

"It's not funny Dec, they were once like us you know." Victoria seemed disappointed in him.

"Na luv, I's just tinkin about how I have to save me brudders arse all da time. Dats it, I tink it's a cryin' shame, honest."

She didn't seem like she believed him and this may have been the first time in his life that he truly cared what a woman thought.

"When did you give my little Priscilla a gun? Why the hell didn't you tell me! I outta whip your ass Finnegan O'Sullivan!" screamed an irate Agatha Foggybottom.

"What gun? What da hell ya be talkin bout woman?"

Priscilla approached her father. Her head was held high and she was clearly looking to brag about her accomplishment.

“She has a gun like you two, only smaller” insisted Agatha.

Finnegan looked at Declan. He must have had a look of confusion on his face because Declan gestured that he had no clue what she was talking about either.

“Priscilla luv, what is she talkin bout?”

“Well Daddy, I liked your design and all but I found them both simply too big. My version is small, fits in my coin purse here and is just as effective as Declans.”

“When did ya, when did ya get it? Who made it?” Finnegan was confused. If Declan didn’t make it and neither did he, who then?

“I made it myself.”

“When!?!?” yelled Finn, Declan and Agatha in unison.

“Back in Lawrence; the night before we left. I call her the ‘Cricket’. Isn’t she cute?”

It was indeed a small gun but how had she made it? How could it have been that they never noticed it before?

“I didn’t tell you because I thought you’d feel bad about your designs. Plus, I never needed it until today.” Priscilla remarked, kind of matter of fact.

"It's true, had she not been there I'd be one of them" stated Agatha. She gulped, clutching her throat. The thought of being turned into one of them horrified her.

"Oh, dear God, could you imagine Agatha as a Loon?" asked Declan.

The group made a collective shutter at the horror of it.

"You'd be the first one I ate you little bastard!" said Agatha to Declan.

Finnegan held his daughter's weapon and admired it. It was truly a marvel and couldn't be more than three inches long. He was amazed that she could harness the firepower in such a small package. This surprise meant that they could make more weapons using less material and they'd be more practical for normal, everyday use.

"Dis is amazin' luv, absolutely amazing!" The proud father exuded approval.

Declan walked over and asked to see it. He didn't care if was small, he wanted to see it shoot. He aimed it at a tree about 50' away and pulled the trigger. It emitted a beam of plasma much like his but when it struck the tree it went clean through.

"Holy crap kiddo, dis if fan…" Declan was interrupted

as the whole group leapt to the side to avoid the falling tree.

"Could ya be more careful? If I am gonna die I'd prefer to do it on da battlefield an' not by a damned tree!" said Finnegan.

"Dats one helluva cricket ya got der kiddo, much respect!" Declan was very impressed.

"Thank you uncle Declan" answered Priscilla. She was quite proud of herself and was quite happy that her father was not mad. He seemed immensely proud in fact. God only knew what scheme he was concocting now. It made her worry a bit but decided that she would just bask in the knowledge that she had saved Agatha and Stone and was now an actual hero.

"Don't know 'bout you brudder but I need a drink!" said Declan.

"Aye, as do I. Let's check out St. Louis, shall we?"

Chapter 26 – I need a drink!
St. Louis Missouri, June 1865

The crew rode into the outskirts of St. Louis feeling like they owned the world. They were quite proud of their survival success and now they wanted a good hot meal, a strong drink and a good night's sleep.

The town looked as though it was untouched by the Loons disease. Even when they spoke to people about it, they generally had no idea of what they were speaking of.

"Maybe it's over" said Victoria. "We did take out a lot of them along the way. Maybe that last group was the last of them."

"Somehow I doubt it luv. Sometin that spreads dat fast and easy is only days away from being here. We need ta get movin' at first light" said Declan.

"I agree. Sound advice, perhaps the first time that has ever happened with you" teased Agatha.

"As much as I'd like ta stay and chat Agatha; Victoria and I have a date at the tavern."

There was a tavern just ahead and Declan was going to stop in. Normally Agatha would have passed but it seemed that Finnegan was going to stay with the kids and therefore she was going to get her some whiskey.

"You go and get yer drink on, just keep your wits about you. All three of them that is! I may be in no condition to save your butt if'n you get in trouble, again" returned Agatha.

Finnegan pulled the wagon into a small courtyard near the town hotel and waved them on. He was going to get some sleep and would watch after Priscilla and Jonathan.

"Where are you going young man? Get yer butt back here."

"I am gonna get a drink at the saloon with Declan" protested Jonathan.

"No Sir you are not. Your gonna get your skinny butt in that hotel and get some sleep. 'Have a drink' he says. Sheessh" Agatha was not going to even entertain it. She was not his mother but she had accepted the job back in Victoria's house and was therefore not hearing anymore nonsense. "Go on, get some sleep boy."

Finn put his arm around Priscilla and Jonathan Stone. He led them in with a smile. He had a lot of respect for Jonathan, even more now that he had seen the boy was smart enough not to fight with Agatha.

As Declan entered the bar he got his third; perhaps fourth wind. It looked like any other bar, men playing cards at tables, women and men at the bar. In the corner an elderly man played tunes on a cheap pump organ. The air was pungent with the smell of tobacco smoke, whiskey and a hint of urine. This bar was his kind of place. He foolishly thought to himself, 'maybe I'll get lucky and someone will wanna fight'.

Agatha walked in and was also anxious to get a drink. It had been a long and rough journey so far and she could use a whiskey to settle her nerves before heading to bed. As she approached the bar she noticed a finely dressed gentleman sitting a table with a rather lovely and elegant woman. He was of average height and wore a brown tweed suit. His top hat brim had been pushed upwards leaving his hat to appear as if it would fall off the back of his head at any second. He had a jolly smile with a very smart mustache that was twisted upwards looping back towards his nose. His chin sported an narrow patch of beard and Agatha's heart began to flutter as she stared at him. He sat and leaned back into his chair. It appeared that he was enjoying this too much and she thought that indicated that he was used to a more formal setting. His chair creaked as he leaned back and sipped on a glass of whiskey. She blushed a bit when she noticed that he was now staring at her.

Lord Paddington Aldwych was a very likeable gentleman. He was friendly with most everyone and prone to buying strangers a drink. He was no chump, not by any means, just a very cheerful and kind hearted person. He was very determined to have a good time tonight. He'd been in this town a little too long and it's "Wild West" charm had long since worn off. He was glad that his traveling companion and cousin, the Duchess Eloise von Strombeutel, had agreed to leave for the east coast the following morning. They had been traveling around the eastern half of America and had not found what they were looking for.

He loved the adventure that America had to offer and he had to admit, it was every bit as "wild" as the stories had promised. They had initially hired a law man to escort them and provide security but that had proven to be; how shall I put it; a poor investment. Marshal James Haddix III took his job a little too seriously and one rowdy night in

Lexington, he up and got himself shot. Sad part was it was in Paddington's defense. They kept running into the Irish everywhere and they really did not like seeing an English Lord. Lord Paddington decided that his money was better spent buying rounds. It put everyone in a good mood and they usually did not want to fight him; not even the Irish.

Duchess von Strombeutel sat at the table and surveyed the bar. She was tired and wanted to go back home to Germany. America had been an adventure but she was not here for that; she was here to find something particular and so far, America had been a tremendous disappointment. She had all but given up hope of ever finding it. She did have to admit one thing, it was fun spending time with her English cousin and this kind of adventure would never have been possible in their more "public" roles back home. It was not easy being related to the late Prince Albert or even worse as it was for Paddy; being Queen Victoria's cousin. Here at least, they had a little more freedom.

She noticed a brash looking woman at the bar staring at Lord Paddington, or Paddy as she often called him. At one point she noticed that the two were engaged in a very long stare and then the woman blushed and looked away.

"Oh dear God Paddy, that woman is staring at you! How crass" chastised Eloise.

"Yes dear cousin she is, and I rather fancy it. Do you think that I should go over and converse with her?" asked Paddington.

"Absolutely not, no self respecting gentleman would approach a strange woman at a tavern, especially one devoid of your breeding."

"Precisely dear cousin, that is precisely why I am going to speak with her right away. Seal your lips and give no words but mum." He tipped his hat at her and began walking over to Agatha. His grin was almost unbearable. She thought him quite smug at times.

"Don't you quote Shakespeare to me Sir, he was German!" Eloise quietly laughed. She was actually quite proud of her cousin. Despite being rich and swarmed by vulture-like women; he rarely fell for their charms. This woman seemed different though and she appeared to like him as much as he liked her.

Eloise scanned the rest of the bar. On the opposite side of the bar, a peculiar looking man ordered a drink. He caught Eloise's attention for he had a very long red beard and big mutton chops. He removed his top hat to reveal a spiked red Mohawk, much like one of the Indians they had seen in New York.

'He's probably Irish' thought Eloise. 'I should keep an eye on him; he'll no doubt be looking for trouble with Paddington'. The woman he was with seemed as though she was being accosted by a very large drunkard. Eloise could hear the woman clear as day.

"You touch me again and I'll rip those arms off and beat you with them!" she yelled with great tenacity. Eloise was quite taken aback. She thought to herself, 'American women can be so uncivilized.'

Declan stood at the bar. He had just ordered two glasses of whiskey and a glass of sassafras for Victoria. He was quite nervous and clutched the glasses tightly. He planned on asking Victoria to marry him tonight and the thought of it scared him more than any amount of attacking Loons or even Agatha. He had never thought of the idea until now and it seemed as good of a time as any. They could get infected by the virus or die any day and he did not want to waste any more time. As he gathered the three drinks together he heard Victoria yell.

"You touch me again and I'll rip those arms off and beat you with them!"

Turning around, Declan saw his victim for tonight. He was a huge SOB and very drunk. Fighting a drunk could either be a very good thing or a very bad thing. It was Declan's experience that sometimes a man got the drink in him and would fall at the mere thought of a punch while others would take on super human tolerances for pain and abuse. Those could be fun as long as you could stay ahead of them and didn't break a hand or your knuckles. Declan was about to find out what kind of drunk this man was.

"Get yer hands away from me girl!" Declan usually didn't give warning or challenge, he simply attacked. This time however, he wanted to make a public display for Victoria and he wanted to say 'me girl'.

The giant drunkard turned and looked at Declan. He gave a sloppy, drunken grin and stepped towards his red headed offender. As he made his move he lunged towards Declan swinging his huge sledge hammer like fist in a chopping motion. Declan stepped to the side and the drunkard's hand smashed down on the bar top. The impact was so powerful that several drinks fell to the ground spilling everywhere. Declan's drinks being among them.

"Now you've gone and done it ya bastard." Declan had a wild look in his eyes and was not about to let this slip. He stepped in and threw a left hook catching the man on the edge of his eye socket. The crack was quite impressive but it did not seem to affect the man one bit despite blood flowing down his face and onto his shirt. Declan followed up with an uppercut that jolted the man's head back. His neck cracked and popped like one would pop their knuckles yet he still retained his senses. He looked back at Declan, who was reaching for his knife now.

"Now it's my turn little man!" the giant challenged.

He grabbed Declan in a bear hug and head butted him nearly knocking the sense from him. He saw bright flashing lights and then black for a moment before getting really mad. As he readied to bite the man's nose off a bottle struck the back of the giant's head. It was Victoria coming to *his* rescue.

"Hey, I don't need any help here, got dis completely under control!" protested Declan.

"I can see but it's my rear that he grabbed and it's his hand that I am gonna break" she replied.

Declan debated on proposing at that very moment but feared that the giant drunkard might get the upper hand. Declan bit the man on the nose and tore as hard as he could. As it ripped, warm blood ran down Declan's chin and neck. The giant leaned his head back and howled like an enraged bear. His eyes were intensely fixed on Declan now and Declan now feared for his life. For the first time in his young life, a fight was not going the way he hoped. His arms were still bound and he could not reach his knife. The giant leaned in to bite Declan on the neck when he suddenly reeled back in pain. This time Victoria was to blame. She had taken the knife from Declan's side and jammed it into the thigh of the giant.

The giant howled as he dropped Declan to the floor and turned to face Victoria. He no longer seemed human and she wondered if he might be changing to a Loon. Victoria stood there, knife in her left hand, and her right hand clenched in a fist. She was not afraid. She was going to take this big fella out. He was messing up her evening with Declan and no man disrespected her and left without a broken limb.

The giant stepped forward to her, ready to lunge. Victoria didn't budge, she merely took a fighters stance and prepared for his attack.

As he stepped forward he swung his giant right hand attempting to strike her with a right cross. Victoria stepped forward, rotating her hips and putting her full weight into the strike. Her fist caught the giant right between the eyes.

Declan could have cried. Not because of the pain but because the love of his life had just knocked out the biggest man he had ever seen, with one punch! He was intensely proud of her. As the giant dropped first to his knees, then backwards onto his back, Declan stood there and stared. He took a knee and cleared his throat. He asked her right then and there:

"Victoria Aschenbescher; will you marry me?"

"Get up off yer knees Dec, of course I'll marry you!"

For the first time in his young life, Declan O'Sullivan said the following sentence:

"Drinks on me!"

The bar erupted in a cheer and barrage of hoots and

hollers. Agatha had debated on stepping in but when she saw how intent Victoria was, she stayed back and watched. Declan was like a little brother to her and now he was in love, and engaged. Tonight was a happy time; despite the gore that had preceded the engagement. The poor giant lay there on the floor, covered in blood with his nose hanging on by the right nostril only. He had started it and therefore deserved what he got but she still felt sorry for him none-the-less.

As Declan reached for his billfold he watched Victoria stomp onto the giant's hand. It made a god-awful crunching sound and despite being unconscious, the giant man still grimaced in pain.

"What? I said I was going to break his hand!" protested Victoria. She was a tough woman and kept her word, this would be no exception.

"Quite a show wouldn't you agree?" asked Lord Paddington.

She had almost forgotten the handsome gentleman in all the hustle and bustle. He had watched the fight right next to her but to be honest, he spent more time admiring her than he did on the fight.

"Ah, yes, quite a show indeed. You're English?" asked Agatha.

"Yes dear woman I am. Lord Paddington Aldwych … at your service" said Paddington as he took a deep bow. He held his hat and made a sweeping motion down from the right side, then across to his left.

"Lord is it? You don't say…"

"Yes, but you should simply call me Paddington or Paddy, as my lovely cousin insists on saying."

"What brings you to this shit hole? … I mean town." Agatha was now embarrassed. While the O'Sullivan brothers found her humor and vulgar language amusing, she could not imagine an English Lord thinking the same. She was quite mortified.

"No no, it is in fact a shit hole, I completely agree" corrected Paddy.

As Agatha and Lord Paddington continued to talk, Eloise scanned the room. She felt it was time to retire and it appeared that Paddy would be busy for some time now. She decided to go and speak with the recently arrived Captain Thaddeus McManus. She needed to ensure their departure tomorrow was still on schedule and that the young pilot did not anticipate any delay. She rose from the chair and composed herself. She fixed her dress ensuring that it was impeccably arranged. Even in this remote town that contained less refinement than most of the brothels in London, she wished to present herself as the Duchess she was. Naturally she had never been to a brothel however she imagined them better than this place.

"Good evening Captain McManus. I trust that we are still on schedule for tomorrow's departure?"

"Yes Ma'am Duchess von Strombeutel. We shall depart at 8 in the morning. I anticipate favorable winds and that we should arrive in Boston in three days time" replied Thaddeus.

"Very well Captain. Then I shall see you tomorrow morning."

Finnegan entered the bar in a panic. He had received word from the hotel front desk that his brother had gotten himself in a bit of trouble. While this was to be expected, he still worried about him and had to check on him. He scanned the bar and saw Declan over on the right side of the bar. He had blood all down the front of him and Victoria was wiping his face clean. No sooner had she finished, she planted a huge passionate kiss on him. Declan raised his glass with great enthusiasm to the cheers of his fellow bar patrons. Finnegan continued to scan the area and noticed a very large man sprawled out on the floor to the left of them. He had seen his brother fight and knew that he was very capable of besting an opponent but that was a very large man. He was quite impressed.

As Finn started to traverse the bar to his brother, he noticed a woman and man speaking. The woman appeared to be very cultivated and wealthy while the man seemed to be a soldier. He was wearing a Union uniform. She was quite possibly the most gorgeous woman he had ever seen. She reminded him very much of Esmeralda. Her hair was a lovely dark brown in wide bouncy curls. Her eyes glittered in the light like the reflection of a sunset on a choppy lake. She wore a tan and black dress with a large bustle. Her head was adorned with a small black top hat and black veil. He also noticed that she appeared to be taking notice of him.

He would have to come back to the woman though. First he had to find out what happened with his brother.

"Brother Finn! Have a drink on me! We're engaged!"

shouted an elated Declan.

"Drink on you? Wow, must have been one helluva fight! Wait… did ya say engaged?" Finnegan was completely taken by surprise.

"Yes, engaged!" exclaimed a very proud Victoria Ashenbescher.

"Look at what she did to this big oaf. She knocked him out with one punch brother."

Finnegan looked at the downed man once again and was horrified at the sight. The poor man looked very worse for the wear and his nose gurgled as he breathed. At least he was breathing, that was a plus. Finn wondered if they shouldn't move the man to a different location or call the physician. It seemed wrong to leave him lying there on the floor, much like an animal pelt. It indeed was a night for surprises. Finn noticed that Agatha was at the bar talking to a gentleman. She seemed to be somewhat timid and blushing like a school girl. Everyone seemed to be fine and now it was time to introduce himself to this vision of beauty he first noticed upon entering the bar. She was still talking to the soldier but seemed somewhat distracted. Finnegan hoped that he was the source of her distraction.

"Congratulations to ya both! Seems everyone is happily in luv tonight."

Declan threw back his head and finished off the shot. He poured another just as quick as he finished the previous one. He was going to be busy with Victoria for a while so Finn decided to make his way over to the lady.

Stepping over the still unconscious giant, Finnegan approached her. He tipped his top hat in an attempt to show he had some manners and class.

Duchess Eloise found the tall man walking in her direction amusing. Could it be that he dared to think that he was on equal playing ground with her? He was a good looking man but certainly not of equal breeding as her. Yet, she still found him appealing.

"Good evening madam…"

"Oh dear God, you're Irish!" she said with disgust and with that, she simply walked away.

Finnegan stood there baffled. He was used to that kind of reaction from people but he was more interested in her disappointment. He convinced himself that she was disappointed because perhaps she was in fact very interested in him. Yes, that must be the reason. Perhaps given some time, she could learn to overlook his former nationality.

"Don't take it too personally" said the young Captain. "She's kind of uppity. I heard she's related to Prince Albert fella that was married to the Queen of England."

"You don't say. So what brings you to St. Louis? It's not exactly friendly territory in deez parts."

"Captain Thaddeus McManus at your service, I operate the country's first air train service. I was testing my newest design when I met the Duchess and Lord Paddington" said Thaddeus. "I've got room for a few more passengers tomorrow, heading for Boston. Passage is only two dollars per passenger."

"Boston you say, what about the capitol? Could we make a stop der?"

"No Sir. The Duchess wants to get to Boston as soon as possible but we could head down south after I drop her off. That would be an additional $2, ... per passenger."

"What time can we leave?"

"Eight AM"

"Good dan, it's set. We will be six of us plus some equipment. Is your air train large enough for that?"

"Yes Sir. Got room for 20 passenger's total." He was quite proud and Finnegan was quite interested in seeing this air train. It seemed dangerous but this would give them enough time to get ahead of the loons. Sure seemed better than riding a wagon and having a gun fight every day.

"Explain the 'air' part" Finnegan said, somewhat suspiciously. He was trying to figure out exactly what the Captain was speaking of.

"Don't worry Sir, just be here at eight and prepare to be amazed" reassured the Captain.

"I don't do well with amazed, I do well with a good plan" responded Finn.

"Well then good Sir, should your plan involve reaching Boston and Washington far quicker than you could ever travel on the ground, I am your man. See you tomorrow morning Sir" answered Captain McManus. With that he walked off leaving Finnegan standing there pondering just what the hell an Air Train was.

Chapter 27 – The Air Train
St. Louis Missouri, June 1865

Agatha had been exhausted but the more time she spent with 'Paddy' the more alive she felt. They had been talking back and forth for some time now. Their pasts were almost equally as colorful. Paddington had never killed anyone but the fact that Agatha had, was even more of a marvel to him.

"So whatever happened to Bloody Bill? He killed the man you loved shortly before you were to marry. I am just dying to know what you did to him" said Paddington.

"It's kind of a long story. You sure you want to hear all of it?"

"Surely you jest woman! Of course I wish to hear of it." His enthusiasm was so charming that even though she was digging up painful memories, she did so happily.

"Well, it was over a year ago in '64. I recall hearing from the boys that Colonel Sam Cox was coming to town and he'd be purchasing some extra revolvers. We heard that he was going 'hunting' for that low life Bloody Bill. Well, after the boys did what they do, I approached

Colonel Cox and asked that I be able to join his posse. Don't you know it, that old codger laughed at me?"

"So what did you do then?"

"Why I punched him in the nose" said Agatha rather matter-of-fact.

"You punched a Colonel in the nose? I'll be."

"Yeah, one of his boys ran over and tried to thump me on the head with his rifle so I took it from him and swept his legs out. The other soldier came over and I punched him in the face as well."

"What happened then? All this before you even left to get Bloody Bill?"

"Well, after all of that, more soldiers came in and thankfully Colonel Cox got his wits about him. He yelled to take it easy. I remember him laughing and saying through a bloody nose, 'Ma'am, with that kind of gumption, I'd be honored if you'd join us. We may need all the help we can get.' That was that. I was on the posse."

"Amazing, absolutely amazing! What then?" Again, his enthusiasm was so dangerously charming to Agatha that she continued.

"Well, it was October 26th and the Colonel had located Bill in Anderson, near Albany Missouri. Knowing that Bill loved to ambush mounted detachments; Colonel Cox sent one near the hamlet to lure him out to our position. There were about 300 of Colonel Cox's men including Declan and myself waiting for him."

"Colonel Cox had us dismount and take positions by the timber. He sent poor Lt. Baker ahead to draw Bloody Bill and his gang to our position. He gave us clear instructions; I'll always remember how he said it too. 'This fight will be either victory or death. You must stand your ground.' I was excited to finally get the chance to kill that bastard. He had this coming a long time for what he did to Doc Cooper."

"Did Lt Baker get killed?" asked Lord Paddington.

"No; nearly but no. We watched as he went out of sight and entered their camp. We couldn't see anything. Then, all of a sudden like, we heard gun shots and we knew it had started. Lt Baker came riding back to our position as fast as his horse would go. You could see the fear in the horse's eyes as much as in Lt Bakers. It was as if Satan himself was chasing them with all the creatures of hell in tow. Not far behind the Lieutenant was Bloody Bill and maybe 20 of his gang. They looked like wild men, each rider holding his reins between their teeth and each hand holding a pistol. Colonel Cox reminded us to hold our fire until he gave the word. I counted the seconds as Lt Baker raced towards us. 'Hold ….. hold….. HOLD…' Colonel Cox yelled."

"The second that Lt Baker had passed our position in the timber he gave the order screaming "FIRE" and we opened up on them. Nearly 300 men shooting at 20 was quite a scene. The air was thick with the pungent smell of gun powder and visibility had all but disappeared. Most of Bill's men fell to thundering clouds of dust in the field before them. Bloody Bill and two of his men kept their pace and blew right through our lines, completely unscathed. It was clear to the young soldiers that they were not shooting at a mere man but the devil himself. Bill's horse whinnied and protested as he turned a very sharp corner to come back. The horse's muscles flexed and were glistening with sweat and its eyes showed that even it understood the stupidity of going back for more. Bill pushed forward with an unrelenting psychotic look in his eyes as he planned on attacking our position again. He leaned his head back and let loose the howl of a madman. His psychotic charge came to an end however just 10 feet from me as he fell to the ground. It was hard to see just who had gotten him and many of the young men yelled triumphantly 'I got him, I got him' but when they rolled Bloody Bill's body over Colonel Cox looked to me. He leaned down and removed this very meat clever here from the back of Bloody Bill and handed it to me stating: 'Believe this belongs to you Ms. Foggybottom.'"

"You threw a meat clever into his back? Oh dear God Madame, I hope I never make you cross!" exclaimed Lord Paddington with a chuckle.

"I take no pleasure in taking another's life but that man got every bit of what he deserved." Agatha felt quite good. She hadn't really talked about Doc much, nor about how she had killed his murderer but it felt good to finally get it off her chest. She also was quite pleased that she could speak so comfortably with Paddy. He was completely enthralled by her story and she was equally enthralled with him.

"This story is the best I've ever heard." Lord

Paddington was genuinely amazed by this woman. She was not only easy on the eye but boy did she lead an amazing life. He felt as though he could listen to her all day. She was the embodiment of how he envisioned the 'Wild West'.

"Oh hell, would you look at that. It's day already. The sun is coming up." Agatha was amazed, she had talked with Paddy all night long and now it was time to get up. She scanned the bar and looked for Declan. She and Paddington were the only ones in there aside from the barkeep. The nose-less giant had even gotten up and left, probably wondering what the hell had happened to his nose.

"Well Paddy, I had a great time speaking with you. I will miss you."

"Actually my dear, I overheard your boss booking a passage on our Air Train. It would appear that we shall have three more lackadaisical days in the clouds to converse as we traverse the heavens en route to Boston."

"Who the hell said he was my boss? Wait, an Air Train? Flying?" While Agatha was pleased to hear that she had three more days with Paddy she was suddenly terrified about the thought of flying. How was this even possible? It seemed far too dangerous. She had seen the balloons that they used in the war but couldn't imagine one that would hold all of them and make it to Boston in three days.

Suddenly the two flinched as they heard gun shots out in the street. Approaching the window with caution, they peered out into the orange and purple sunrise lit streets. There was a group of men running east bound who turned occasionally to fire their pistols at the group of people chasing them.

"Oh dear God, they're here already" said Agatha.

"Who?"

"The Loons"

"The what?"

"Never mind, we gotta get to the hotel and get Finn and Declan now!"

Agatha grabbed Paddington by the arm and practically dragged him out of the bar in a rush. Her heart pounded in her chest and she began to sweat on her forehead. She was horrified as thoughts of where everyone was and if she could get them in time filled her head. 'The children, oh dear God, the children' she thought. As Agatha raced out into the street she nearly cried as she saw Finn, Declan and Victoria rushing her way. They were accompanied by the children and looked as if they were all ready to go.

"We got up early. Kinda thought dis was gonna happen and wanted ta be prepared" said Finnegan. "We got a passage booked on an Air Train and I tink it be leavin' early dis morn."

"I grabbed your bag Ms. Agatha. Your stuff's all here" said Victoria. She handed Agatha the tattered old bag with a sign of relief.

Agatha screamed as she was startled by Finnegan. He aimed Tintreach at a small pack of Loons that were rushing towards them. Their would-be attackers were quickly reduced to smoldering piles of half charred bodies and ash. The all too familiar smell of burning Loons overwhelmed them with a nauseating stench. They were getting used to it but it still made them nauseous. The group nervously scanned their surroundings for more Loons when a dark shadow slowly engulfed them.

Finnegan peered over the roof of the hotel and slowly the others followed. All gazes focused on the sky with shock and awe as the "Air Train" blocked out the sun. The Air Train was immense with an oblong shaped balloon covered by a rigid framed insect-like skeleton. Below it, suspended by hundreds of ropes, hung an ornate craft resembling a royal naval vessel. It was magnificent site to see… and it appeared as if it was leaving without them.

"Son of a bitch!" exclaimed Declan.

Despite the appearance, it wasn't taking off from behind the hotel, rather it was approaching them. Finnegan's thoughts raced for a moment. He hoped that it was coming to get them and looking for a place to land. There was an empty lot three buildings over and it seemed like he may touch down there.

"FOLLOW ME!" yelled Finnegan and the group ran over towards the empty lot. Declan fired at some Loons running towards them. Priscilla fired her "Cricket" to the right and Declan fired behind them. The streets were becoming very crowded as the Loons appeared to be coming out of the walls. They could feel the world collapsing in on them and desperation was taking hold of their fears.

The Air Train hovered barely ten feet above the

ground and a long plank with horizontal boards was lowered like a bridge to safety. They ditched most of their belongings, aside from the weapons and Victoria's tool bag, and rushed aboard the Air Train. Finnegan helped everyone board while Declan kept firing; barely keeping the Loons at bay. The sound of both weapons crackled loudly in the morning chaos. Bright flashes of light shot out into the crowd of approaching Loons and splintered their deadly way amongst their victims. All over the city the sounds of Loons and their victims could be heard.

"Good Lord, what is this madness?" screamed Captain Thaddeus.

"Good Sir, perhaps this is a discussion best had at a higher altitude!" suggested Lord Paddington.

"Best idea I've heard since Declan's proposal last night!" replied Victoria.

"Leave it to the Irish to turn the entire town mad! What in God's name did you do last night?" asked a perplexed Eloise. She acted disgusted but deep down inside; she was quite thrilled to see her tall Irishman again. The way he wielded that weapon around, shooting their attackers, defending his family, it was all quite attractive to her. She blushed at the thought of the others noticing her emotional reaction.

Thaddeus adjusted a cluster of levers frantically and the steam engine roared into action. A large plume of steam rose into the air with a wonderful hissing sound. At the tail end of the engine, numerous pipes passed through larger stove pipes and on to even more. It was quite an engineering marvel. As the engine roared and hissed into action and the Air Train rose from its hovering position. Finnegan and Declan continued to fire into the crowds of Loons. Jonathan was on the opposite side firing his pistols as he stood next to Priscilla, who fired her "Cricket." The city seemed as if it were being swallowed into the depths of hell. Smoke filled the air and the sounds of chaos, pain and suffering drowned out even the noisy steam engines. Despite the relief of escape and safety, they could not help but feel an overwhelming sense of guilt as they left so many innocent people behind.

"You all just got recruited to becoming my crew. I didn't have time to get all of them so I am a few hands short. Mr. O'Sullivan; your assistance please."

"So it's free passage for us den is it?" asked Declan

with a smug look on his face. He looked around, surprised of their reactions. “What? … If I am gonna work den I sure as hell ain’t payin!”

As the Air Train ascended into the heavens Finn and Declan received their instructions with Captain Thaddeus. Agatha breathed a huge sigh of relief as she held Priscilla and Jonathan closely. Her maternal instincts were being overworked on this journey and could hardly believe they had all made it out alive and unscathed.

“Daddy … come quick!” yelled Priscilla. She stood there with her weapon clenched in her hand, pointing at a robust crew member. His head and body shook as if convulsing and he began to make a sound resembling a growl. He was changing right there in front of them. Finnegan looked at the man making eye contact and was horrified to see his eyes becoming a blood red. Finnegan knew he did not have much time to react. If the man completed the transformation he would be too strong for them to fight off and their weapons would be too powerful to use without potentially shooting the Air Train down. He did the only thing that he thought he could do, he charged the man attempting to throw him overboard. In doing so, he ended up falling overboard himself. As Finnegan tipped over the side of the large wooden railing, he felt a hand grab his foot and leg, saving him from plunging to his death.

"Ya need ta lay off da big lunches ya fat fook!" teased Declan as he hauled his terrified brother back onboard.

"Tanks brudder. Dat was a close one. Ms. Agatha, would you be so kind as ta check all the members of this vessel for signs of the Loon virus? Just don't push dem o'er board until we know for sure, OK?"

Chapter 28 – The Senator's army
Richmond Virginia, June 1865

As Senator Tinkersmith pulled his wagon into the streets of Richmond Virginia he felt a sickness in his stomach. For all his faults and disappointments, Gideon was still a good boy. He really had hoped that he would have grown into the man that he wanted him to become. Now however, it seemed it was too late. He had lost his only son to the very disease he himself had created. The Senator felt guilty however he felt he had to look at the big picture, the destruction of the Union and the preservation of the Confederacy.

The only thing that mattered now was to meet with Gen Johnston and deal with those Yankees once and for all. When this was all over they'd be running this country and he could finally set things right.

Richmond was a broken city. General Sherman and his troops had taken the city only a few months ago however they left it to continue on south to Raleigh. Fortunately, Gen Johnston had navigated his army west, around Sherman and now re-occupied the city of Richmond with nearly 30,000 troops.

Senator Flavious traveled River Road eastbound straight into the heart of Richmond. As he approached Armistead he was stopped by plain clothed men with rifles.

“State yer business mister!” warned one of the men as he pointed his musket in the face of the Senator.

“My name is Senator Flavious Tinkersmith of the Confederate States of America. I am here to see Gen Johnston. Bring me to him at once!”

“Yes Sir, we’ve been expecting you.”

The two men remained on guard while another group of 6 led him to a large brick factory building. They were various ages and all looked as though they’d been through hell a few times and back. Senator Flavious wondered just how many battles they’d seen and if they were capable of handling one more. ‘Never mind that’ he thought, we’ve come too far. This was going to work, there was no other alternative. These men would fight soon and would win this war, he was certain of it.

The Senator walked through a set of double doors and into a rather lavishly decorated parlor. It certainly did not look this luxurious from the outside. Textured red wallpaper covered the walls which displayed gilded golden frames with lovely works of art. The furniture looked to be French and was so ornate the Senator wondered if they could even stand up to regular use. The wooden floors were covered by a large number of oriental rugs, ornately woven displaying magnificent designs. The ceiling boasted a magnificent oil painting of Bible scenes resembling the Italian greats. The sweet smell of pipe tobacco gently danced through the air and teased his senses. It was a sweet smell, resembling cherries and bourbon. Senator Tinkersmith turned his head as he heard the sound of ice cubes being stirred in a glass. The glorious sound of liquid and ice was almost more than he could bear. He was so parched that he'd drink just about anything at the moment.

"Senator, do have bourbon and a pipe with me."

"Don't mind if I do General. It's been a long journey here."

"Lost your whole entourage?"

"Yes … and my son Gideon as well. Those monsters came out of nowhere; there were just too many of them."

"I thought that you had this planned a little better. Seems you've weakened the southern states rather than the northern ones. Your little experiment appears to have gone a tad … awry." It was apparent that General Johnston was neither amused nor inclined to follow Tinkersmith into battle. The General seemed to be pondering surrender. He looked defeated and beaten.

"General, we must act now and strike while the opportunity presents itself."

"Does it present itself? Or does it appear that way so we can have one last colossal failure before the demise of our country?"

"Why General, your lack of courage disappoints me. I thought you more of a soldier than a coward."

"How dare you, you… you bloated political snake! You haven't spent one day in the hell I've endured the past 4 years. I have thirty thousand men out there ready to fight for me and you want me to tell them they can't go home but rather have to go and fight for you now? And how dare you speak of cowardice. This audacity coming from the man that left his 12 year old son in the wilderness to be eaten by the very monsters he created! If this is the leadership of the Confederacy's future then perhaps we deserve to lose."

"General Johnston, we have a destiny that we cannot ignore. Not for a child, not for soldiers, not for another 4 years of hell. We cannot return our nation to the hands of Northern oppression. We simply have to muster your troops and set to Washington as soon as possible. We are so close. If we can defeat General Grant then we will have won. General Lee will come back and we can finish what we started all these years ago. What of Jefferson Davis, have you heard from him yet?"

"He was being held at Ft Monroe but my detail has not returned yet so I do not know his current status. I sent 300 men, posing as refugees, to rescue him. I should have heard from the messengers by now."

"General, we must march on Washington tomorrow. It will work, I guarantee it."

"I have little faith in the promises of politicians Senator. I only trust three things: my rifle, the abilities of my men and the knowledge that God has not yet finished with having me suffer."

"Then trust in your men's abilities and let them show

you what they can do. They've fought so hard for so long that it would be a waste to give up now when we are so close."

"I hope you are right Senator, I hope you are right." The General gulped the last bit of his bourbon and set the glass on the table rather loudly causing the guard on the other side of the door to peek in.

"Is everything alright Sir?" asked the nervous soldier. His eyes went from the General to the Senator and then back again. He seemed as though he was hoping for a reason to shoot the Senator. He did not like this man and feared what was coming next.

"Captain Caranci, assemble my Command and Staff. We march on Washington tomorrow. In a few days time the Yankee bastards will meet their end once and for all."

"Yes Sir" answered Captain Caranci. He headed out towards the neighboring buildings. The Senator could hear rousing cheers and hopeful banter amongst the men.

"See General, they can feel it too."

"I hope you are right Senator. Otherwise, those sounds of cheering men will be replaced by the sounds of their grieving widows. Like most politicians, I am sure you are prepared to make that sacrifice."

"Yes General, I am" came the heartless reply. The look in the Senator's eyes showed even less sympathy than the icy words that slid off his tongue.

The following morning, the last remaining force of the Confederacy began their march towards Washington DC. The force of nearly thirty thousand men was cheerful and optimistic that victory would soon be theirs. What they did not know of was the horror that approached from the west. The manifestation of Senator Tinkersmith's cruelty was approaching fast and not even he had an idea of just how bad things would get.

Several hours into the march Captain Caranci noticed two riders approaching at a very rapid pace. They were riding as if their lives depended on it and he worried of the news they brought.

"Lieutenant Buchta, get over there and check on those riders" ordered the Captain.

"Yes Sir"

Captain Caranci saw the men speaking and then all three returned to the column in a somewhat hysterical state.

"They're all dead Sir! All of Fort Monroe is dead, the entire post!"

"How is that possible? What happened?"

As the two riders calmed down enough to speak, they rode up to the front and briefed General Johnston. The Loons had infected the garrison of Fort Monroe and the two riders were all that was left of a 300 men detail and of a 4,500 man Union garrison.

What they described was a graphic scene of violence and horror.

"When we arrived in the town of Phoebus we could see the fort on fire. Smoke was billowing out of several of the main buildings and houses. We assumed that they were under attack, we just didn't know from whom. All of the town's people were hiding in their homes and had their windows and doors boarded up. They were terrified Sir."

"Slow down son, let's start from the beginning" said the General. "How about we have a drink by that tree over there and enjoy some shade."

The two soldiers, General Johnston and Senator Tinkersmith walked over to the tree and had a seat under the welcomed shade. An adjutant brought over a bottle of bourbon and the two men shook as if alcoholics waiting for a drink. The General took the first cup and offered it to the soldier.

"No thank you Sir. I's need ta keep my whits about me. You have no idea how they be" protested the soldier.

"How who can be Private?" asked General Johnston.

"Like I said Sir, when we got to the fort all we could really see was smoke. The town looked as though it were boarded up. The shutters on the windows were all scratched up and bloody. There were even bodies lying in the streets. Not just bodies of men fightin' but of women and children. They had been ripped apart and looked like they'd been eatin' on by animals."

General Johnston cringed and looked as though he would be sick. His glance turned to a very nervous looking Senator Tinkersmith, then back to the terrified soldier.

"Captain Lindfors got his binoculars ta see what was going on. Then he said what he wer seeing and I thought he was jokin' us. He said that the soldiers were fighting themselves. They were ripping each other apart, clawing and tearing at each other like they were madmen… or animals."

"We thought we could just wait it out and then attempt to rescue the President but our detail came under attack as well. I'll never forget it Sir, we were attacked by town folk. It wer men, women and children; all of them just as crazy and depraved as what the Captain had described. Their eyes were blood red and they howled and moaned like crazy folk. I shot until my bullets were gone and then I took off on my horse. It was the most horrible thing I've ever seen and now they're all dead."

The soldier was in a state of shock and had clearly been through a hellish ordeal. He knew that this 'ordeal' would be heading their way.

"Gentlemen, your service with the Confederate Army is finished. See the Quartermaster for your pay and head home to your families" General Johnston said with sincere sympathy. The two men did not hesitate nor did they bother with the money. They simply left and as fast as they could.

"Why the hell did you do that?" yelled Senator Tinkersmith.

"Do you want those kinds of stories circulating

through the men? We are likely going to have to fight those monsters and I'd just as soon not have the men terrified before we get to that point."

"Good point. At least the Loons do not have weapons. It should be easy to fight, right?

The General looked at the Senator and turned away in disgust.

"Damned politicians" was all he could answer with.

Chapter 29 – What a view
Harrisonburg West Virginia, June 1865

Finnegan closed his eyes and enjoyed the warm sunlight as it shone on his face. He felt relaxed as he thought to himself, 'I can get used to this'. This Air Ship was absolute luxury as they floated through the heavens eastward. There were no bandits, no Loons; it wasn't even hot up here. He had a few minor jobs to do but nothing too strenuous. It sort of reminded him of their first boat voyage back in '51. Of course, falling overboard would be more painful in this case, but the trip was quite enjoyable.

While "underway" Declan and Priscilla had built a personal flying apparatus from scrap parts and one of the plasma generators from Tintreach. It was quite impressive but they had not had the opportunity to test it out yet and Finnegan was becoming anxious to do so. The thought of flying on one's own accord, like a bird, thrilled him. If he and Declan had built it, he might be hesitant trusting his life to it but Priscilla had led the charge which provided him with a high degree of confidence. Well, as safe as flying could be that is. One wrong move and he could find himself barreling towards the ground.

“Pa, when are we gonna get there?” Priscilla asked.

“Captain Thaddeus said another day sweetheart. Feel free ta nag him though, he likes it I tink.”

“We should be there by nightfall tomorrow young lady” replied Captain Thaddeus. The young man was starting to grow on Finnegan.

“So how did you come up with the idea for this?” asked Finnegan.

“I served with the Army balloon corps in ’63 in Yorktown Virginia. While there, I had the pleasure of working with a German Baron who served as an observer. He was a brilliant fellow, that one, the Baron von Zeppelin. He had this idea to make a ship, very similar to this one but wasn’t much of a builder. When my boss, Mr. Crowe resigned; the whole project was kind of forgotten. I decided to try and build it myself. The engine is what I am most proud of. The others talked a lot but couldn’t ever get it to work. It’s a water gas using a water gas shift reaction. Basically I pass high-pressure steam over hot coal. I improved the chimney system which keeps the coal super-heated which in turn maintains a high supply of gas. It creates a thermo-chemical reaction by applying hydrogen in the steam to carbon monoxide in the gas. After it gets cooled and scrubbed by passing through the water vapor, it produces pure hydrogen gas. I don't need a whole lot of coal and I can power this beauty for several days. Heck, I may even be able to get it to cross the Atlantic some day. That would be quite the feat, don't you think, to cross the Atlantic? Heck, I could even put my name next to Magellan."

Lord Paddington added "You are quite an inventive young man Thaddeus, I applaud your ingenuity. America can sure use more men like you. In fact, perhaps when this is all finished, perhaps you'd entertain a visit to Great Britain and display your invention to Her Majesty, Queen Victoria. With the right financial backer, we could have us a very lucrative business here".

"Yes, this is truly a marvel of the modern world, why I shou…."

The Duchess was interrupted by Declan. He leaned over the side of the ship, looking down at the ground below. "Oh dear God! Look at how many of dem der is! It's an Army of Loons. There must be tens of thousands of them" said Declan.

The group looked over the side in horror as the army of Loons ran eastward. There were so many that they could not even begin to guess their numbers. Everywhere you looked you saw Loons running. It was like observing an ant hill only they moved as one terrifying collective.

"Where are we right now?" asked Agatha.

"By my calculations, we should be directly over Harrisonburg West Virginia. We are to head north east now towards Boston" answered Captain McManus.

"We have to keep east and warn da President. If we keep dis pace, we could get about a day ahead of dem. Dis could be enough time to prepare dem." Finnegan stated.

"I suppose we could divert our course, long enough to drop Mr. O'Sullivan off."

"Thank you Duchess. We have da opportunity ta save countless lives."

"Guess you are gonna get to use our flying apparatus quicker than you thought" Declan chimed in.

"I want to use it! Let me test it out!" shouted a very excited Jonathan Stone.

"Yeah, ah maybe not buddy."

"Why not?" the young man protested.

"Think of the shotgun recoil effect when you were in the tree. Then magnify it tenfold" added Agatha. "Probably not a good idea buddy. Hell, you could be the first person on the moon if things went wrong!"

"We will have good Thaddeus drop Declan and I off, then he will continue on to Boston with you all" said Finn.

"I ain't leaving you two knuckleheads behind. You wouldn't last a day without me to take care of ya" said Agatha.

"You madam are gonna take da others ta safety. I can't have anything happen to me girl."

"Don't get yer knickers in a bunch Finn! Just saying that you may need help" returned Agatha.

"I realize me friend but dis is sometin' I have ta do. I can't risk the rest of ya" said Finnegan.

It was a quiet ride from that point on. The once cheerful crew of the Air Train now looked as though they'd lost their favorite dog. Priscilla pleaded with her father but gave up after she realized he was determined to help. It was obvious that whoever waited eastward would need the warning and the firepower that her father and uncle possessed. She decided to focus her thoughts on the flying apparatus factoring in all the necessary calculations. He would have a steep learning curve but if anyone could do it, she felt that her father could.

Victoria and Declan were off in a corner of the ship. Their foreheads touched, hands holding the other's shoulders. They quietly whispered to each other. Priscilla wondered what they were saying but figured it was somehow related to love. She did not find all of that mushy stuff appealing and wondered why so many to-dos were made of it.

The Air Train sailed quietly eastward. Jonathan Stone leaned against the railing at the front of the massive ship. He was looking off into the distant horizon, unsure of what he was looking for but staring intently none-the-less. The young boy's posture stiffened as he sat up straight and focused on the horizon. He leaned forward as his eyes widened and his jaw dropped.

"What is that?" he asked. "Captain, come here! What is that?"

Off in the distance they could see smoke rising against the horizon. There were faint echoes of cannon fire gently breaking the silence of their flight. It appeared as though a great battle was already underway. Finnegan wondered if the whole world had gone mad. He wondered if they were too late and if it were even worth stopping them. They had been at each other's throats for nearly five years now. Would it ever end? Would it take something like the Loons disease to finally end this madness?

"Thaddeus, what town is that over there?"

"Should be Fredericksburg Virginia and just north, where they are fighting is likely Falmouth." answered Thaddeus.

It was a large battle and it appeared as though it had just started. Finnegan had to determine which side was the North. He searched the smoke filled horizon for the dark blue uniforms. As the Air Train approached the battlefield he noticed that the northern section of the battlefield was in fact the Union troops. Finnegan searched for the command cell and located it in the back of the formations.

"I don't think that I can get you that close Finnegan, not without running the risk of the ship taking fire. If that were to happen, we'd drop like a sack of flaming potatoes." He knew Thaddeus was right and that he would have to get there some other way. Perhaps he could be lowered by rope and then run to the battlefield. 'That would take too long' he thought. With some reluctance, he decided to use the flying apparatus and carry Declan with him.

"Get a rope" ordered Finn.

"What ya got planned there brudder?" asked Declan.

"We are gonna test this puppy right here and right now."

"I was afraid you'd say that. Fook it, why not! If I am ta die today, might as well be strapped to a flying Irishman!" joked Declan.

Finnegan donned the flying apparatus and looked at Priscilla.

"I never thought about the weight of two men. It should be able to hold you both but only for a very short time, and your gonna have difficulty controlling it. You're gonna have to get to the ground quickly and drop him off" warned Priscilla.

"It's the quickly part that worries me" joked Declan.

"Alright brudder; I'll go over the side with the rope and you climb down after the pack is started. You'll have to carry both guns and I'll hold you."

"We are so fook'n dead. Dis is never gonna work."

"Just wait to slide down when I've got da pack started and we'll be fine."

Thaddeus hung the rope over the side of the ship. The end of it was tied in a big loop for Finn's foot. As Finnegan climbed over the side he placed his right foot in the loop and prayed for a miracle.

"I am gonna lower you down about 10 feet and then tie the rope off" shouted Thaddeus.

Declan watched, like the others, in quiet disbelief. He was nervous and had little faith this would work. Not only did they have to get safely down, they still had the battle and the Loon army to deal with.

"Why the hell aren't we going' to Boston?" Declan asked with sarcasm. "Ah yeah, 'cause we're O'Sullivans and logic don't play much into o'er nature."

By the time Thaddeus had lowered Finnegan to roughly ten feet, he and Declan tied off the rope to the frame. He watched as Finn started up the flying apparatus. 'So far so good; no explosion!' they thought. Finn gently started to rise and then let off the thruster causing the rope to go taut again.

Declan slung both weapons over his neck and shoulder, said a prayer and then slid down the rope to his brother. As Finnegan grabbed his brother in a hug they made eye contact and laughed.

"I figured it would be better to face you dan to have ya spoonin' me" joked Declan.

"Tanks brudder. Let's just hope dat I can keep hold of ya."

"Ready?"

The two brothers sighed.

"Yeah, let's do it"

Chapter 30 – The Great Battle of Falmouth
Falmouth Virginia, June 1865

As General Johnston and the last Confederate Army approached the northern outskirts of Fredericksburg Virginia he was very surprised to see a large formation of Union soldiers marching southward. He felt as though someone had punched him in the gut. Despite what you may think, war was not something that he looked forward to. He cared for the men in his charge and watching them die sickened him to the core. These were the decisions that great men had to make however and he had sworn an oath to lead the Confederacy to victory. He was optimistic that they would be successful today. Despite his plans however, it appeared that Washington DC would not be reached today without a fight first. The great battle would be fought here and now. Fate would choose her champion this day and he was now more determined than ever that he would prevail.

He quickly surveyed the terrain for the best place to form his troops. He had not enjoyed any real success during the war and was now hell bent on this being his moment of glory. This was his last chance to show everyone his caliber. He had never faced General Grant on the battlefield before and was eager to knock the luster off that bastard's collar.

They were approaching a one mile wide peninsula area that bent the Rappahannock River and he figured that this would be a good place to form his lines. There would be only one place the Union forces could cross and it was all marsh. His boys would pick them off easily while they tried to cross and his cannons would push them back or press them forward. The tiny, one mile area was protected by the river and should give his army a good spot to sit and pick off the Union troops.

On the other side of the river General Grant sized up his options. President Lincoln had decided to ride a horse instead of sitting in a carriage which served as a distraction to Grant but he would have to deal with it. Lincoln wanted the men to see him with them in hopes that they would be inspired. He figured that the men needed to see him in order to adjust to his new, "look", but also to know that he was in fact still alive. The men seemed to be excited about his appearance and some even joked about their new war machine.

As they approached the city of Fredericksburg General Grant expressed his surprise with a boisterous laugh and an exasperated look on his face. He could hardly believe what he was seeing. Across the river the Senator's army was forming ranks on the other side of the Rappahannock River. "Mr. President, it appears our early departure was in fact a great idea." General Grant would much rather fight here in rural Virginia than in the streets of Washington. At least here there should be no civilian casualties.

President Lincoln surveyed the area and consulted with General Grant on a plan of attack.

"Indeed my old friend, indeed. So, what do you think General?"

"He's taken up by the river and expects us to attack by crossing the marsh there. If we did that, we'd suffer pretty heavy casualties. We'd be better off moving our cannons within range and opening up a few holes. We'll keep the troops back, just out of range and wait for them to break. We'll let the cannons do the work. It really is no surprise now why General Johnston hasn't won a battle yet. His men will be torn to pieces."

"Major Moses; move your artillery into position near the wood line there and over there on that ridge. Wait for my command to begin firing."

"Yes Sir" answered the Major.

As the troops moved into position President Lincoln made one last attempt to resolve the confrontation peacefully. He sent an envoy flying a white flag of peace to offer terms. The terms were quite simple, complete and total surrender. The envoy was to remind them about Lee's surrender as well as Jefferson Davis's imprisonment.

Senator Tinkersmith sat on his horse and watched nervously. The muscles of his horse twitched as if the beast sympathized with him and shared his anxiety. He watched as an envoy of Union soldiers approached. They were flying a white flag. He did not want to even entertain the thought of discourse. He was disgusted by the whole ordeal to this point and knew that once the origin of the virus was discovered, he would need to be in charge. Anything else would lead to his neck being stretched by a hangman's rope.

"I'll give $50 to the man that shoots them out of their

saddles!" yelled Senator Tinkersmith.

Before General Johnston could protest and call his soldiers off, they opened fire filling the air with a grey haze and the pungent smell of gunpowder. The envoy of four soldiers who had come in peace now lay dead on the crimson stained earth, shrouded by a thin cloud of dust. He had given his answer to their terms and now both sides prepared for battle.

President Lincoln choked back his anger and disgust of these cowardly and dishonorable men. If he had known the depth to which Senator Tinkersmith and General Johnston would sink, he never would have sent those poor men. He grabbed his megaphone and addressed the troops.

"Gentlemen, it is apparent the caliber of men that we face today. These cowards would shoot down innocent men with hopes of peace and killing them in cold blood. This battle will be the last of this tragic war. We are one wretched day away from peace and the restoral of the Union. Today we close this horrible chapter of our great country's history and begin to write a new. Let us end it with distinction and honor. Let us write it with the courage and dignity that these Rebels clearly do not possess."

The troops of the Union Army cheered loudly. Their optimism thundered over the field and river to the ears of the Confederates. It was a sunny day and the sky was blue as if God himself had unobstructed the view in order to watch the events as they unfolded.

General Grant looked to the Confederate lines one last time before he gave the order to fire. Thundering like the wrath of God, the cannons disrupted the tension of the moment letting the world know that it had begun. General Grant had forty eight cannons and he planned on using them until the barrels melted. The weaker he could make them with artillery, the fewer of his men would have to die. He had seen enough death and he prayed to God that today would be the last he must endure for this lifetime.

The cannon balls disrupted the earth and the bodies of the Confederate ranks with devastating effect. General Johnston was now beginning to see that he had taken the wrong position. He had made a smaller target and taken away their option for movement. He watched as his lines began to take heavy casualties. They fired back at the Yankees with their cannons but they were not inflicting adequate damage and he was greatly outmatched.

Fighting the urge to curse the heavens, General Johnson noticed something above the horizon to the left. He thought he was losing his mind as a huge balloon with a boat below flew towards the battlefield. As he focused his eyes he noticed that it looked as though two men were dangling below it before falling from the sky. They fell nearly 20 to 30 feet until a large blast of smoke and fire discharged from the one man's backside and he began to rise. The man was actually flying! It did not look very graceful; in fact it looked much like a bumblebee that was injured, flying in a wavy almost drunken pattern. He watched in amazement however as the men flew towards President Lincoln's position.

"Damn Yankees! What the hell have they got up their sleeves now?!" cursed General Johnston.

"Did you see that General? Was that what I thought it was?" asked a bewildered Senator Tinkersmith.

"It would appear that they have a few surprises for us Senator. We could be discussing this, among other things had you not blurted out an order to my men. I should have shot you myself right there and then and will do so should you try it again."

The miraculous sight of seeing a flying machine and flying men inadvertently caused a cease fire as both sides watched in utter amazement.

President Lincoln and General Grant were in awe as well as they watched the enormous Air Train approach their position. Lincoln knew that it could only be one man, Mr. Thaddeus Lowe. He knew of Thaddeus Lowe's plans to build the machine but he, like many others, thought it was impossible. Clearly they had been wrong as the proof hovered in plain sight, nearly blotting out the sun. As if the Air Train was not impressive enough the flying men approaching him nearly made him fall off his horse.

"Should I have one of my men shoot them Mr. President?" asked General Grant.

"No! Dear God, no. I must speak to these men at once. If that is Thaddeus Lowe then these men are on our side."

Thaddeus McManus, former apprentice to Thaddeus Lowe, watched as his two passengers clumsily flew towards the Union command position. He could hardly believe the wondrous sight before him. He felt a great deal of pride for his accomplishment of building the Air Train.

Thaddeus Lowe and Graf von Zeppelin both thought it was impossible and yet here they were. This however was something entirely different. This was two men actually flying. Well, one was flying at least. The other was hanging on for dear life.

"You could try ta fly a bit straighter ya know. This floating around crap is startin ta make me sick" protested Declan.

"Quit yer cryin' little brudder. We'll be der soon and den you get ta shoot people" answered Finnegan.

Declan was indeed looking forward to getting on the ground. The marvel of flight was greatly outweighed by his unsettled stomach and the fear of crashing to the ground or even possibly through it. Surveying the area below, he figured that the two armies had perhaps an hour at best before the Loon army would be here and then all hell would most definitely break loose.

As Finnegan touched down both he and Declan raised their arms hoping to convey they were not aggressive. The fact that they hadn't shot at them was a good indication but they did not wish to risk it. Several Union soldiers approached them with rifles aimed and shouting instructions for them to keep their hands up.

"That is quite a contraption you have there, young man. I never thought I'd see the day when a man could fly through the air. Thank you by the way, you've successfully created a cease-fire." stated President Lincoln.

"Thank you Mr. President but we haven't the time for pleasantries. There is an army of Loons coming this way. We flew over dem earlier. I figure dat ya have maybe an hour until dey get here. When dey do, you'll need everyone here to fight dem. Ders likely 20 thousand, perhaps more."

Lincoln looked at General Grant. He knew about the Loons but he did not know that they were organized and en route as an army.

"We are going to need those southerners to fight with us if we hope to contain this virus today" said General Grant.

"Wit all due respect Sir, yer gonna need dem Southerners just ta stay alive" added Declan.

"Hopefully we will get them to talk this time without shooting our messengers. How do you feel about flying over there and delivering a message for me young man?"

"Mr. President, did ya say shoot at da messenger?" Finnegan was unsure but willing to do what he could.

It appeared at least, that their flying spectacle had inspired a peaceful moment of intrigue on both sides.

"Do ya want me to come wit ya brudder?" Declan looked concerned.

"Na, if dey be wantin to shoot me dan I be wantin ta shoot back. Can't do dat if I am carrying yer fat arse!"

The two brothers laughed as Finnegan started the engine of his flying machine. It was quite the spectacle. Finn took Tintreach and headed off towards the Confederate command cell. It was truly amazing how well the pack flew without his brother. It was fast, very responsive and he cut through the smoke filled air as if strapped to the front of a locomotive. He did not know what awaited him and the echoes of President Lincoln's sentence taunted his courage, "... without shooting our messengers." He hoped that it was an isolated incident. Either way, he had Tintreach and would at least put up a good fight.

Senator Tinkersmith watched with both amazement

and horror as the flying man approached their position.

"Should we shoot him Sir?" asked a bewildered soldier.

"Yes..."

"NO, do not shoot, I repeat, do not shoot. The first man that shoots will take a round to the back of the head by my own hand so help me GOD!" General Johnston wanted to make himself perfectly clear this time. He was not going to let this idiot politician cause the death of any more of his men.

"Senator, give an order like that again and I'll put a bullet in you myself. Am I perfectly clear?"

"That man is working for the Union, therefore an enemy. He's coming this way with some sort of weapon and unless you shoot him, we may all be dead!" protested the Senator.

"The Yankees were just as hesitant as we are now which means he brought them a message. Now he's risking his life to come to our position. I will hear this message. You Sir should feel free to wade in the river and wash your trousers."

"Wash my trousers? Pray tell Sir, what do you mean?"

"You've soiled your trousers more than once today; perhaps you'd like to freshen up!"

"I'll see you hang for that you insolent bastard! …" screamed the Senator.

"Gentlemen please; you can box each other afterwards if you like. It is unsettling to the men and our messenger approaches" warned the young Captain.

The Captain was right. General Johnston wanted to know who this man was and of his message.

Finnegan did not like the look of the scene that he was approaching. The two main men seemed to be in a hot argument and he wondered if the argument was who would get to shoot him first. The anticipation was turning his stomach in knots. He worried about Priscilla and the others. He worried that this was all one horrible mistake. He worried about how much time he had before the area would be infested with the Loons.

As Finnegan approached the head men the soldiers surrounding them moved out of the way clearing a spot for him to land. His hands gripped Tintreach tight, turning his knuckles white.

"Advance and be recognized" shouted the young

Captain.

"Da names Finnegan O'Sullivan and I have grave news I'm afraid."

"What news do you bring us and how could it be graver than war?" asked General Johnston.

"There is a virus dat turns men, women an' children into murderous lunatics. We've been calling them Loons. They are very fast an' very violent. We flew o'er dem a few hours ago and I recon dey'll be here in about an hour or less."

"We know something of the Loons; don't we Senator?"

"This man is a lunatic himself. Everyone knows you don't trust an Irishman, especially one that flies!"

There was rumbling in the crowd of soldiers as they nervously mumbled to each other. Finnegan could not tell if it was in response to the Irish comment (many of the soldiers there were Irish) or if regarding the Loons. He decided that he would just have to lay the plan out there and hope that they agreed.

"You are going to have ta join with dose Yankees if ya want ta survive. I figure ders 'bout twenty ta tirty thousand of dem. Da only way we'll hold dem off is if we join forces."

"Fight with those murderous Yankees? I'd sooner die!" shouted the Senator.

"You won't just die Sir. I hear that you become one of them. My cousin told me about it in Richmond. He said that your eyes turn blood red and that you stay in constant pain 'cause you howl and moan all the time." The young soldier seemed as though he was reciting some fairy tale but Finnegan knew he was spot on.

"Dat is exactly how it is. I've been fighting dem since Missouri" added Finn.

"How do we know this isn't just a trap?" asked Captain Felt.

As Finnegan tried to explain once again he was interrupted by the sound of yelling and gun fire from the Union troops.

"I knew it, it's a trap!" yelled Senator Tinkersmith.

"It's no trap Senator; they're firing to their right. Someone is attacking their flank!"

"You have to get yer Army tru da marsh and join the fight" pleaded Finnegan. He knew that Declan was over there and he had to hurry.

"We should just let the Loons take care of them, and then we won't have to."

"They'll be annihilated and den you'll be next ya fool. You can stay here and be cowards dat die an hour from now or ya can join the fight and perhaps win. Yer choice General, I just hope ya make da honorable one" said Finnegan with disgust.

He started the engines of his flying apparatus and took off towards the location where he left Declan. If the Confederates were going to join, they had all the convincing he was going to give today. He hoped that they would come to their senses but he could not wait any longer. As he roared through the air he searched for his brother. Declan was not difficult to find, he just had to head towards the bright flashes of light. Declan seemed to be having a splendid time. The Union troops had formed their lines to the West and were firing everything they had at the Loon army. It was like shooting into a tidal wave though as the Loons poured onto them with such a force that Declan seemed to be the only open area. Finnegan shot into the Loons with Tintreach and hoped that this would not be the end of their journey. As Finn landed to the ground he slowly made his way closer to his brother's side. If their weapons would hold up and they stood side to side, they may be able to hold out. Declan obviously had the same idea and within moments the two brothers stood side by side, firing blasts of plasma into the hordes of attacking Loons. They could not see anything but Loons. The sound was deafening as the electric crackle of Tintreach splintered and electrified the onslaught of Loon attackers. The Loons howled and screamed in pain, driven by a madness that would not be swayed by anything. Their blood red eyes sought out their targets and they pushed on even after waves of them fell to smoldering piles of ash and burnt flesh. The Loons amassing near Finnegan and Declan actually had to climb over the bodies of their fellow assailants just to get towards the brothers. The air was thick with the stench of burning flesh and all hope seemed lost.

"HOW MUCH LONGER DO YA TINK DESE WILL HOLD UP BEFORE WE RUN OUTTA JUICE?" shouted Declan over the noise?

"NO CLUE BRUDDER!"

"FIRE DAT PACK UP AND GET DA HELL OUTTA HERE" ordered Declan.

"NOT A CHANCE LITTLE BRUDDER. I AM HERE WIT YA NO MATTER WHAT YA SAY." Finnegan was insulted to think that his brother would have him leave him here to die. What kind of coward did he take him for?

"STUBBORN SON OF A BITCH!"

"SURE HOPE DOSE REBELS QUIT CRAPPIN' DER PANTS AND GET DA HELL OVER HERE TO HELP" Finn looked around and noticed that the Union forces had collapsed their ranks to a much smaller column and were actually helping them by firing into the Loon ranks. Finn and Declan were singlehandedly holding off thousands of attacking Loons. Finnegan felt an overwhelming sense of accomplishment, not only for their bravery but for the success of their weapons. If they lived, he thought, they surely need not "sell" the weapons capabilities; they were advertising themselves quite vehemently this day.

President Lincoln watched in horror as the Loon army swarmed onto his men like ants smothering honey. His stomach was twisted and sick at the thought of their plight. Some of his men desperately pleaded for him to escape before the opportunity was no longer an option but he would not leave them. He had resigned himself that if it were God's plan for him to come back from the dead then it was also his plan to stay here until the end. He hoped that his presence would be motivation enough to the men but he knew that they were fighting for their lives and needed no more motivation that that. He looked over at General Grant and noticed a twinkle in the chiseled General's glance. He stroked his beard as if contemplating something brash.

"Well Sir, I ain't sitting back here and watching them slowly be destroyed." With that, General Grant yelled a few commands to his officers and led a cavalry charge to the left flank of the Loon army. Before President could protest, his attention was turned to his left at the sight of the Confederate Army, also leading a similar charge. Their entire Army was in a feverish rush to the Union left flank. Before he knew it Blue and Grey were standing side by side, united against a common enemy. All the differences over the past 15 years seemed to have been placed on hold while his fellow Americans desperately battled against the odds.

"President Lincoln! President Lincoln!" a young woman's voice pierced the air behind him. As President Lincoln turned away from the battlefield, he was facing the massive Air Train. A young woman leaned over the side attempting to hand him something. He whipped his horse into action and rode over. The Air Train floated only ten feet above the ground and the pilot looked extremely nervous and he fiddled with various levers, occasionally looking up.

The young woman tossed him a small weapon, barely bigger than that blasted Derringer Booth had used on him. He held it in his hand and marveled at its design.

"Just flip the switch on the side and watch out! Go help my father please!" yelled Priscilla.

"Thank you young lady! I shall do just that" he replied with a youthful vigor.

Lincoln turned his horse towards the battlefield. He felt a sense of freedom, even optimism. Even if they should fail today, he had at least accomplished one thing. America was united, even if for only this brief moment in her turbulent history. He let out a yell catching the men by surprise. The adrenaline coursed through his veins and he charged into the thick of the battle. His entourage of soldiers had a tough time keeping up with him and were quite inspired. It was a glorious sight to the men. As they fired as fast as they could, the men saw not only General Grant leading a charge but their President as well. He fired Priscilla's "Cricket" into the foray and prayed for the best.

As Lincoln charged into the heat of battle he was quickly reminded that it had been some time since he last rode like this. He was uncertain and at times quite clumsy. He did not let this deter him however and chose rather to focus on firing this amazing little weapon. He merely aimed and pulled the trigger. A short, six inch beam of light shot from the gun and killed its target with a single shot. As the blast of light hit a Loon, he marveled at the horrific sight of its effectiveness. The Loon was instantly incapacitated and then the wound smoldered and disintegrated at a rapid rate. The Loon was reduced to a smoldering, half disintegrated pile of flesh within the span of several minutes. It was horrific. President Lincoln would remember the face of each individual he sent to their maker this today. It was intensely surreal and while he was glad to have this power he could not help but worry about the future.

Meanwhile, Finnegan and Declan watched the Air Train rise into the sky again, into safety. They were both extremely relieved. Neither wanted to die on this battlefield but they certainly did not want anything to happen to their loved ones.

As the Air Train ascended into the safety of the heavens, Priscilla watched the bright flashing spot where her father and uncle fought for their lives. Tears streamed down her cheeks and she looked over at Victoria. She was in a similar emotional state of worry. The two stood there, looking over the edge of the ship into the dismal horror that unfolded below them. The Loons seemed to be gaining ground, despite the reinforcement of the Confederate troops.

On the far west of the raging battle, Lucy searched for her father. She had a very tough time focusing herself with all of the commotion going on. She felt every bullet hurled into a Loon and in turn, they reflected her ever growing rage. She did not care about the battle or the soldiers that they faced today. She only cared about one thing, she had to find that bastard and make him pay.

Harley stood on the shoulders of his ‘transportation’ and scanned the chaos. He too felt an overwhelming urge to find this Senator. He was affected by the psychic connection but he wanted to find the Senator as well. He had suffered his own losses and desperately wanted revenge. He had lost the only family he had ever known, his circus. It was his calling in life and now it was gone thanks to one scheming, murderous politician.

Through the smoke and chaos they saw him. Harley knew it was him. He wasn’t sure how but he knew without the shadow of a doubt. Before he could say anything to Lucy she shouted.

“Good job Harley. Let’s get that bastard!”

With that, the main force of the Loon army split from the battlefield and charged the Senator’s position. The thrill of zeroing in on their target was electrifying. They ran as fast as they could and their grunts synchronized rhythmically like some horde driven by a primal force. They ran faster and faster, completely forgetting about the army to their left.

The President and Generals Johnston and Grant watched with a tremendous sense of relief as the Loon army broke and gave chase to Senator Tinkersmith. They could see the coward attempt to flee but in vain. As he was torn from his horse they watched a female Loon rip his arm off. She began to beat him with it and he fell to the ground. She sank into the pit of attacking Loons only to surface seconds later with the Senators detached head in one hand and his entrails in the other. The mass of Loons raised their heads back and released a most gruesome howl.

"QUICKLY MEN! We haven't much time. Form ranks! FORM RANKS!!" General Grant yelled. He knew they only had moments until the fury of the Loon army was redirected back towards them.

"Mighty fine job there Mr. President!" exclaimed Finnegan as he rushed over. "I see you are rather fond of my daughter's creation."

"Yes Sir I am. When this is all said and done, you and I have some serious business to discuss" proclaimed the President.

"Sir! One of the Loons is coming this way. It's a child

Sir!" yelled one of Grant's Captains.

Before Declan could warn them that it didn't matter he heard the young Loon speak.

"Please do not shoot me! I am not like the others. I can help control them and get them to stop!"

It was Gideon. He was awake from his coma and seemed more in control of himself than even Lucy or Bobby. Declan quickly grabbed Gideon and brought him over, shielding him from the soldiers.

"We can trust dis one … I tink. Boy, how is it dat ya don't act all crazy like da others?"

"Somehow I am different, perhaps a mutation of the effects on the proteins. I'd have to study it more but…."

"You said you can control dem, well now's yer chance to make good on dat. Dey be commin' dis way lad" Declan interrupted.

The men seemed to be bracing for a giant tidal wave. They anchored themselves to the ground and grimaced with the anticipation of impact. As the Loons came closer their sprint slowed to a jog and then to a walk. They came to a complete stop within ten feet of the terrified army. While they did not attack, it was apparent that they wanted to, desperately. Something however, was holding them back.

“I knew it! Who’s da man now?” Finnegan looked at the exuberant Declan and motioned him to relax.

“Sorry brudder but if I hadn’t grabbed him, well, we’d be knee deep in smokin’ Loon guts again” retorted Declan.

Through the Loon army two Loons approached. It was Lucy and Bobby. Lucy seemed outraged.

“GIDEON! Stop this at once! We must destroy them. Destroy them all for what they’ve done us!” screamed Lucy.

“No sister, for what Father has done to us. You have seen to it that he has paid, now let us end this.”

The two met in the narrow, uneasy space between armies. One hell bent on destruction, the other praying for survival.

“If we can control the collective, then we can round them all up and keep them from hurting any more people. We can buy some time to develop a cure. We could save all of them, maybe even ourselves. I created this and I was too weak to stop father from unleashing its cruelty. I will not be that weak again. I must do this sister, *WE* must save them."

President Lincoln slowly walked through the nervous crowd to the two siblings. He was not sure what but he felt that he must say something. The entire situation seemed like it could disintegrate at any moment.

"You are a very wise young man. I can assure you that they will be well cared for and we will dedicate every resource to helping discover a cure. These people are our fellow Americans. I have a duty to protect them just as much as I do my own family. It would appear that we will require your help as well young lady. Can we count on you?"

Lucy looked at Bobby. He got a smirk on his face and spoke to her telepathically.

'What are you grinning about?' she asked.

'A few months ago I wasn't good enough to live; now I have the President of the Union kissing my ass. It's pretty amazing if you ask me' replied Bobby.

Lucy lowered her head as she turned to face President Lincoln. She looked defeated almost but Lincoln could tell that she was finally feeling a sense of relief. She looked up at him and held the moment. All eyes and ears were on her, anxiously awaiting her reply.

"Alright, I'll help."

Thc soldiers released a deafening roar of joy, nearly startled Lucy enough to break the fragile hold she held over the Loons. It seemed that with her 'surrender', her energy seemed to be fading as well.

Bobby stepped closer to her and put his arm around her. He comforted her and did his best to help keep the Loons at bay. He knew that this "round up" effort would mean splitting the two up to cover more ground. He did not relish the idea of being away from her but he did like the idea of ending this madness.

"So, my Irish friends, please forgive me but I have forgotten your name" stated Lincoln somewhat embarrassed.

"It's Finnegan and Declan O'Sullivan Sir."

"Yes, Mr. O'Sullivan, I shall need to speak to your pilot friend. It would seem that a few more of those Air Ships would be very helpful at rounding up the Loons as quickly as possible. Speed will be essential and I'm guessing that is the fastest way about."

"Aye Sir, and we can equip dem wit our plasma weapons. Um, assuming dat is sometin on yer mind." He felt slightly embarrassed, fearing he may have over stepped his bounds.

"Yes Mr. O'Sullivan, your weapon creations are most exquisite. We shall have to speak about those as well."

Declan could smell the money. In fact, he could even taste it!

"Lucy, we are going to need your help moving these Loons to a holding facility we have just west of here in Richmond. General Grant, have your men assist Ms. Lucy any way that they can. Please keep in mind gentlemen, this is not over. Do not let your guard down or provoke the Loons in any way. The consequences will surely mean death, if not from the Loons themselves then from my hangman at the gallows."

High above the battlefield in the safety of the Air Train, Agatha studied the ground with great anxiety.

"What the hell is going on down there? They stopped fighting but surely it can't be over. What the hell is going on?"

"I think that it is finally over Ms. Agatha. I think that

your country has just survived the worst plague since the Black Death" Sir Paddington answered with an extremely reassuring tone.

"I wonder if the President wants a lift?" said Mr. McMannus matter of fact like.

Optimism flooded the air and for the first time in a very long time they felt like anything was possible.

Chapter 31 – A new frontier
Washington DC, September 1865

President Lincoln was a nervous wreck. He searched the Oval Office frantically rushing from one side to the next, looking between books and papers, under the chairs, even under his desk.

"Blast it! Where is my speech?" he yelled.

"Relax dear. Its right here where you left it" said Mary.

"You my dear are a life saver and a wonder."

"I don't know why you are nervous, it's not like you haven't done this before" said Mary.

"I know, I've never been afraid to speak to a crowd but I also didn't look like this before either" protested Lincoln.

"You look so handsome. In fact, I dare say it is an improvement" she jested. She sat in her favorite chair, calmly knitting. Her gaze remained on her work and she only revealed a slight smirk as she teased her beloved husband.

"Very funny, you know how I feel."

"I know but I had the horrible fortune of experiencing

a world without the great Abraham Lincoln and it nearly drove me mad. I am certain that the general public feels something similar."

"I hope that the general public is not in love with me"

"Ah, there you go. Humor is the best medicine. Now practice your darn speech." Mary was not saying this just to cheer him up. As she sat down on the overly comfortable chair, her thoughts drifted back to that horrible night in April. The sound of the shot resonated in the booth and was deafening. The vision of his body slumping over, lifeless, still haunted her to this day. It was that sight and sound that woke her each morning and several times throughout the night. In the days that followed, not knowing where his body was; were unbearable. She headed as far away from Washington as she could; returning back to their home in Chicago. Even there she could not shake the nightmares that plagued her every waking moment. Her dreams were hellish and ate away at the fabric of her sanity. Were it not for Mr. Cox coming to Chicago himself to deliver the news and to fetch her, she feared she would not be sitting here today. She watched her husband pace the length of the room, quietly muttering the words of his speech. His right hand was folded behind his back, the left held the mass of notes that comprised his speech. He paced, back and forth, back and forth. In a different time perhaps, she would have scolded him for making her nervous. This was different and she welcomed any semblance of her husband that she could get. He was indeed different than before and it was very hard for her to look him in the eyes without focusing on his … mechanical enhancements. She used to hold his head in both hands when she kissed him but now could not bring herself to touch the left side of his face. She knew that he noticed but she did her best to mask her thoughts. She was happy to have him back and would learn to accept these changes in his appearance.

Suddenly there was a knock on the door and an aide peeped in.

"Excuse me Mr. President but we need to leave. Your Air Train is ready to head down to Falmouth."

"Excellent. Mary, you are going to love the view, and our new Air Train."

"Would this be the one commissioned by Mr. McManus? I rather like the young man, very bright. Full of promise that one." Mary stated. She had become somewhat of a patron of Mr. McManus. It was she that convinced the cabinet of the importance of such advances in technology. "The sky was no longer the limit" was a phrase that she had coined. She was rather proud and was very anxious to take her first air-born journey.

As the entourage of staff members exited the White House, they gazed in amazement at the sight that hovered before them. It was a magnificent sight. Her balloon glistened in the sun with a silvery glow. The ship below was ornate, a masterpiece in fact. It resembled the design of the royal ships of the English Navy. It was as if God himself had selected the finest ship ever made, carefully removed it from the water and attached a giant oval shaped balloon above her masts.

"Gentlemen, I present to you the Aeronautical Force Super Ship, model 1 or Air Force 1 for short. She is the first of the newly created Aeronautical Corps of the War Department" stated President Lincoln proudly.

There were many gasps and bewildered looks as many of the staff had heard of the ship but not yet seen it. Now they took a moment and soaked in the masterpiece that hovered before them. A young man in uniform at the helm of the craft tipped his hat and motioned for the group to approach.

"GOOD AFTERNOON LADIES AND GENTLEMEN!" yelled the pilot.

The group approached the craft and climbed on board. A long plank was extended to a platform with wooden slats for traction. As the President and his entourage boarded the craft, President Lincoln addressed the pilot:

"Captain McManus, so good it is to see you again!"

"Aye Sir, the honor is all mine" responded Thaddeus.

"I see that the ship has survived General Lowe's barrage of tests and met his approval."

"Aye Sir, it has" answered Thaddeus.

"Excellent, let's be off to Falmouth shall we?"

With that, Thaddeus addressed the crew with orders and the team sprung into action like the finely tuned machine that it was. The helium engine sprang to life pumping pure helium into tubes that fed smaller balloons located inside the main balloon. Smaller bags lined the lower half of the balloon and filled as the engine roared into action. Each bag was equipped with a valve system so that gases could be added or leaked in order to better control the flight. At the tail end of the ship, two massive propellers spun providing horizontal movement of the ship.

Priscilla sat underneath the canvas pavilion and fidgeted with her leather shoulder harness. She had asked her father to fashion one for her to hold "Cricket" and her newest, somewhat larger weapon. She hadn't come up with a name for it but much like Cricket, it was small and very powerful. All of the other women there wore fancy dresses and bonnets. Priscilla felt somewhat out of place but then again, she was one of the honorees and therefore it didn't matter what the others thought. They should be aspiring to be more like her.

She looked at her father and uncle. Both were wearing their finest outfits complete with ascots, spats, high collars and top hats. Her father wore his newest top hat, one that he had specially commissioned for this event. It had custom brass work on it that truly looked spectacular. He had a booth area where people could approach him and speak about the flying apparatus. Although he was among the honorees, he looked quite nervous. He would be conducting a demonstration today after the President's speech.

To his left, her Uncle Declan stood. He looked like a million dollars as well. He and Victoria had married just two weeks earlier and he was still glowing. Priscilla was incredibly happy for both of them. Declan was to conduct a demonstration of Tintreach and Slán for the crowd. An old barn was to be today's target and Declan was prepared to make quite a spectacle.

Priscilla hadn't heard from Gideon in a while. The two had started up a friendship via letters. She found his ideas quite fascinating and vice versa. He was in a secret facility somewhere working on the cure for the Loons disease. Judging by the delay from the post office to the time he read it, she figured the facility was within a day's ride. She did not actually want to know where it was however, she simply worried that her friend was being properly taken care of.

Lucy and Bobby were still off with the 3rd Pennsylvania Calvary guard rounding up Loons for containment. Among the thousands of infected citizens, they had found hundreds of Loons that were just like them; infected with the Loons disease but not out of control. With each find, they were recruited into the LVCU "Loon Virus Containment Unit" or "Nighthawks" as they preferred to call themselves. This was good because the virus spread faster than the two could travel and with each new member to the Nighthawks, the faster they could be dispatched to help contain the spread of the virus.

Priscilla had heard that the virus was nearly contained and reports of it spreading had all but disappeared. She wondered if they would find a cure for the Nighthawks. While they were able to control themselves and still function within the confines of their society, the general public was terrified of them. Random acts of violence were even reported as many people knew the horrors of a normal Loon and did not trust the Nighthawks. She knew that President Lincoln had intended on addressing this and hoped that he could convince the general public that they were not a danger. They were in fact heroes and directly responsible for saving the country.

As Priscilla's gaze drifted from her father, she stopped at a large crowd of ladies practically swarming a dashing couple. Lord Paddington Aldwych and “Lady” Agatha Foggybottom had also recently married and were thoroughly enjoying the attention they received. Agatha, despite her new status and fancy dress with matching hat, still had that meat clever attached to the back of her belt. Priscilla had asked her why and the profoundly simple reply seemed legitimate: ‘Because I will likely need it again.’

Jonathan Stone was now Master Jonathan Stone-Aldwych and future heir to Lord Paddington’s title and estates. That was the one condition of marriage for Lady Agatha; that they adopt Jonathan. Naturally Lord Paddington did not object as few men did with Agatha. He was happy to finally have a son and Jonathan had proven to be quite the impressive and inspiring young man. He would no doubt make a fine English gentleman. He would just have to perfect his accent. This American twang would simply not suffice.

As the crowd hushed, all heads turned north as they stood in awe of the approaching Air Ship. It was breath taking. A photographer flashed his cameras and began hustling to prepare for the next shot. The crowd began to bustle with anticipation of the day's events.

As the ship approached the landing area, just behind the speaking platform the fever was nearly out of control. Grown men and women giggled with glee like little school children. A pride and sense of wonder seemed to overcome the crowd.

As President Lincoln walked the lowered plank to the speaking platform he was greeted by several thousand elated citizens. This day was one that they had all waited for, a day of peace, a day of hope and a day of promise. President Lincoln took the stand as well as a moment to survey the crowd. He saw the hope in their eyes and truly wished that he could deliver what they sought, what they all needed. He took a deep breath and prepared to give a modified version of a previous speech earlier in the year.

"Ladies and Gentlemen! The President of the United States!"

As the applause subsided Lincoln took another deep breath and began:

> *"Four score and seven years ago our fathers brought forth on this continent, a new nation, conceived in Liberty, and dedicated to the*

proposition that all men are created equal."

"We have finally closed the last chapter of this tragic civil war, having tested whether this nation or any nation so conceived and so dedicated, can long endure. We have shown that it can and shall endure. We are met on a great battle-field of that war having come to dedicate a portion of that field, as a final resting place for those who here gave their lives that that nation might live. It is altogether fitting and proper that we should do this for both Confederate and Union soldiers. For if it was not for the combined force of these bold Americans, united with purpose, we would not be sitting here today with optimistic gaze towards our futures."

"But, in a larger sense, we cannot dedicate -- we cannot consecrate -- we cannot hallow -- this ground. The brave men and women, living and dead, who struggled here, have already consecrated it, far above our poor power to add or detract. The world will little note, nor long remember what we say here, but it can never

forget what they have accomplished. It is for us the living, rather, to be dedicated here to the unfinished work which they who fought here have thus far so nobly advanced. It is rather for us to be dedicated to the great task remaining before us -- that from these honored dead we take increased devotion to that cause for which they gave the last full measure of devotion -- that we here highly resolve that these dead shall not have died in vain -- that this nation, under God, shall have a new birth of freedom -- and that government of the people, by the people, for the people, shall not perish from the earth."

~applause from the crowd~

"We congregate here today with a new breed of man amongst us, a breed that currently works diligently towards securing this grateful nation by sequestering the last of the infected citizens. This group of heroes, having donned the nickname of 'Nighthawks', are true American heroes and will be treated as such -- for they are the true saviors of our Union. Not only for those survivors of the

disease but also for those infected and soon to be cured."

~applause from the crowd~

"We have been blessed as a nation with ingenuity and an adventurous spirit. As you can clearly see, my health has been restored thanks in part to a new technology called bionics. This technology will be used to help those crippled survivors of the war and restore their mobility, their function and hope where it once was lost. We cannot, and will not, forget their sacrifices nor leave them incapable of functioning in our society."

As the President finished saying this he gestured to his right. From behind a tent four war veterans emerged, each with a mechanical prosthetic limb. While their appearance was quite frightening to some of the audience, all applauded dutifully.

"We also celebrate today the ingenuity and creative genius of a family that has contributed so greatly to the future prospects of this great nation. We shall be treated today with demonstrations of a

few incredible inventions by Mr. Finnegan O'Sullivan, Mr. Declan O'Sullivan and Ms. Priscilla O'Sullivan. I present to you, the O'Sullivan family of Hartford Connecticut."

The crowd applauded wildly and Finnegan stepped up first. He spoke as eloquently as he could as he recounted the adventures of the group and how they ended up at the Battle of Falmouth. He then asked Declan to explain the weapons and do his demonstration while he prepared for flight. Declan's presentation went over very well as he blasted the old dilapidated barn leaving little more than rubble and smoldering ash. The crowd was awed with a childlike delight and amazement.

As Declan stepped down his glance caught his older brother and the two shared a moment of pride in their accomplishments. Finnegan took the stand and began to recount the amazing genius of his daughter and how she had built, with Declan's help, the Flying Apparatus. The crowd was skeptical to say the least but anxiously awaited his demonstration. As Finnegan started the thrusters and increased the throttle, he lifted off of the ground. The crowd went wild with a feverish excitement. Finnegan was really hamming it up by this point and flew directly over the crowd several times causing ladies to duck in fear. Some of the gentlemen shook their fists at him displaying their disapproval. Finn did not care; he was showing the world something that did not exist before his daughter took an age old dream and turned it into a reality. Man had dreamt of flight since cavemen observed birds and she would be forever remembered as the first to accomplish it.

President Lincoln concluded the day by introducing the newly commissioned Colonel in the Union Army, Thaddeus McManus. He was the youngest Colonel in the United States military and was now the chief engineer and pilot for the newly formed Aeronautical Corps of the War Department. The commander was his old mentor and original head of the former Army Balloon Corps, Thaddeus Lowe. Mr. Lowe had been re-commissioned as a Brigadier General. It was the genius vision of Thaddeus Lowe and Graf von Zeppelin that inspired Thaddeus McManus to build the wonder that hovered before them. President Lincoln continued:

"My fellow Americans, this is but the tip of the iceberg. I have petitioned Congress and they have emphatically approved plans to increase the number of ships in our Aeronautical Corps. By the end of this year we shall begin construction of the first Air City. It shall be a floating city that hovers just above Washington. As you can see, we will rebuild this country and exceed our founding fathers expectations." proclaimed President Lincoln.

It was a truly magnificent day and all that left were brimming with the prospects and promise that the future held. No one even seemed to be bothered by the President's new and improved look. In fact, many spoke of purchasing bionic improvements of their own.

Meanwhile, 6,770 miles away, a ship swiftly approaches a harbor in feudal Japan. At the helm is a man who has already inspired terror and respect of the crew. The fire in his eyes gleam with the grim determination of rebuilding what was once his. He would bring this world to its knees and annihilate anything that stood in his path. As the stranger's ship began to dock he was met by a group of Samurai demanding to know who he was.

The stranger merely grinned with eager anticipation.

He had wanted a good fight and the thought of testing his skills against real Samurai was something he had dreamt of since he was a little boy. He leapt from the bow of the ship, flipping through the air. In one fluid motion he had severed the heads of two Samurai. He landed in a crouched position with his sword extended high and behind him. Blood dripped off his blade and it shook as if possessed with a hunger for more. The other Samurai attacked and the stranger made quick work of each one. His movements were well rehearsed and as fluid as the most intricate of machines. When all Samurai lay dead at his feet only the one messenger remained, trembling in terror.

"Who.....who are you my Lord?"

"I am Emperor Myamoto Musashi. Bring me to your former Emperor. We have business to discuss."

About the Author:

David Lee is the principal artist at Hatton Cross Steampunk. His Steampunk art has been featured in numerous art exhibits to include Dr. Grymm's 2011 "Steampunk Bizarre Exhibit" in the Mark Twain Museum, CT. He's been a guest artist and panel presenter at numerous conventions on the east coast to include the Steampunk World's Fair and AnachroCon. He has been chosen to be an "Attending Professional" at DCon 2013.

His "Gentleman's Flying Apparatus" aka "The Morgan Aeronautical Destroyer of Satan's Arrogance" was nominated for "Best non-goggle accessory" in the Steampunk Chronicle's 2012 Readers Choice Awards. He is also a contributing "DIY" author for the Steampunk Chronicle website. David's most recent Steampunk creation is the "Gentleman's Armored Battle Carriage" (a Steampunk tank) which will be making numerous appearances in 2013 as well as his Steampunk drivable Dalek, aka "Dalek Steam".

With all that David Lee and Hatton Cross Steampunk have going with Country in Ruin:1865, he continues to push the envelope with some very ambitious projects to include a Steampunk Séance Machine with interactive show, a web comic with illustrator SE Ripley, book two of his Steampunk western series "World in Ruin:1870", a musical production, as well as numerous DIY projects for the Steampunk Chronicle website.

David's personal motto is "Anything worth doing is worth overdoing!" and applies this to his Steampunk creations, his writing.

For more information, please visit David at:

www.hcsteam.net

ISBN: 0615763677
ISBN-13: 978-0615763675

Finnegan O'Sullivan - 1865 Falmouth, VA

Declan O'Sullivan - 1865, Falmouth, VA

Priscilla O'Sulivan - 1865, Falmouth, VA

ISBN: 0615763677
ISBN-13: 978-0615763675